Butsko scanned the inlet with his binoculars from left to right and then back again, when suddenly he heard something. He spun around. The sound had been like a foot stepping on a twig and came from the woods below the summit.

"I heard something," he said.

"It's probably one of them land crabs," Sergeant McCabe said.

"There ain't no land crabs up this high."

Ka-pow! A shot crackled over their heads.

"Get down!" Butsko yelled.

The men of the Second Squad already were down, but they got down lower.

"Japs!"

Death Squad

by
John Mackie

A JOVE BOOK

Excepting basic historical events, places, and personages, this series of books is fictional, and anything that appears otherwise is coincidental and unintentional.

The principal characters are imaginary, although they might remind veterans of specific men whom they knew. The Twenty-third Infantry Regiment, in which the characters serve, is used fictitiously—it doesn't represent the real historical Twenty-third Infantry, which has distinguished itself in so many battles from the Civil War to Vietnam—but it could have been any American line regiment that fought and bled during World War II.

These novels are dedicated to the men who were there. May their deeds and gallantry never be forgotten.

DEATH SQUAD

A Jove Book/published by arrangement with
the author

PRINTING HISTORY
Jove edition/November 1983

ISBN: 0-515-07110-2

Jove books are published by The Berkley Publishing Group,
200 Madison Avenue, New York, N.Y. 10016. The words
"A JOVE BOOK" and the "J" with sunburst are trademarks
belonging to Jove Publications, Inc.

PRINTED IN THE UNITED STATES OF AMERICA

ONE . . .

It was night on Guadalcanal, and Bannon lay in his foxhole, holding his M 1 tightly and peering ahead into the moonlit jungle. Word had been passed along that Japanese soldiers had infiltrated the American lines, and GIs had been found in forward positions with their throats cut. Sporadic bursts of gunfire could be heard, and occasionally a Jap would shout a taunt or laugh maniacally.

It was eerie and frightening. Bannon didn't mind fighting Japs he could see, but now the night was full of phantoms, and any shadow might conceal a Jap soldier with a knife in his teeth, creeping forward to kill another GI.

"I see something," said Frankie La Barbara, lying next to Bannon.

"Where?"

"Over there." Frankie pointed with his index finger.

Bannon narrowed his eyes and examined the dark patch of jungle indicated by Frankie La Barbara. "I don't see anything."

"Keep watching. Something's over there."

Bannon thought Frankie was seeing things. Moonlight and shadows made you see things that weren't there.

Deep in the jungle to their left they heard a Japanese voice: *"I coming for you, Maline! I kill your ass!"*

"I ain't no fucking Marine!" Frankie shouted.

"Sssshhhh."

Shots and screaming erupted to their right. A mortar shell

1

exploded behind them, brightening the jungle and sending clods of earth flying into the air. Then it became dark and silent again. Bannon blinked, trying to get his night vision back.

"That son of a bitch," Frankie said.

Bannon had a headache and wished he could smoke a cigarette. He'd slept the night before, but he'd gotten no sleep at all tonight, and it was two in the morning already. He and the rest of the Twenty-third Infantry Regiment had landed on Guadalcanal three days before, and they'd been fighting hard ever since.

Suddenly a machine gun opened fire in the patch of jungle in front of them. Bannon and Frankie ducked quickly as bullets stitched across the top of the foxhole.

Frankie pulled a grenade from his lapel and yanked out the pin. "I told you a Jap was there," he said, hurling the grenade into the jungle. They held their heads low and waited a few seconds; then the grenade exploded, making the earth tremble and sending trees crashing to the ground.

"How'd you like that one!" Frankie shouted.

"Keep your voice down," Bannon told him.

"You think they don't know where we are? They know where we are and they know what we had for breakfast!"

"I said keep your voice down."

Frankie muttered something and rested his helmet against the side of the foxhole. He was a six-footer like Bannon, with muscular shoulders and arms in contrast to Bannon's lean, rangy build. Frankie was from New York City and Bannon had been a cowboy in Texas before the war.

Bannon heard footsteps behind him and spun around, raising his M 1 to his shoulder. "Who goes there!"

"Butsko."

Bannon recognized his platoon sergeant's voice and lowered his M 1. Butsko, a big gorilla of a man with a scarred, mangled face, materialized out of the darkness.

Butsko cradled his carbine in his arms as he crawled into the foxhole. "Who threw the hand grenade?"

"I did," Frankie said.

"Whatja see?"

"There's a Jap machine gun out there."

Butsko looked into the jungle. "Let's go take a look."

2

Bannon and Frankie glanced at each other, because they didn't feel like venturing into a jungle infested with Japs, but if Butsko told them to go, they had to go.

Butsko grunted as he crawled out of the foxhole, and Frankie and Bannon followed him. The ground was covered with damp leaves and clods of earth. Mosquitoes and other insects buzzed around their heads. All the men were covered with blisters and bumps from insect bites.

They made their way across the floor of the jungle, with Butsko in front and Bannon and Frankie side by side behind him.

"Maline, you die!" shouted a Jap somewhere in the jungle.

Somebody to their right fired a rifle. Another Japanese mortar round landed not far away. Bannon wished it would get light soon, so that he could see what was going on.

Butsko stopped, and so did Bannon and Frankie. They listened to the sounds of the jungle at night, to leaves rustling in the wind and insects chirping. Bannon wondered if a Jap was lurking in the grove up ahead, waiting for them to come closer so he could open fire.

Butsko moved forward again, followed by Bannon and Frankie. They threaded around the thick trunk of a tree and came to the area where Frankie's hand grenade had landed. Butsko made motions with his hand and they fanned out, holding their rifles ready to open fire instantly. The air smelled of gunpowder, and a mist of smoke hung over the ground.

"Looka here," Frankie said, waving something in the air.

Bannon crawled closer, and it looked like the leg and haunch of an animal. Butsko took it from Frankie's hand.

"You threw a grenade at a pig, you asshole."

"I toldja something was in here."

Butsko threw the leg over his shoulder.

They heard the whistle of a mortar round over their heads and ducked down. The mortar round exploded into the American lines and was followed by three more. Bannon watched the explosions light up the sky and fill it with flying debris. Then everything became quiet again. Butsko peered into the jungle.

"I wonder where he is."

"Where *who* is?" Frankie asked.

3

"The Jap with the mortar." Butsko sniffed the air and grimaced. "He's probably not too far away. Let's see if we can find the son of a bitch."

Bannon didn't think it was a good idea, because the jungle was crawling with Japs, but he never argued with Butsko, who had a ferocious temper once he got going.

"Don't make no unnecessary noise," Butsko said.

Butsko got to his feet and walked in a crouch into the jungle. Bannon and Frankie followed him, peering into bushes and looking at the tops of trees for movement that could indicate the presence of Japanese. After moving only a dozen paces, Butsko stopped suddenly and dropped to one knee. Bannon and Frankie kneeled beside him. Butsko was examining footprints in the mud.

"These are fresh," Butsko murmured. "And they're deep. They must have been carrying something."

"The machine gun," Frankie said. "I'll bet they were carrying that machine gun that just fired at us."

Butsko looked ahead in the direction the footprints were going, and a faint smile passed over his lips. "They can't be far away," he said. "Keep quiet and follow me."

They crept through the jungle stealthily in a single file. Rotting foliage stank and mosquitoes continued to buzz around their heads. Vines hung from the trees, looking like snakes. The moon cast phantasmagorical shadows on the ground, and the trunks of the trees were slimy with dew. Bannon's feet itched and burned at the same time, and he was sure he was getting jungle rot. He wondered if he'd ever see the hot, dry prairies of Texas again.

Butsko stopped, examined the tracks on the ground, and moved out again. Bannon knew that few sergeants on Guadalcanal would go out looking for trouble like this, but Butsko had a pathological hatred for Japs. He had been on the Bataan Death March and escaped from a Jap prison camp in the Philippines. The experience had warped his mind a little.

They heard a faint metallic sound and halted suddenly. Butsko pointed to the ground, and they all got down on their stomachs. Bannon stared at a big yellow worm that glowed phosphorescently in front of him. Then the stillness was rent by the sound of a machine gun opening fire a short distance

4

away. It was so close, they could see the muzzle flashes through the foliage.

Butsko beckoned with his finger and they drew closer to him. "They're right over there," he said. "Let's go get them, but don't fire until I give the word."

They arose and moved quickly through the jungle, not worrying about making noise because the machine-gun blasts drowned everything out. Damp leaves slapped Bannon's face, and branches scratched him as he tried to keep up with Butsko. The machine gun stopped firing and the three GIs came to a sudden halt. They heard Japanese being spoken in low voices and knew the machine-gun squad was only a few yards away. Then the machine gun opened fire again. They could see its flashes clearly, and the flashes illuminated the three men in the gun crew.

Butsko dropped to one knee and tore a hand grenade from his lapel. He nodded to Bannon and Frankie, who also removed hand grenades and pulled the pins. Butsko reared back his mighty arm, and Bannon and Frankie did likewise. They threw their grenades at the same moment and pitched forward onto their faces, waiting for the grenades to explode.

The Japanese soldiers shouted in alarm and tried to flee, but they only got a few steps before the grenades detonated. The jungle roared and Bannon saw one Jap, with his arms and legs akimbo, being blown into the air.

"Hit it!" Butsko yelled.

The three GIs jumped to their feet and charged into the little clearing where the machine gun had been set up. There was a big hole in the ground, and the Japanese machine gun lay on its side near the shoulder and arm of a Japanese soldier whose torso was a few feet away. The air was filled with acrid smoke, and one Jap lay on his stomach, moaning. His back was a bloody mass. Butsko raised his carbine and bayonet and plunged it downward toward the Jap's neck. The bayonet severed the Jap's spinal cord, and its tip came out the front of his throat. The Jap stopped moaning. Butsko pulled out his bayonet.

"One less Jap machine gun to worry about," he said.

He walked toward the gun. It was a Nambu light machine gun, with bayonet affixed at the end and a bipod on the barrel, like the American Browning automatic rifle. The ammunition for the machine gun had been blown up by the grenades, but the weapon itself still appeared to be in good firing order. Butsko flicked his carbine on automatic and fired two bursts into the chamber of the machine gun, mangling its innards and making certain it couldn't be used again.

"Let's get out of here," Butsko said.

The GIs slipped into the jungle and it soon swallowed them up. They entered a denser growth of foliage that blocked out the moonlight, and they could barely see. Butsko found a waist-high boulder and sat down next to it.

"Take a break," he said.

Bannon and Frankie sat down on the moist leaves. Rifles and machine guns fired far away, but they felt safe in their little corner of the night. They took deep breaths and rested their rifles on their legs.

Bannon looked at Butsko, who slowly turned his head from side to side, listening and searching for the presence of Japs. Butsko never really relaxed, never stopped being a soldier. Bannon was a corporal, a squad leader in Butsko's platoon, and always felt inadequate around Butsko, who was a fantastic soldier. Frankie was a private in Bannon's squad, a complainer and a goldbrick, but he could always be relied upon in tough situations.

"We'll never find that mortar out here," Frankie said. "There's too much jungle. Why don't we go back, Sarge?"

"You wanna go back, go back," Butsko replied. "I'm going after that mortar."

Frankie didn't dare go back alone, and he knew Butsko was counting on that. "How're you gonna find the mortar out here?"

"They're probably using trails to get around fast, and there ain't that many trails around here. All we have to do is sit next to one of the trails, and the fuckers'll probably walk right by us. And if they don't walk by us, maybe some of the other Japs out here will. I know all the trails around here."

Just like him, Bannon thought, *to know all the trails around here. He's probably reconnoitered the area on his own time, just in case.* The jungle was no-man's-land, but that didn't stop Butsko.

"Okay, let's go," Butsko said.

6

He stood, stretched, and moved into the foliage, stepping high and bringing his feet down softly so as not to make noise. Bannon and Frankie followed him, walking the same way. Bannon didn't feel in as much danger with Butsko as he would have without him, because Butsko saw and heard things that no one else did, and Butsko was worth three or four men in combat.

They came to a narrow trail. Butsko looked up at the full moon in the sky and then around at the treetops. He bent his knees and searched the bushes at the side of the trail. Motioning with his head, he led Bannon and Frankie toward the Japanese lines.

Frankie didn't like Butsko's impromptu patrol at all. He wished he could be back in his little foxhole, copping some Z's and dreaming of hookers and chorus girls in New York City. More than anything else, he wanted to survive the war. He was not interested in becoming a hero.

They heard sporadic sounds of fighting in the distance as they moved along the trail, but around them were only insects and birds. Frankie squashed a mosquito against his nose, which already had mosquito bites all over it. He'd once had a love affair with a girl who'd been a Rockette at Radio City Music Hall, and she'd told him that he'd had a perfect Roman nose, but if she saw it now, she wouldn't think so. *This fucking Army is ruining me*, Frankie thought.

A metallic *whump* came to them from not far away, and the three of them stopped cold on the trail. No one had to say anything: it was the sound of a mortar. Sure enough, seconds later, there was an explosion in the distance as the mortar round landed inside the American defense perimeter. Then they heard another *whump* and another explosion far away. Butsko smiled in the moonlight. "I toldja they were around here," he whispered. He stared in the direction of the mortar, trying to estimate its distance. His ears were sharp and his judgment usually was pretty good. He figured it was three or four hundred yards away. "Let's go, and keep your eyes open."

They moved down the trail toward the Japanese lines and after a while came to the intersection of another trail. Butsko took a left, and they proceeded swiftly through the jungle as

7

the sound of the mortar became closer. They came to another trail, and Butsko held out his hand, then got on his hands and knees and brought his eyes close to the earth.

Bannon and Frankie joined him, and they saw more tracks. Butsko had been right: The Japs had been using trails to get around quickly as they harassed the GIs in front of them.

"Maline, you die!" shouted a Jap somewhere in their vicinity.

Bannon's hair stood on end and Frankie jumped to his feet. Butsko pulled Frankie's pant leg and Frankie kneeled down again.

"Be quiet," Butsko whispered. "He's right around here. You two find yourselves a place to hide off the trail. I'm gonna get the son of a bitch."

"I kill you, Maline!" the Jap yelled again.

Butsko trembled with excitement, because he could almost smell the blood of the Jap with the taunting voice. He removed his bayonet from his carbine and passed the carbine to Bannon.

"Hang on to this for me."

Bannon nodded and took the carbine.

"If any Japs come by here, just let 'em have it."

"Hup, Sarge."

Holding his bayonet blade up in his fist, Butsko moved away in a crouch and in seconds was lost in the darkness. Bannon and Frankie stepped off the trail and found a little depression in the ground to lie in. They dropped down, only a few feet from the edge of the trail and stretched their rifles in front of them.

"I pity that poor Jap out there," Frankie said.

TWO . . .

"Maline, I fuck your sister!" shouted the Jap in the jungle.

Butsko closed in on him, his bayonet in his teeth, creeping through the dense foliage and gently moving branches out of the way with both his hands. The Jap had switched positions twice already, and Butsko had adjusted his direction to the sound of the Jap's voice. Butsko's heart beat faster and his skin tingled with excitement. There was nothing he hated in the world more than Japs, and nothing he'd rather do than kill them. Every few steps he halted and listened, to make sure no Japs were following him and that he wasn't being led into a trap. His saliva covered the blade of the bayonet in his mouth and dripped down his chin as he walked with his knees bent and his ass low to the ground, clearing a path through the jungle with his hands.

Butsko realized the Jap hadn't said anything for a few minutes. Either the Jap was moving to a new position or he'd heard Butsko. Butsko decided to pause and listen. He crouched down near the trunk of a tree and cocked his head like a parrot on a branch, trying to pick up sounds.

The jungle was silent around him. The Jap wasn't moving, nor was he shouting taunts toward the American lines. *He must have heard me*, Butsko thought. *But if I stay quiet, he'll think it was just his imagination or an animal wandering around. I'll have to wait him out.*

Butsko had been in the Army fifteen years and was accus-

9

tomed to waiting. He just sat at the base of the tree, held his bayonet in his hand, and listened to the symphony of the jungle. He could sit there perfectly still until dawn if he wanted to, but the Jap would have to move sooner or later. The Jap was far from his own lines—too close to the Americans. Time was on Butsko's side.

Butsko figured he was within fifty yards of the Jap and knew that Jap was as good as dead. There was no way he could get away. Butsko imagined the slanty-eyed, yellow-skinned bastard out there, slinking around. Maybe the Jap had been one of the guards in that prison camp in northern Luzon where Butsko had been incarcerated for two months. The guards had kicked and punched the shit out of him, and many times he'd thought they'd kill him, but he'd never knuckled under to them. He'd dreamed that someday he'd get his hands around the throat of a Jap and squeeze until his eyes popped out. He'd thought of slashing Japs with knives and shooting them with guns. He fantasized about driving a tank over them and crushing their bones. Hatred of Japs had kept him alive, and now it was his prime motivation in life: He lived to kill Japs.

Butsko heard a sound ahead of him and pricked up his ears. Was the Jap moving? Butsko looked at his watch; it was half past three in the morning. Dawn would come in a couple of hours. Was the Jap getting ready to leave? Butsko heard another sound and deduced that the Jap was indeed moving. Clearly the sounds were footfalls. He heard the rustle of branches and leaves. The Jap was being careless; he didn't think Americans would be lurking in the vicinity.

With a ragged smile Butsko moved to intercept the Jap. He slid silently through the jungle, pausing every few steps to listen, and then eased forward again, his bayonet in his mouth. The Jap was moving parallel to the American lines, evidently looking for a new spot from which to hurl his insults.

"Maline, I coming for you!" the Jap shrieked, and then laughed maniacally.

Butsko knew that the Jap's voice was scaring the shit out of a lot of GIs, but it didn't scare Butsko at all. It only made him madder and more determined. He'd killed dozens of Japs since landing on Guadalcanal with the Twenty-third Infantry Regiment, but the more he killed, the more he wanted to kill.

If he had his way, every Jap in the world would be killed slowly and painfully for what they did to him and his buddies on the Bataan Death March and in that POW camp in northern Luzon.

"Maline, I cut you up!" the Jap shouted.

The Jap had stopped again to hurl more threats, but Butsko kept going, gliding silently through the leaves and branches as gracefully as a ballerina, although he was a big, bulky man.

"Maline, I coming for you!"

Butsko could hear the Jap not more than ten yards dead ahead. Dropping to his knees, Butsko crawled through the underbrush, a few inches at a time, making no noise whatsoever. The Japanese soldier laughed hysterically, keeping American GIs awake, but he wouldn't do it much longer. Butsko's mouth went dry as he closed the distance between him and the Japanese. A horde of ants covered his left hand and bit into his flesh, but he brushed them away casually and kept going. He slithered over a rotting log and through a puddle of water. Peering ahead, he made out the silhouette of the Japanese soldier making all the noise.

"Maline, you die!"

The Jap was wearing a soft-billed cap with long flaps covering his ears and neck. His rifle was slung over his shoulder and he kneeled on the ground, cupping his hands for a megaphone as he shouted and laughed. He was about twenty feet away, and Butsko thought he should get within ten feet at least.

Holding the bayonet tightly in his teeth, Butsko crawled forward. A wave of anxiety swept over him, because he didn't want the Jap to get away after all the effort he'd expended. Closer and closer he crawled, the front of his uniform soaking with mud. His shoulders ached from the tension. Just a few feet more.

Then the Jap soldier arose, turned around, and walked backward toward Butsko! The Jap evidently was going to change his position again, and Butsko took the bayonet from his mouth and held it blade-up in his fist. He crouched and watched the Jap move in his direction through the jungle. The Jap was tall and thin and wore glasses and a mustache. He was headed straight for Butsko, and Butsko thought it was too good to be true.

The Jap came within three feet of Butsko, and Butsko leaped

11

forward, ripping upward with his bayonet with one hand while trying to cover the Jap's mouth with his other hand. The Jap shouted in alarm at the sudden sight of Butsko, and a split second later Butsko's bayonet sliced into the Jap's gut. The Jap howled in pain and terror as Butsko's knife cut him wide open. His guts spilled onto the ground as he fell backward, grunting and whimpering, and Butsko pulled his bayonet back, trying to keep his footing on the Jap's slippery intestines.

The Jap landed on his back and Butsko kneeled over him. The Jap was still alive, trying to push his stomach together with his hands, his eyeglasses crooked on his head and his tongue sticking out of his mouth.

"How're you feeling, champ?" Butsko asked with a murderous grin, waving the blade of the knife back and forth in front of the Jap's eyes.

The Jap looked at the knife as he gasped for air. He didn't have the energy to scream anymore, and an expression of pain and panic was on his face. Butsko placed the point of his bayonet against the Jap's jugular vein and winked.

"Looks like you're the one who's gonna die, huh?"

The Jap barely heard him, because he'd already gone into shock. Butsko pushed his bayonet forward, and its point cut open the Jap's jugular. Blood spurted out and Butsko ripped to the side, slicing open the Jap's windpipe. Blood foamed out of the Jap's mouth, and the Jap went limp on the ground. Butsko wiped his bayonet on the Jap's shirt, pushed it into his scabbard, and turned around, making his way back to Bannon and Frankie La Barbara.

Frankie looked at his watch. "He's been gone nearly forty-five minutes. Do you think something happened to him?"

"Nothing happened to him. Relax."

"How can I relax when there are Japs all over the place?"

"Ssshhhh."

Frankie snorted and chomped the gum in his mouth nervously. He felt like a sitting duck out there in the jungle. A Jap might be creeping up on him at that very moment, and he spun around at a sound behind him, but it was only a dead twig that the breeze had knocked to the ground. He felt himself becoming angry at the Japs, the Army, and the whole world.

It didn't seem fair that a handsome intelligent guy like him should have to be crawling around on hot, sweaty Guadalcanal.

Next to him Bannon was listening to the jungle. He hadn't heard the mortar for a half hour and wondered if the Japs had pulled out. It'd be light before long, so it'd make sense for them to leave around that time. The jungle had become quiet. Even the Jap who had screamed insults was quiet, and Bannon wondered if Butsko had got him.

Bannon peered through the underbrush at the trail that passed by the shallow depression that he and Frankie were in. It was moonlit and peaceful. Nobody would be able to come close without Bannon spotting him first. Sweat dripped off his nose, and he wiped it away with the back of his hand. It'd be nice if he could see that mortar squad coming by. He had one hand grenade left, and there'd be one less mortar squad in the Jap army.

"Hello, boys," said Sergeant Butsko.

Bannon and Frankie spun around. Butsko crouched in the underbrush beside them. He'd crept that close and they hadn't heard him.

"Jeez," Frankie said, "you shouldn't sneak up on people like that!"

"You should keep your eyes open, fuckhead."

Butsko hopped like a frog into the shallow spot where Bannon and Frankie were lying.

"Did you find the Jap with the big mouth?" Frankie asked.

"Do you hear him anymore?" Butsko replied.

Bannon gazed at Butsko with admiration. "You really got him, Sarge?"

Butsko nodded. "Cut him from asshole to elbow, just about." He looked at his watch. "I think we spent enough time out here, and I don't hear that mortar anymore. We might as well go back."

Butsko picked up his carbine and snapped his bayonet onto the end. He motioned with his hand and Bannon and Frankie stood. Butsko looked both ways on the trail, then stepped onto it and headed back toward the American lines. Bannon and Frankie followed him.

A faint breeze was blowing now, rustling the leaves on the trees and keeping flying insects away. Bannon felt a chill from the perspiration drying on his body. He hoped he could get a few hours sleep before reveille in the morning. He didn't think he could get through another full day without any sleep.

The trail twisted and turned through the jungle. It was so narrow that branches and leaves on both sides of the path touched their shoulders and elbows. A caterpillar dropped onto Frankie's nose, and he flicked it away. Bannon looked up at the sky and saw the full moon shining. He wondered if the moon looked like that over Texas that night and if his girl friend, Ginger, was looking at it too. It would be nice if she was, but she was probably working as a waitress in some honky-tonk and all she could see were 4-Fs winking at her. Sometimes Bannon wished he'd never met Ginger, because if he'd never met her, he wouldn't have to suffer the anguish and pain of not being able to see her.

They moved around a bend in the trail and saw directly in front of them four Japanese soldiers, one of them carrying a mortar tube and another carrying the mortar base plate.

The three GIs and four Japanese soldiers stopped cold in their tracks, astonished to see the enemy directly in front of them. Butsko was the first to come to his senses as he lunged with his rifle and bayonet at the Japanese soldier closest to him.

"Get them!" shouted Butsko.

The Japanese soldier closest to Butsko was carrying the base plate, and he raised it in front of his chest to protect himself from Butsko's bayonet, which struck the metal hard and cracked in half. The Jap tried to clobber Butsko in the head with the base plate, but Butsko dodged back, whacked the base plate out of the way with the butt of his carbine, and lashed out with his foot, kicking the Jap in the balls. The Jap goggled his eyes and cupped his groin with both his hands. Butsko would have liked to finish him off with his bayonet, but it was no good any longer, so he smacked the Jap in the face with his rifle butt, flattening his nose and knocking a few teeth down his throat. The Jap sagged to the ground and Butsko stomped on his head a few times.

Bannon found himself in front of a Jap who was so shocked by seeing American GIs that he fired a wild shot over Bannon's head. Bannon fired a straighter shot from the hip, which hit

14

the Jap in the stomach and spun him around, but before Bannon could fire another shot, a third Jap jumped in front of him and tried to stick him with his bayonet.

Bannon parried the blow with his rifle and bayonet, swinging his rifle butt around to crack the Jap in the head with it, but the Jap danced back, leaned to the side, and tried to plunge his bayonet into Bannon's stomach. Bannon managed to parry that lunge, too, and this time pushed his rifle butt straight at the Jap's face. The Jap dodged to the side and Bannon followed his movement, punching him in the mouth with his rifle butt and knocking his jawbone loose. Still game, the Jap tried to block Bannon's next blow, but he wasn't seeing clearly and couldn't do it. Bannon's bayonet and rifle crashed through the Jap's guard, and the bayonet buried itself up to the hilt in the Jap's stomach. The Jap dropped to his knees, trying to push the bayonet out of his stomach with his hands. Blood flowed like ribbons between his fingers, and Bannon pulled his bayonet out. He raised his rifle a few inches and pulled the trigger, shooting the Jap in the face. The Jap's head exploded and he fell forward, lying motionless astride the trail.

The fourth Japanese soldier dropped his box of mortar ammunition and ran for the hills at the first sight of the GIs. Frankie La Barbara raised his M 1 to his shoulder and fired, but the Jap kept running. Frankie fired again, and that shot brought the Jap down. Frankie ran after him to finish him off. It was too dark for him to see the wounded Jap roll over and pull a Nambu pistol out of its holster. The Jap took aim with a trembling hand and squeezed the trigger. The Nambu fired and the bullet whizzed past Frankie's ear. Frankie shot his rifle from the hip, pulling his trigger as he charged the wounded Jap. His first bullet grazed the Jap's shoulder, making him flinch, but the second bullet hit him in the chest and the third in the stomach. Frankie stood over the Jap and fired down point-blank at his heart. The Jap's chest exploded at the impact of the bullet, and then the Jap lay still.

Frankie returned to the trail, seeing Butsko and Bannon looking down at the other three Japs.

"Well," Butsko said, "I guess we've had a pretty good night. Let's take this mortar stuff back; it might come in handy for something."

Butsko picked up the tube, Bannon got the base plate, and Frankie lifted the crate of ammo to his shoulder. The three GIs walked down the trail toward their lines, leaving behind four dead Japs in the pale moonlight.

THREE . . .

It was morning and Colonel William Stockton sat in his office, smoking his pipe and drinking a cup of coffee. Stockton was tall and lean, white-haired and fifty years old, the CO of the Twenty-third Infantry Regiment, and he was looking over his plans for an offensive against the Japanese on the west bank of the Matanikau River. His men were on the east bank, and his left flank had advanced into the jungle where the Matanikau turned southeast. This meant that his left flank had driven a wedge into the Japanese lines, and if he wheeled to the right, he could assault the west bank of the river, which would place him in a favorable position for an assault on the Japanese-held ridge line to the west.

There was a knock on his door.

"Come in!" he said.

The door to his office opened, and Major Gordon Butler, his chief of personnel, poked his head in. "Got a minute, sir?"

"Sure, come in, Butler."

Major Butler, a bald, roly-poly man with metal-framed glasses, entered the office, a folder full of papers under his arm. He sat on a chair in front of the desk and opened the folder in his lap.

"Sir," he said, "I've been looking at the records of the men in your new recon platoon, and I thought I should recommend that you put an officer in charge of them."

"What for?"

"Well, sir, I think it's best that you have an officer in charge of a group of men like that."

"They seem to be doing all right by themselves, don't they?"

"But they've only been here at Headquarters for two days. I think a situation may develop before long that will require an officer's judgment."

"Like what?"

Major Butler was beginning to feel frustrated. He knew that the new recon platoon was Colonel Stockton's pet unit, because they'd advanced farther than any other unit in the regiment during the first big battle on Guadalcanal. Before becoming the recon platoon, they'd been just another rifle platoon in the Second Battalion.

"Well, sir," Major Butler began, "as I said, I've been going over the records of the men in the recon platoon, and they're an awfully unstable bunch. I mean, the platoon sergeant, Sergeant Butsko, has been in trouble almost from the first day he joined the Army, and he's been in the Army fifteen years. You know about his court-martials. You know that he killed a civilian in a fight in Australia just before we shipped out."

"Major Butler," Colonel Stockton said, a tone of annoyance in his voice, "I know all about Butsko, and I agree with you: He's a tough egg. If he weren't in the Army, he probably would have gotten the electric chair years ago. But this is an army, not a garden party. In an army you need men like Butsko. I don't want to put an officer in that platoon because there isn't a lieutenant in this Army who could handle Butsko, and on top of that, there isn't a lieutenant in this Army who knows more than him."

"But, sir, the Army psychologist who examined him in Australia thought he was insane."

"Really? Do you think that psychologist could have attacked the Japs the way Butsko and his platoon did on the first night we hit this island? If Butsko is insane, then I wish I had more men who are just as insane as he is. If I did, I'd be on the other side of the Matanikau right now."

Major Butler cleared his throat. "But, sir, you *do* have more men who are just as insane as Butsko, *and they're all in the recon platoon*. I don't know what trick of fate brought that bunch together, but that platooon is like a time bomb waiting to go off. You've got a man named Shilansky who was a bank robber, of all things, before he came into the Army. You've got another man named La Barbara who was a racketeer. There's another character named Jones who reportedly goes berserk on the battlefield, although he's a moron the rest of the time. One of the men is a gun-happy Texan named Bannon, and you've got a crazy Apache Indian named Longtree who spends all his spare time sharpening his bayonet and talking to himself. There's an ex-movie stuntman named O'Rourke who likes to swing from trees, and I could go on and on. Sir, I know you're fond of that platoon, but someday they're gonna screw up real bad. A group of men like that has to screw up real bad someday. They fight with everybody who's not in their platoon, and when there are no strangers around, they turn on each other like wild animals." Major Butler took a deep breath. "Sir, I strongly recommend that you put an officer in charge of them before they do something to embarrass the regiment and you."

Colonel Stockton turned his pipe upside down and tapped the burnt tobacco out of it. "All I know is that platoon is full of fighters, and I don't care what their personalities are like. I appreciate your concern for the regiment, but that platoon is staying just the way it is."

Major Butler knew when Stockton had his mind made up, you couldn't budge him. And he definitely had his mind made up about the recon platoon. "Very well, sir. You know best. I'll let you get on with your work." Major Butler stood and turned toward the door.

"One more thing, Major."

Major Butler faced Colonel Stockton. "Yes, sir?"

"If there are any more tough guys in the regiment who're getting in trouble all the time, transfer them to the recon platoon. I'm sure Butsko will be able to whip them into shape."

Major Butler wanted to tell Colonel Stockton that he was making a terrible mistake, but he just saluted and said, "Yes, sir." He did an about-face and walked out of the office, closing the door behind him.

Colonel Stockton reached for his pigskin tobacco pouch and filled his pipe again. He thought Major Butler was way off base about the recon platoon. They were just a bunch of rough-house boys, that's all. So what if they made a little trouble

19

once in a while? They hadn't committed any serious infractions of rules. Colonel Stockton had faith in his recon platoon. He didn't think they were as bad as Major Butler made them appear.

It was ten o'clock in the morning and the sun shone like a ball of fire in the sky. The air was filled with the sound of shovels and pickaxes striking earth as the men of the Twenty-third improved their fortifications. The Japs weren't attacking, and Colonel Stockton had left for a meeting with General Vandergrift. It was the first major lull in the fighting since the regiment had landed on Guadalcanal.

The bunkers and foxholes were being dug throughout the dense jungle, but the foliage was so thick, men could disappear for a few winks of sleep or a surreptitious cigarette. Guards had been posted to look for infiltrating Japs, although it was doubted that the Japs would try anything like that during daytime. The Japs liked to fight at night, but the men of the Twenty-third were gaining skill at fighting in darkness, and fewer Japs were getting through after the sun went down.

Men cursed and laughed as they hacked the dirt and the tangle of roots beneath the surface. It could take hours to dig a few feet, and then you had a hole whose sides bristled with cut roots. You hoped your sergeant wouldn't make you dig deeper, but he always did, and you worked until your bones ached and your body was covered with sweat and insect bites.

In one section of the regiment's area, hidden by huge leaves and a tangle of underbrush, Privates Homer Gladley and Morris Shilansky, who did not particularly like each other, crawled side by side, without rifles and bandoliers of ammunition to weigh them down.

They heard digging and clatter all around them as inch by inch they made their way toward a wall of khaki tarpaulin straight ahead. They could see only patches of the tarpaulin through the underbrush, and their mouths watered as they drew closer. The tarpaulin sheltered crates of food, and they had been sent on this special mission by Butsko, who had decided that he and his men hadn't been getting enough to eat.

Gladley had been chosen for the mission because he was

the platoon chowhound and therefore had the most motivation to get the food. Butsko picked Shilansky because he'd been a crook in civilian life and presumably had expertise in this sort of activity. It had been hoped that Gladley's passion for food wouldn't cause him to bungle the mission and that Shilansky wouldn't get caught, as he'd been caught so many times in civilian life. Shilansky had been told by a judge to join the Army or go to jail, so he'd joined the Army and often wondered afterward if it might not have been better to go to jail.

Both were big men, but Gladley was the biggest in the platoon, with enormous round shoulders and a head like a basketball. He had blond hair and a few freckles on his face.

Shilansky was a few inches shorter than Gladley and not as wide, but he was muscular and strong, with a swarthy complexion and a hooked nose. His eyes were slanted and he had a gloomy intense personality. He had no friends in the platoon, and that seemed to be the way he liked it.

Gradually, Gladley and Shilansky drew closer to the tarpaulin. They'd scouted their objective earlier in the morning, and only one sleepy guard had been outside, sitting on a crate of C rations and smoking a cigarette. The guard was stationed there because guards were traditionally assigned to watch rations and equipment, but nobody seriously expected anybody to steal anything on the front lines, hence the man's lax attitude.

Gladley's mouth watered as he dug his fingernails into the dirt and crawled closer to the tarpaulin. He thought of all that good Spam, the beans, and the delicious sweet fruit salad slithering down his throat and making his belly feel good. His nose twitched and his lips trembled. They were almost there.

Shilansky stared at the tarpaulin and recalled the day he had robbed the bank at Needham, Massachusetts, with Moe Gumble and Donnie Rapoza. There had been the same excitement, the same suspense, and afterward the big payoff, fifty thousand dollars, and during the Depression that had been a lot of money. He'd taken his share to Boston and for six months had been the king of Scollay Square, but then something had gone wrong in that bank in Lowell, and the next morning he'd found himself before a judge.

They reached the edge of the tarpaulin and silently rose to

their knees. They removed their sharp bayonets from the scabbards, sliced into the fabric, and cut an opening four feet high. Separating the edges, they saw crates of food directly in front of them. All they had to do was reach in and take a crate apiece. It was too good to be true.

Gladley gingerly took down a box of Spam while Shilansky selected a crate of C rations, because crates of C rations had cigarettes inside, and everybody in the platoon needed more cigarettes. Gladley nodded to Shilansky, and they both dropped down to the ground, crawling back to the edge of the underbrush and carrying their crates at their sides so the crates wouldn't scrape along the ground and make noise.

Gladley was overjoyed. It had been so easy. He imagined a fire and his helmet full of chunks of sizzling Spam, the air redolent with succulent odors. So vivid was the fantasy that he began to drool like a child. He licked his lips as he crawled over the floor of the jungle.

Shilansky was as cold as a block of ice. He was always that way after a holdup. You couldn't relax until you had the swag in a safe place. He was a mass of coiled steel springs as he held his crate of C rations under his arm and made his way through the tangled vines and branches.

"Hey, there's somebody in those bushes over there!"

"Where?"

"There!"

Ka-pow—a bullet was fired and it whistled through the leaves near Gladley and Shilansky. They jumped to their feet, hiked the boxes of food onto their shoulders, and ran as fast as they could.

"Halt!"

Ka-pow—another bullet was fired and it whizzed past Shilansky's left ear. When he jumped up he'd seen soldiers and jeeps and tents, for he and Gladley had been right in the middle of the headquarters area.

"Halt!"

Shilansky and Gladley sped through the jungle, dodging around trees and jumping over foxholes in which soldiers looked up at them in amazement.

"Stop them!"

22

But nobody made an effort to stop them. It was obvious that they were not Japs but two GIs who'd stolen some chow, and more power to them. Some MPs from Headquarters were hot on their trail, firing bullets over their heads, but it was hard to get off clear shots because Gladley and Shilansky were fast-moving targets, and the MPs were afraid of hitting innocent bystanders.

Shilansky and Gladley hotfooted it through the jungle, kicking out their legs underneath them and glancing to their rear to see if they'd lost the MPs, but the MPs were coming on strong. Shilansky and Gladley ran around an artillery piece, jumped over a foxhole containing a fifty-millimeter-machine-gun squad, and dodged around a coconut palm tree. Finally they approached the encampment of the recon platoon and exploded into the clearing. Butsko looked up from sharpening his bayonet and realized what must be happening.

"Throw the chow in the bushes over there and keep running," he said.

Gladley and Shilansky dumped the crates off their shoulders and ran off to the left. Moments later the MPs stampeded into the clearing.

Butsko pointed with his bayonet to the right. "They went thataway!"

The MPs ran to the right, and seconds later the clearing was still. Everybody watched Butsko as he walked to the bush and pulled the crates of food out.

"Longtree, start a fire!" he said.

The jeep stopped in front of General Vandegrift's headquarters near Henderson Field, and Colonel Stockton swung his long legs to the ground. He stood, looked around, adjusted his steel helmet on his head, and marched to the front door of the fragile wooden building. He was followed by Major Cobb, his operations officer, and Lieutenant Harper, his aide.

Colonel Stockton entered the orderly room, full of Marine officers and NCOs sitting at desks. General Vandegrift was a Marine, and most of the American troops on Guadalcanal were Marines. The men of the Twenty-third had arrived to reinforce the Marines, and more Army men could be expected in the

23

weeks to come, but Guadalcanal was still predominantly a Marine operation in October of 1942.

"I have an appointment at noon with the general," Colonel Stockton told a major.

"He's expecting you, sir. Go right in."

Lieutenant Harper went first and opened the door to General Vandegrift's office. Colonel Stockton marched in and approached the general, a slope-shouldered, jowly man, who sat behind the desk.

"Colonel Stockton reporting, sir!"

General Vandegrift returned his salute. "Good to see you, Colonel. Have a seat."

"Yes, sir." Colonel Stockton held out his hand and Lieutenant Harper placed a sheaf of papers in it. "The reason I asked for this meeting, sir, is that I've developed a plan to clear the Japs out from the west bank of the Matanikau and I'd like to show it to you."

Colonel Stockton stood and spread out his maps and diagrams on General Vandegrift's desk.

"As you can see, sir," Stockton said, "my regiment is dug in on the east bank of the Matanikau, but the river turns here, and in the engagements we've had with the enemy during the past few days, some of my units have managed to push into the open jungle past the line of the river, so if I wheel to the right from the jungle, I'll be able to take the west bank of the Matanikau with a frontal assault combined with a flank attack."

General Vandegrift wrinkled his nose and nodded his head. "It might have been a good idea a few days ago, but not any longer. According to my intelligence reports, the Japs have been landing reinforcements at night, and you probably have more Japs in front of you right now than you'll be able to handle."

"The Tokyo Express," Stockton replied, referring to the nighttime convoy system used by the Japanese to reinforce its garrison on Guadalcanal. "Can't the Navy stop them?"

"They can't stop what they can't find. There's an awful lot of ocean to cover, and when it's dark you can't see very far. If we knew where they were landing, we could hit them before they got ashore, but we don't know where they're landing. We know that some of them are coming ashore between Tassafa-

24

ronga Point and Cape Esperance, which is just ahead of your sector, but that's fifteen miles of beach, all held by the enemy. Of course *we're* being reinforced too. When you get more men, then perhaps you can put your plan into operation."

Colonel Stockton looked at the map that showed the length of shoreline between Tassafaronga Point and Cape Esperance. Tassafaronga Point was about three miles from the Matanikau River. "I've got an idea," he said. "I could send my recon platoon behind enemy lines and have them scout the shoreline between Tassafaronga Point and Cape Esperance. It's very possible that they can locate the landing point of the Tokyo Express and radio the coordinates to us and the Navy, and we can hit them with artillery from the sea and land."

"I don't know," General Vandegrift said. "It'd be awfully dangerous behind enemy lines. The Japs presumably guard their landing point very carefully. How would you get your men in and how would you get them out?"

Colonel Stockton placed his fists on General Vandegrift's desk and leaned forward. "Let me work out the details of this," he said. "I'll present my complete plan to you by sixteen-hundred hours today. Would that be all right?"

"Sure," General Vandegrift replied. "If you think you could work something out, I'd be glad to see it. If it's any good, I'll give you the green light."

Colonel Stockton stood straight and tossed a salute. "See you at sixteen-hundred hours, sir."

In a small clearing deep in the jungle, several men from the recon platoon sat around a fire, roasting chunks of Spam on the end of sticks. The odor was like ham cooking, and it reminded Homer Gladley of his mother's kitchen on the family farm in Nebraska. He licked his lips as he watched the Spam sizzle on the end of his stick. If he had cloves and a piece of pineapple to put on the Spam, it would have been even better, but he was satisfied with the plain Spam. He would have been satisfied with anything edible just then.

Other men in the platoon sat or lay under trees, wolfing down the food. Some wore bandages on their faces and arms, and others had their wounds uncovered to let the air get at them. It was hot and their uniforms were plastered to their

25

bodies. Insects were everywhere, but the men were getting used to them. They didn't even bother to swat the bugs anymore.

Bannon and Frankie La Barbara sat under a tree, smoking cigarettes. They both had their helmets off and their rifles lying beside them. Frankie stared at the grass at his feet, wondering when the fighting would start again.

"You know," Frankie said, "they ought to pull us off the line after what we've been through. We need a rest."

"We're getting a rest."

"I mean someplace way behind the lines. Someplace where you don't have to worry about snipers and shit."

"There's no place on this island like that."

"Well, they should evacuate us to Hawaii for a while. Let somebody else do some fighting. We've done enough."

"Yeah, sure."

Frankie spat at the ground. "Fuck you, Bannon."

Bannon ignored him. He ran his fingers through his sandy hair and felt an insect crush between his fingers. "Shit!" he said, pulling the bug out of his hair, but some of the goo remained behind. "Son of a bitch." He wiped the stuff off his fingers.

Butsko erupted through some bushes nearby, a khaki bag slung over his shoulder. "Mail call!" he yelled.

Everybody jumped up and crowded around him, and the men who'd been cooking Spam waved their sticks in the air.

"Calm down, you fuck-ups," Butsko growled, dropping the bag on the ground and opening it up. He took out the bundle of mail and untied the string, reading the name on top. "Shilansky!"

Morris Shilansky pushed through the crowd, his big hand wide open. "Hup, Sarge!"

"Holgate!"

One by one the men pressed forward and got their mail, ripping open the envelopes, sometimes tearing the letters nearly in half in their eagerness. They dispersed throughout the clearing to read the letters, and some read them standing up next to Butsko. No one noticed that Butsko himself had not received mail.

Frankie had letters from his mother and wife, and Bannon

26

had one letter from his girl friend, Ginger Gregg. Bannon sat next to Frankie and opened the letter. It was unlined pink paper and written in Ginger's elegant handwriting. He scanned the letter quickly, gulping the basic information down, and later he'd read it over and over again, meditating on every sentence, caressing the letter in his hand as if it were Ginger herself.

It was a short letter, only one page. She said she loved him and missed him. Things were slow at the saloon where she worked because so many of the guys were in the service. Some girls were taking up the slack by working at cowboy jobs on ranches, and she was thinking of doing that. It was getting cool in Texas. She missed him especially in the mornings.

Bannon stared at the letter and thought of Ginger. He felt annoyed by what she said about missing him in the mornings. She was always horny in the mornings. He wondered if she was being faithful to him. He knew that she'd always screwed around a lot, and it would be hard for her to stop, but on the other hand he believed that she loved him. Maybe she thought she could screw some 4-F and it wouldn't really matter, but it would to him. He couldn't bare the thought of her sleeping with somebody else. It made him physically ill.

"Get bad news?" Frankie asked.

"Naw, I'm all right."

"You don't look all right."

Bannon punched the palm of his hand. "I'm sure that little bitch is fucking around on me."

"Well, from what you told me about her, I wouldn't be surprised."

Bannon's eyes bulged out of his head. "What do you mean by that?"

Frankie smiled. "Hey, take it easy."

"I said what do you mean by that?"

"Well, women like to fuck. You know that. You think you got troubles? My little baby hasn't even written to me, and I can just imagine what she's doing. I'll break her fucking legs when I get back to New York."

"Yeah, but it's different with you, Frankie. You're married."

"So what?"

"How do you expect your girl friend to be faithful when you've got a wife?"

"Are you kidding—after all I've given that little bitch?"

"Yeah, but there's one thing you can't give her."

Frankie thought of his girl friend, Cindy, who was a Radio City Music Hall Rockette. She was the best fuck of his life, and he believed that was because she was a dancer and she knew more about how to move.

"I'll kill her," Frankie muttered.

"Calm down."

"I am calm. You calm down."

"I'm calmed down."

But Bannon wasn't calm. He felt like jumping out of his skin. Getting up, he put on his helmet and slung his rifle over his shoulder.

"Where you going?" Frankie asked.

"I'm not going anywhere."

"You look like you're going someplace."

Bannon walked away aimlessly. He glanced around at the men in his platoon and they looked like they were from another planet. *What the hell am I doing here?* he wondered. *I had a life once, and now all I got is this fucking war.* He reared back his foot and kicked an empty can of Spam halfway across the clearing. Butsko, who'd been napping under a bush, opened one eye.

"Siddown, Bannon," he snarled, "before I knock you down."

Bannon found a quiet spot away from everybody else and sat down. *I can't take this shit much longer,* he thought.

"Hiya, guys!"

Everybody turned around and saw Jimmy O'Rourke walk into the clearing. A short, powerfully built man, he had been shot in the arm by a sniper during their first few hours on Guadalcanal. Before joining the Army, he had been a stuntman in Hollywood.

"Who do I report to?" O'Rourke asked.

"Butsko," somebody said.

"Where's he at?"

Butsko pushed himself to a sitting position. "Who wants to know?" He didn't know O'Rourke, because O'Rourke had been wounded before Butsko took over the platoon.

28

O'Rourke walked toward Butsko. "Private Jimmy O'Rourke, Sarge. They just released me from the hospital."

"What happened to you?"

"I got shot."

"You look awfully good for somebody who got shot."

"The bullet didn't hit anything. My shoulder's still fucked up, but they sent me back anyway."

"Can you fire a rifle?"

"Yup."

"What do you mean, *'Yup'*?"

"Yes, Sergeant, I can fire a rifle."

"That's all you have to do around here. Get yourself something to eat. You do as you're told and you'll be all right. If you don't, I'll kick your ass. Got the picture?"

"I got the picture, Sarge."

"Take a walk."

"Hup, Sarge."

O'Rourke wasn't hungry, because he'd eaten just before leaving the hospital. He'd expected everybody to celebrate when he returned to the platoon, but nobody seemed to give a shit, and that disheartened him. His eyes fell on Craig Delane, the rich guy from New York. Delane was O'Rourke's favorite person in the platoon, because he thought Delane was the only one with any class, and more than anything else, except a desire to survive the war, he wanted to have class. He sat down next to Delane.

"Hi, Craig," he said.

Delane despised O'Rourke and just about everybody else in the platoon, but he was nice to everybody because he didn't want any trouble.

"Hello, there," Delane replied in his patrician New York accent. "How do you feel, old man?"

"Pretty good. My shoulder still hurts but it's not so bad. Where'd that sergeant come from? He looks like Frankenstein's big brother."

Delane lowered his voice. "He's tough. Watch out for him. If you do something wrong, he'll punch you right in the nose."

"He can't do that!" O'Rourke said. "Sergeants aren't supposed to hit privates."

"Well, he does."

"Why don't you guys report him?"

"You try it sometime and see what happens to you."

O'Rourke sniffed. "Maybe I will. I don't take no shit from anybody—you know me."

"Yes, I know you, O'Rourke."

"I heard you guys have had a lot of hard fighting since I've been gone."

Delane nodded. "Yes, we have."

"Everybody in the hospital was talking about you guys. In a way I'm sorry I missed all the fun."

"It wasn't fun," Delane replied.

O'Rourke stared into Delane's face, and now for the first time realized that Delane looked different. Delane had become older somehow, and his eyes had dark pouches underneath them. Delane had lost weight also.

"Gee," O'Rourke said, "things sure seem different around here."

"Yes, they're different all right. Did you see Longtree at the hospital?"

"No. Was he hit?"

"Yes. In the stomach. It was pretty bad."

"My God. Anybody else?"

"Jonesy got it too."

"He dead?"

"I don't think so. How come you didn't see them in the hospital?"

"Well, you know it wasn't like a regular hospital. Some of us were in tents and some of us were lying on the ground. An awful lot of men got wounded. They're dying like flies. I was lucky. I wasn't hurt that bad and I got a Purple Heart."

Delane said nothing.

"Gee," O'Rourke said, "You sound like you're a little down in the dumps, Delane. Cheer up, it's not so bad. We'll get through this, me and you, somehow."

"Don't be an ass," Delane snapped. "If you'd seen what I've seen, you'd know that most of us will never leave this island alive."

"Shit," O'Rourke said, "you think like that and it'll happen to you. You got to start thinking positively."

"I'm a little tired. I think I'm going to lie down."

Delane reclined on the grass and closed his eyes. He really wasn't very tired, but he didn't feel like talking with O'Rourke. Before, he'd been able to tolerate O'Rourke, but now he didn't have the patience. *I'm sick of all these people,* Delane thought, *and I'll never get off this island alive anyway, so what's the point of trying to be nice to them?*

FOUR . . .

Seven miles from the Twenty-third's encampment, nestled in a wooded valley, General Hyakutake, the commander of all Japanese forces on the island, sat behind the desk in his tent, sipping sake from a tiny cup.

Opposite him, sitting ramrod-straight on a folding wooden chair, was Colonel Tsuji, Hyakutake's chief of operations. Tsuji had planned the series of Japanese attacks three days earlier that had resulted in serious setbacks for the Imperial Army.

"The situation is not good," General Hyakutake said grumpily. "If the Americans attack, I don't know how we can hold them off."

"They won't attack," Tsuji said, trying to imbue his voice with confidence. He was a slender man with a Fu Manchu mustache and had been nicknamed "God of Operations" for his brilliant staff work in the battle for Malaya, but his reputation had become tarnished on Guadalcanal. "They're still licking their wounds from the battle three days ago."

"So are we. We must hope that the Americans don't try anything ambitious before we build up our strength. I shudder to think of what would happen if the Americans attacked tomorrow morning."

"They won't get far, because the jungle will stop them. The terrain is on our side."

"How many men did you say arrived last night?"

"Five hundred, sir."

"And we're expecting five hundred more tonight?"

"Yes, sir. Plus ammunitions and supplies."

General Hyakutake leaned forward. "Tsuji, it is absolutely imperative that there be no interruption in these resupply operations."

"There will be no interruption, sir. The men and supplies land at night. The enemy can't see them."

"I've been worried about spies, Tsuji."

"Spies, sir?"

"Yes. Spies."

"What spies, sir?"

General Hyakutake narrowed his eyes. "Tsuji, we can assume that the Americans know that we're being resupplied, can't we?"

"Yes, sir."

"If you were an American, wouldn't you try to do something about it?"

"Yes, sir, but the Americans are not an intelligent people. We can't assume that they analyze situations as clearly as we do."

"Maybe not, Tsuji, but I don't want to take any chances. There are natives in these jungles who may report to the Americans. We know there are Australian spies on all these islands. And perhaps Americans might have infiltrated our lines just as we infiltrate theirs."

"What do you suggest I do, sir?"

"Organize a force that will make certain our landing area remains secure. If there are any natives in the vicinity, evict them. Comb the jungle ceaselessly for Australian spies and American patrols. Make sure there are enough men in the force to repulse any attack the Americans might launch against our landing area from inland. Take care of this at once."

"Yes, sir."

Butsko came out of the jungle, appearing more like an animal than a man. He was grizzled, filthy, and smelly. Guards at regimental headquarters didn't know what to make of him,

33

because he looked so unsoldierly, yet he was a hero in the regiment and his platoon often was referred to as the Rat Bastards because they had killed so many Japs on Guadalcanal.

Butsko ascended the steps to the wooden building and threw a snappy salute to some officers standing near the doorway. He entered the orderly room, his carbine slung barrel down on his shoulder, and approached Sergeant Major Edwin Ramsay from Scotch Plains, New Jersey.

"Hello, Sergeant," Butsko said.

"Hello, Butsko. How's it going?"

"Can't complain. The old man wants to see me?"

"Go right in."

Butsko opened the door and entered Colonel Stockton's office. Colonel Stockton sat behind his desk, shuffling papers. He looked up and smiled. "Hello, Sergeant Butsko."

Butsko was unnerved by this friendly greeting. According to military protocol, he was supposed to advance to the desk and report, but now he didn't know what to do.

"Have a seat, Butsko."

"Yes, sir."

"I'll be with you in just a moment."

Colonel Stockton puffed his pipe and continued to peruse the papers on his desk. Butsko never had been in a situation where his immediate superior was a colonel, and he still was trying to adjust to it. Somehow it didn't seem right, but he knew Colonel Stockton liked him, and he liked Colonel Stockton in return. They were two career soldiers and they understood each other.

Finally Colonel Stockton looked up from his desk. "I've got some work for you, Butsko. I want to send the recon platoon behind enemy lines to find out where the Tokyo Express is coming in. Come behind my desk here."

Butsko arose and lumbered behind Colonel Stockton's desk, where he looked down at a map of Guadalcanal.

"The Tokyo Express," Colonel Stockton continued, "is landing somewhere between here and here"—he pointed to the stretch of beach between Tassafaronga Point and Cape Esperance—"and they've got to be stopped. We can't stop them because we don't know where they're coming in. I want you to locate their debarkation point and radio it in to us. Got that so far?"

Butsko turned down the corners of his mouth. "That's an awful lot of beach to cover."

"Break up your platoon into its four squads. Each squad will have three or four miles of beach to cover. That shouldn't be too much. The Navy will be ready to strike as soon as you leave. When you tell them where to go, they'll get there fast and wipe out whatever they can find. Think you can handle it?"

Butsko looked down at the map. "Yeah, I think I can handle it."

"Your men have never done anything like this before. You think *they'll* be up to it?"

Butsko shrugged. "They'll be up to it as much as anybody else in the regiment."

"Have a seat, Butsko."

"Yes, sir."

Butsko ambled around the desk and returned to his chair. He was surprised that the colonel didn't have a picture of his wife on his desk. He didn't know that Colonel Stockton's wife had run off with a young captain years earlier.

"There's something I have to talk with you about, Butsko," Colonel Stockton said. "I've been under pressure lately to put an officer in charge of the recon platoon. What do you think about that?"

Butsko frowned. "We don't need no officer."

"Are you sure?"

"Yes, sir. He'd only get in the way."

Colonel Stockton smiled. "Do you feel that way about all officers?"

"No, sir. Officers have their place in the Army. But in the recon platoon—we just don't need one."

"I don't know whether you need one or not, but to tell you the truth, I don't think there's an officer in the regiment who could handle the recon platoon."

Butsko grinned. "I agree with you there, sir."

"Well, results are what counts in this man's Army. If you can perform this mission effectively, I'll be able to keep your platoon just the way it is, but if you don't, I'm afraid I'll have no choice but to assign you an officer."

Butsko nodded. "Whatever you say, sir."

"When will you and your men be ready to leave on this mission?"

"We can go right now, sir."

"Good. Plans are being made for your jump off at oh-one-hundred hours. You'll travel by submarine into Japanese waters, and the sub will leave your men off at four separate spots along the Japanese shoreline. Each squad will carry a field radio for contact with my headquarters here. You'll take enough food with you for a week, when you'll be picked up by the PT boats again at night. Any questions so far?"

"What about ammo, sir?"

"I didn't think you'd need much because you should avoid contact with the enemy."

"Yes, sir, but they might make contact with us. I wonder if we could be issued them nice Thompson submachine guns. They're small and light but they put out a lotta firepower, and we'll need a lotta firepower if we ever run into Japs."

"All right," Colonel Stockton said. "I'll see to it that you get submachine guns. Anything else?"

"Not just yet, but if I think of anything else, I'll tell you."

"I'm sure you will, Sergeant Butsko. Come look at this map again, because I want to go over everything with you in detail."

Colonel Stockton pointed to the map and began explaining the operation in detail, and Butsko bent over the desk, listening carefully and taking notes in his dog-eared notepad. The discussion was all business; both men were pros at war. Butsko's questions were sensible and his suggestions pertinent. Colonel Stockton felt confident about the operation. If anybody could find the Tokyo Express, it was his recon platoon.

The sun was sinking behind the horizon on Guadalcanal. In the field hospital Pfc. Sam Longtree, the full-blooded Apache Indian, lay on his cot with his eyes closed, but he was not asleep. He was formulating a plan to escape from the hospital.

He'd been there for nearly four days because a Jap had stabbed him in the stomach with a bayonet. Upon arriving at the hospital, Longtree had lain outdoors for a couple of hours, feeling no pain because he'd been shot full of morphine by the medics. Then they'd operated on him, cleaned out his wound, and sewed him back together again. Since then he'd been on this cot, getting medicine and feeling restless. It was dishonorable for an Indian warrior to be on his back for so long while a war was taking place. Since his youth he'd heard the old men talk about warriors who'd gone on fighting although they were seriously wounded, and those same old men would spit contemptuously into their campfires if they knew that he, the son of a chief and the grandson of the great Mangus, was lying in bed like an old woman while his friends were fighting hard.

Longtree didn't think he was hurt that badly. He was a big rough Indian and since youth he'd been taught to disregard pain. That afternoon he'd gotten up and walked around, and he'd felt all right, but an orderly had caught him and sent him back to bed. A little pimply faced medic in a white jacket. What did he know of the warrior's way?

Longtree listened around him, and all was quiet except for snores and the occasional mumbling of soldiers shot full of drugs. Longtree thought the hospital was an evil place and that the doctors were full of shit. Back in Arizona the medicine man would have put some leaves on his stomach and said some prayers and he would have been all right. Longtree missed being with his people and his young wife, but also, very strangely, he missed the white eyes in his platoon. They were his fellow warriors and he had come to love them. He thought them very fine warriors, even though they were white eyes, but it was well known among his people that the white eyes could produce great warriors too. He especially liked Corporal Bannon, who was from Texas, his part of the world. Corporal Bannon was an exceptionally fine warrior, very brave, a dead shot with a rifle, and Bannon appreciated Longtree's skills at fighting and reading the ground. And Sergeant Butsko was surely a great warrior, capable of much cruelty, but very fair. Longtree also loved Frankie La Barbara, who was clearly a maniac, but maniacs were considered magical people by the Apaches.

Longtree had never told Bannon, Butsko, or Frankie La Barbara what he thought of them, because warriors do not speak of such things. Great warriors show nothing but a fierce face. Longtree missed his fellow warriors and was determined to get back with them by hook or by crook.

Longtree pulled the sheet off himself silently and sat up in bed. He focused on his ears, listening for the sound of footsteps, and then felt light-headed and dizzy, but he shrugged that off because he knew that as soon as he moved around and got some energy his strength would return. He heard no footsteps or anything suspicious. The hospital was not guarded, because soldiers were needed in the trenches. Wearing only his shorts, he stood up. His belly was stiched horizontally and ached somewhat, but he willed himself to overcome the pain. Stealthily he moved toward the door of the big walled tent.

He pushed aside the flap and looked outside. The full moon was shining brightly and stars twinkled in the sky. He saw medics and soldiers moving around the other tents, but other than that the coast looked clear. Stepping out into the moonlit night, he tiptoed through the hospital compound, looking for a solitary soldier wearing a uniform that would fit him. The moonlight shined on his straight black hair as he crossed some open space and plunged into the shadows at its far side. Crouching, he looked around for a uniform.

There were no GIs around the part of the hospital compound where he was hiding. He thought of moving into the jungle and finding a lone soldier in his foxhole, punching him out and stealing his clothes, but it occurred to Longtree that a trigger-happy GI might shoot him, so that wasn't a good idea. Then he remembered the hospital admitting area. There were lots of GIs milling around there and lying on the ground, awaiting treatment. That would be a good place to get a uniform.

Longtree slunk in that direction, pushing branches and leaves out of his way with his long fingers, ducking and dodging as he moved through the dense foliage. His route was long and circuitous, because he didn't dare show himself, and finally, after fifteen minutes of slow progress, he arrived in the bushes next to the admitting area.

He peered through the brush and saw soldiers out on the ground. There were so many of them that some lay in shadows, and he thought he could get their clothes unseen, because his

38

skin was dark and would blend in with the night. He wore khaki undershorts that also would provide camouflage.

He spotted a GI lying in the shadows. The GI appeared to be out cold, and he was wearing his cartridge belt with bayonet, canteen, and first-aid pouch. Longtree thought he could get that man's clothes. He looked like a big fellow. The clothes probably would fit.

Longtree crept toward him, not making a sound, even making his breath shallow so no one would hear the passage of air between his teeth. A medic entered the area, stepped over some men, and left. Farther away, a soldier on a cot was being carried into the operating tent.

Longtree moved forward again and, after several minutes, found himself in the bush next to the wounded man he'd selected. The man had a big bandage on his head and appeared to be out cold. He reached out of the bush and felt the man's pulse. There was no pulse. He was dead.

With a shrug Longtree grabbed the dead soldier's combat boots and dragged him into the bush. He was a stout old soldier with the stripes of a tech sergeant on his arm. Longtree untied the dead soldier's boots and pulled them off, then quickly undressed him. The boots were small, but Longtree didn't need boots, because he could walk barefoot at night and no one would know the difference. The man's shirt had been bloodied from his wound, but that didn't bother Longtree; he put it on and buttoned it up. He pulled on the soldier's pants and fastened the cartridge belt around his waist. Now he felt like a warrior again. The soldier's helmet lay beside the stretcher, and Longtree crawled out to get it and put it on. Then he stood, squared his shoulders and walked away. He didn't even look back at the hospital compound. It was an evil place and he wanted no part of it.

A lively crap game was taking place in the recon platoon area. A blanket had been laid on the ground and Frankie La Barbara held the dice in his hands, rubbing his palms together, trying to heat them up. None of the men had any money and they were playing for payday stakes, using pieces of paper to represent dollar bills.

Frankie took the dice in his right hand and shook them next to his ear. "Let's go, you little hot babies," he said, "Daddy needs a new pair of shoes. How much is four and three, dice?"

He tossed the dice onto the blanket and they rolled in the moonlight as the gathering of soldiers watched them intently, hoping they'd come up snake eyes. The dice stopped and showed five and three.

"Eight's my point!" Frankie La Barbara shouted, scooping up the dice and shaking them next to his ear. "Eight, don't be late," he begged. "Eight me, don't hate me. Eight, rate, kiss me Kate!"

He threw the dice and they came up with a six and a four.

"Fuck!" said Frankie, picking them up again.

"I bet he makes it," said Napoleon Denker from the Second Squad, who thought Frankie was lucky and decided to bet on him.

"Put your money where your mouth is," replied Tommy Shaw, also from the Second Squad.

They both threw their bits of paper to the ground. Frankie chewed gum frantically and shook the dice again. "Eight, be my fate," he said. "Eight, clean my slate. Eight, be my date. Eight, fill my crate."

"So throw the dice already," grumbled Morris Shilansky, who wore a clumsy bandage on his broken nose.

Frankie tossed the dice again, and his eyes goggled as he watched them roll across the blanket. They came up a two and a one.

"Shit!" said Frankie.

"You lose!" said Tommy Shaw to Napoleon Denker.

"Whataya mean I lose!" replied Denker. "I didn't lose. He didn't crap out yet."

"But he didn't make his point on that throw."

"I wasn't betting on that throw. I'm betting on him as long as he's got the dice."

"You didn't say that."

"You didn't say anything about it either."

Tommy Shaw had been a professional boxer before he joined the Army, and he didn't take any shit from anybody. "I don't give a fuck what you say, asshole, I won and I'm taking my dough."

"Like shit you are."

Shaw grabbed for the pieces of white paper, and Denker jumped on him, catching him by the neck. Shaw elbowed Denker in the jaw, but Denker refused to loosen his grip, so Shaw threw an uppercut, one of his favorite punches, and it connected with the tip of Denker's jaw. Denker went flying straight up in the air like a rocket and then fell to earth again, flat on his back.

"Jesus Christ," Frankie complained, "you can't even have a little crap game around here without somebody going nuts! This isn't a fucking rifle platoon! This is a fucking looney bin! I'm sick of this platoon! I wanna be in a platoon full of normal people! I wanna be in a platoon where you can have a decent crap game so's I can take my mind *off this fucking war!*"

"Shut up, Frankie, and throw the dice," Bannon said.

Frankie glowered at him. "Who are you telling to shut up, hillbilly!"

Bannon sighed, because he knew he was about to get into it again with Frankie La Barbara. "You."

"Oh, yeah?"

"Yeah."

The thunderous voice of Butsko came rolling across the platoon area. "Knock it off over there!" Butsko stomped toward them, his face a mask of fury. "Jesus Christ, I can't even leave you guys alone for a minute without some shit starting up! You're like a bunch of fucking kids." He looked at Napoleon Denker lying out cold on the ground. "What happened to him?"

Everybody looked away guiltily. Nobody said anything.

"I just asked a question!" Butsko roared.

Frankie held out the palms of his hands and smiled. "Well, you see, Sarge, Denker just fainted."

"Fainted!"

"Yeah, he just lost a big pot and he fainted."

Butsko's foot lashed through the air, but Frankie dodged to the side as Butsko's size-twelve boot whistled past his ear. Frankie jumped back to get out of range.

"Jesus," Butsko said wearily, "I don't know what I'm gonna do with you guys. You're the worst bunch of fuck-ups I ever saw in my life."

"Halt—who goes there!"

"Now what?" Butsko asked.

A sentry was challenging somebody on the platoon's perimeter. Everybody turned in that direction.

"Pfc. Longtree," said a voice in the jungle.

"Advance to be recognized!"

The bushes rustled and Pfc. Longtree materialized, barefoot and in pants that were too short.

Butsko stared at him in disbelief. "What are you doing here! I thought you were dead!"

"I ain't dead," Longtree replied. "At least I don't think I'm dead. I'm reporting for duty, Sarge."

"Where're your fucking boots."

"I ain't got no boots."

"What happened to them."

"I lost 'em someplace."

Butsko looked Longtree up and down and wrinkled his brow. Longtree's uniform clearly didn't fit him, he had no boots, and he wore tech sergeant's strips on his shoulder. Something fishy was going on.

"Where's your orders?" Butsko asked.

"I ain't got no orders, Sarge."

"What happened to them?"

Longtree looked up at the sky in the hope that the Great Spirit would help him. "I never got any orders."

"You mean you're AWOL?"

"Uh-huh." Longtree grinned in an effort to charm his platoon sergeant.

Butsko tore off his own helmet and threw it on the ground. "I can't take you guys anymore!" he screamed. "Every time I look around, you're doing something wrong? You're wearing me out! You're making an old man of me before my time!"

Frankie La Barbara stepped forward. "Take it easy, Sarge. You're liable to blow a gasket."

Red-faced, Butsko turned toward Frankie. *"Don't you tell me what to do!"*

"Sorry, Sarge."

Butsko faced Longtree and pointed at him. "I oughta call the MPs on you."

"Aw, don't do that to me, Sarge," Longtree said.

"Sarge," said Bannon in his slow Texas drawl, "he's the best scout in the platoon."

"Huh? What you say?"

"He's the best scout in the platoon."

Butsko remembered that Longtree was indeed the best scout in the platoon and that he'd be useful in the mission behind enemy lines. In fact he'd be more than useful. He'd be indispensable.

Butsko sighed. "He's in your squad, Bannon. Get him a pair of boots and if he doesn't have those phony stripes off his uniform in one hour, I'm gonna take his fucking Indian head off. Got it?"

"Hup, Sarge," Bannon said, still talking softly. "What'll we do about his orders?"

"I don't know. I'll have to talk to the colonel about it. Right now I have more important things to think about. We're going on a trip tonight."

"A trip?" Frankie La Barbara asked excitedly. "You mean they're sending us back to Australia?"

"No, you asshole, they're sending us behind enemy lines to get some information and maybe get our asses shot off. Strike the tents and prepare to move out. I want a meeting of all my squad leaders in frunna my tent right now. Let's go—move it out!"

Colonel Tsuji sat on a pillow in his tent, trying to meditate in front of a photograph of Emperor, but he wasn't getting very far. He was unable to drag his mind off the ignominious events that had taken place three nights earlier, when all his carefully made plans produced a crushing defeat and humiliating retreat for three Japanese regiments on Guadalcanal.

Until three nights earlier, Tsuji had believed that he was indeed "God of Operations," but now his confidence in himself was badly shaken. Never had his plans resulted in such a catastrophe. In order to avoid anything like it happening again, he would have to calm and strengthen his mind through meditation. But he couldn't meditate because he kept thinking of that disastrous night. What had gone wrong?

Tsuji couldn't sit still anymore. He stood, took a pack of

43

cigarettes off his desk, and lit one up. Then he paced back and forth, trying to find the flaw in his plans. The key blow was to have been struck against a green American regiment that had come up on the line that day, but somehow the green Americans not only held, but they actually advanced several hundred yards into Japanese territory. It was possible that there were more American soldiers than a regiment. Perhaps the intelligence was wrong. If so, that would explain everything. *Yes,* Tsuji thought, *it is absolutely necessary to have reliable intelligence.*

Sergeant Kaburagi drew aside the flap in the section of the large tent where Colonel Tsuji had his office. "Sir?"

"What is it?"

"Captain Mizushima is here to see you."

"Send him in."

"Yes, sir."

Sergeant Kaburagi stepped out of the way, and seconds later a short, molelike officer with a dark complexion appeared in the passageway. He wore a mustache and was bowlegged. Colonel Tsuji didn't like the look of him.

Captain Mizushima marched to Tsuji's desk and saluted. "Captain Mizushima reporting, sir!"

"Sit down."

"Yes, sir."

Captain Mizushima sat on the chair in front of Colonel Tsuji's desk, who sat behind his desk, shuffling papers and looking for Mizushima's personnel file. He found the file and glanced over it again while Mizushima sat at attention before him. Tsuji made no effort to put Mizushima at ease.

On paper Mizushima looked very good. He had fought as a young lieutenant in the Philippines and had distinguished himself in combat on numerous occasions. He was said to be intelligent, in possession of a fine analytical mind, and was utterly fearless. He had arrived in Guadalcanal only two nights before and was awaiting assignment when his folder had been pulled for the job Tsuji was going to assign him.

"Well, Mizushima," Tsuji said, "I see you've had experience fighting the Americans before."

"Yes, sir."

44

"How did you find them?"

"They could not stand up to us, sir. They abandoned most of the island of Luzon shortly after we landed in the Philippines and holed up like rats in Corregidor. Then their great General MacArthur left them. It was most dishonorable. It is hard for me to feel much respect for the Americans. They're even worse than the Chinese, if you can imagine that."

"It's difficult to imagine anything worse than the Chinese," Tsuji said, "but the Americans have been giving us a surprising amount of trouble here on Guadalcanal, although I suspect most of the trouble is the fault of our own shoddy intelligence work."

Captain Mizushima raised his eyebrows. "The trouble could not have been the fighting ability of the Americans, because they have none. You should have seen how docile they were when we marched the American prisoners to the prison camp we had in northern Luzon. They were like cattle. Many didn't even have the strength to complete the march. We had to shoot them like dogs alongside the road. It was a very nasty business. As I said, it's very hard for me to have much respect for American soldiers."

"Hmmm. Yes." Tsuji raised his handkerchief and wiped perspiration from his brow. "Well, we've selected you for a special mission, Captain Mizushima."

"Yes?" Captain Mizushima said, his tiny eyes bright with anticipation. "What is it?"

"Basically it will be patrol duty."

Mizushima's eyes became dull. "Patrol duty, sir? I had thought that I would be assigned to command an assault company."

"This assignment is far more important, Mizushima. We assign ordinary captains to assault companies as a matter of course, but to an officer like you we give the more critical assignments."

Mizushima's eyes lit up again. "Yes, sir. What is this patrol duty?"

"Come over here to the map."

Both men stood and approached the map of Guadalcanal that hung on the wall. Mizushima came up to Tsuji's chest, but he was sturdily built, like the trunk of a tree. Tsuji felt a personal distaste for the man, but evidently he was a good officer, and one mustn't let personal considerations overrule military necessity.

Tsuji stopped beside the map, held his hands behind his back, and addressed Mizushima. "As you know, we receive our supplies here at night, because the waters around the island aren't very safe during the day. You yourself came here at night, so you know what I'm talking about. Our nighttime resupply system is our lifeline, and we cannot permit it to be interrupted under any circumstances. Right now we are trying to build up our forces here so that we can mount major operations against the Americans, and General Hyakutake is concerned that the Americans might take action to interdict our supply system. We must assume that they know we receive our supplies and replacements at night, and we can further assume that they'd give anything to know where we unload, so they could strike us there from the sea. Therefore, General Hyakutake believes the Americans might have spies working behind our lines to determine where our unloading sites are. He's concerned about native spies, Australian observers, and American patrols. Your mission will be to lead a company of men back and forth across our coastline and keep it clear of the enemy. The men who will compose your company have been selected already and are awaiting your orders. We want you to leave with them tonight and begin patrolling this area. We will give you enough supplies for a week and resupply you as needed. Any questions?"

"What should I do if I find spies?"

"Bring them here for questioning if you can. We need better intelligence concerning the Americans, and the best way to get it is from the mouths of the Americans themselves."

Captain Mizushima stiffened and held his hands straight at his sides. "If they are out there, we shall get them, sir."

"Very good. Do you have any more questions?"

"No, sir."

"Sergeant Kaburagi will take you to your company. Good luck, Captain Mizushima."

"Thank you, sir!"

Both men saluted each other. Captain Mizushima turned and marched out of Colonel Tsuji's office. Colonel Tsuji returned to his desk and lit another cigarette. He thought Captain Mizushima hideously ugly, but he'd seemed to be a capable, straightforward officer. Colonel Tsuji was confident that if American spies were in the landing areas, Captain Mizushima could be relied upon to find them.

FIVE . . .

The recon platoon struck their tents and packed their bags, then had chow with the rest of Headquarters Company. After chow they went to Supply for the Thompson submachine guns, ammunition and hand grenades. Each squad was issued one SCR-300 backpack radio. Finally the platoon was issued seven days of C and K rations, plus bottles of little pills to purify water for drinking.

The recon platoon marched in a column of twos across Henderson Field to Lunga Point, where they'd arrived in Guadalcanal. Lunga Point was the debarkation spot for supply and troop ships, and the beach was covered with stacks of crates waiting to be hauled into the interior. Butsko told his men to take a break, and they sprawled out everywhere, trying to catch a few winks of sleep before the submarine arrived.

Butsko sat by himself and rested his back against a pile of crates. He looked at his watch; it was 2100 hours. The submarine would arrive in three hours to take them away. It didn't disturb Butsko to be so early. When you got to your jump-off point early, you didn't have to worry about arriving on time. The men could use the time to rest. They probably wouldn't get much rest for the remainder of the night.

Butsko took out a Camel and lit it up. Puffing, he thought about the mission that lay ahead. He'd reorganized the platoon so that each squad would have a nearly equal number of men. He'd decided that he would travel with the second squad.

The men alternately smoked cigarettes and dozed as they waited for the submarine to arrive. Bannon lay on his back and stared at the stars in the heavens above. Next to him sat Craig Delane, the SCR-300 radio on his back. Bannon had assigned Delane the radio, and Delane wasn't happy about it, because he thought the job was beneath him. He felt like a coolie.

Not far away Frankie La Barbara chatted with Tommy Shaw, the heavyweight boxer, who had been assigned to the first squad as part of Butsko's reorganization. Frankie and Tommy Shaw found that they had a lot to talk about because Shaw had lived in New York periodically and had fought in Madison Square Garden and St. Nicholas Arena.

"If I hadn't been drafted, I woulda had a shot at the title," Shaw said. "Believe it or not, I was ranked number sixteen in the world by *Ring* magazine when I was drafted, and in a couple more fights I woulda landed in the top ten." Shaw held his big right fist in the air. "I was on my way to the championship, and the Japs spoiled it all for me."

"You think you coulda taken Joe Louis?"

"I don't know," Shaw said thoughtfully, "but after three or four more fights I woulda give him a run for his money. One punch can change a whole fight around, you know. And Joe Louis can be hit. Max Schmeling knocked him out. If I coulda got a clear shot at him I woulda knocked him right on his ass."

"How many knockouts you got, Shaw?"

"Twenty-eight out of thirty-seven wins."

"How many losses."

"Nine," Shaw said in a low voice, "and one draw." His voice grew louder. "But those fights were all at the beginning of my career. I didn't learn how to fight as an amateur; I learned as a professional. I won my last six fights in a row, all by knockouts."

"Shit," Frankie said, "when we get outta this fucking Army, maybe I could be your manager. I know people who're very big in the fight game. I'll bet I can get you a title shot. You might have to lay down someplace first where it don't matter, but then you'd get your shot."

49

"What do you mean, 'lay down'?"

"You know, take a fall."

"You mean throw a fight?"

Frankie shrugged. "Yeah."

Shaw pulled his chin in to his chest. "I ain't throwin' no fight!"

"Why not?"

"Because I ain't!"

"Then how do you expect a title shot?"

"By beating everybody I go into the ring with!"

Frankie chuckled. "I can see that you don't know how the boxing game works. You see, there are certain guys who control the whole . . ."

Butsko's booming voice interrupted him. *"Keep your voice down, La Barbara, or I'll put my boot right down your throat!"*

"Hup, Sarge." Frankie looked sheepish and wiped his nose with the back of his hand. "Jeez, I can't get over that guy," he whispered. "He used to work in a factory before he joined the Army, and now he can tell a guy like me what to do."

Shaw had narrow suspicious eyes and a lantern jaw. "Were you in the rackets before you got drafted, Frankie?" he said in a low voice.

Frankie winked. "You're fucking A."

"The Italian mob."

"Right."

Shaw thought for a few moments. "Well, maybe I'll look you up when I get out, Frankie."

"Just ask for me down in Little Italy. They all know me down there. Even the cops who walk the beats know me." Frankie smiled and placed his hand on the boxer's shoulder. "You stick with me, Shaw, and I'll take you all the way to the top."

Frankie took the butt of his cigarette out of his mouth and snuffed it out in the sand. Then he field-stripped it, ripping off the paper and scattering the tiny crumbs of tobacco to the wind. Working the bit of white cigarette paper into a tiny ball between his fingers, he tossed it over his shoulder and wondered how much of a percentage a manager takes out of a fighter. Was it ten, twenty, or fifty percent? He didn't want to ask Shaw

50

because he didn't want Shaw to know that he didn't know. But surely there must be a lot of money in being the manager of the heavyweight champion of the world.

Frankie looked at Shaw, who was muscular, tall, and had big hands. *Jesus, maybe he can beat Joe Louis,* Frankie thought.

The waves crashed monotonously on the shore and the men slept fitfully, muttering and jerking on the sand or laying still with their mouths open as if they were dead. Butsko pored over his maps, trying to memorize principal terrain features between Tassafaronga Point and Cape Esperance and working out contingency plans in case something went wrong.

At thirty minutes after midnight Butsko heard a commotion out on the water and looked up to see the faint outline of a submarine. He hadn't seen it surface, and now its crew was running around on the deck, preparing to launch rubber boats.

Butsko stood and strapped on his full field pack. *"All right, you guys!"* he yelled. *"Up and at 'em!"*

The men groaned and rolled over, disheartened to see they were waking up on the beach in Guadalcanal and not at home with their wives or girl friends. They grumbled and burped, assembling their equipment and watching four rafts being rowed to shore by sailors.

"Bannon!" Butsko roared. "Get your men ready! You'll go first! McCabe, if there's room, your men will go on this trip too!"

Bannon moved the First Squad down to the beach, and Sergeant McCabe assembled the second squad nearby. A breeze was blowing and the boats approached shore on wide, rolling swells. Bannon peered at the submarine in the distance, sitting in the water like a long deadly stiletto.

The rubber boats neared shore and sailors in dark uniforms jumped out and dragged them up on the wet sand. A young man wearing a dark officer's cap jumped off one of the rubber boats and looked around. "Who's the officer in charge here?" he asked.

Butsko stepped forward. "I'm in charge here, but I ain't no officer."

The young officer was surprised that Butsko didn't salute

him. "I understood there was to be an officer in charge of the men coming aboard."

"You understood wrong," Butsko told.

Frankie muttered under his breath, "The situation is normal: Everything's fucked up."

"Shaddup, La Barbara!"

Frankie closed his mouth. Butsko looked at the young officer. "Well, what are we waiting for?"

The young officer took a document out of his shirt pocket and unfolded it. "Is this the reconnaissance platoon of the Twenty-third Regiment?"

"It is," Butsko said.

"Isn't there a Captain Butsko here?"

Frankie laughed like a hyena.

"Shaddup, La Barbara!"

Frankie put his hand over his mouth.

"It's supposed to be *Sergeant* Butsko," Butsko told the young officer, "and that's me. Who're you?"

"Ensign Collins."

"Let's get on with it, Ensign Collins. The sooner we get moving the sooner we'll get done."

"Right," said Ensign Collins. "Load your men into the boats, Sergeant Butsko. It looks like we'll have to make two trips."

"Right."

The first two squads climbed into the rubber boats and sat down. Each boat had a crew of two sailors with oars, and the GIs looked them over curiously. Bannon remembered landing here at Lunga Point four days before. It had been the worst day of his life, but that night had been even worse than the day.

"Everybody okay?" asked Ensign Collins.

Nobody said anything.

Collins jumped into the boat with the First Squad. "Who's in charge here?"

"I am," said Bannon.

"Your name?"

"Corporal Bannon."

"Shove off," said Ensign Collins.

The sailors pushed off with their oars, and the rubber boats rode over the swells. Rowing furiously, the sailors pulled the

52

raft away from the beach and into the deep water. Then the sailors settled down and rowed in smooth strong strokes. Bannon looked back at Guadalcanal, so peaceful that evening. He looked ahead at the submarine floating in the water. He'd never been on a submarine before and had no idea what one was like. He thought it odd that some men were fighting the war from underneath the sea.

The sailors rowed the boats over the water, which reflected the moon in a long squiggly line. The boats drew close to the submarine and sailors aboard it threw lines out. Homer Gladley caught the one thrown at the boat carrying the First Squad and tied it to a cleat as sailors aboard the submarine pulled them alongside.

"Move your men onto the sub," said Ensign Collins.

"Yes, sir." Bannon cupped his hands around his mouth. "Move it out!"

A group of sailors was waiting to pull the men up. Frankie La Barbara was closest to the submarine and he held out his hands. Two sailors grabbed him and yanked him aboard. Frankie caught his balance on the gently moving deck and looked at the cannon mounted two feet away. Then he turned around and saw more sailors on the conning tower. Some of them held binoculars to their eyes and were scanning the air and sea around them.

"Move below, men!" one of them said. "Don't dawdle up here."

"That way," said a sailor, pointing to a hatch.

Frankie climbed down a ladder into the bowels of the submarine. It smelled oily and brass fittings gleamed in the light of bulbs affixed to ceilings and walls. A group of sailors and officers looked at Frankie as if he were a geek, and Frankie felt self-conscious as he gawked at all the dials and controls. The complexity of the submarine intimidated him. He thought a person would have to be very smart to serve on the crew of a submarine.

The rest of the men in the First and Second squads descended into the bowels of the submarine, and among them was Bannon, who was fascinated by the gadgetry.

"You men move aft," said an officer.

"What's *aft*?" asked Frankie La Barbara.

53

"That way." A sailor pointed toward the rear of the submarine.

The first two squads made their way through the narrow passageway to the enlisted men's mess and sat at the tables.

"Jeez," said Frankie La Barbara, "this is like living in a sardine can."

The cook working in the kitchen nearby scowled. He didn't like the idea of dirty dogfaced soldiers sitting in his clean mess hall.

"Can we smoke in here?" Frankie asked.

"No," said the cook.

"Well, fuck you," Frankie said.

Bannon turned to Frankie. "Shaddup."

"Why is everybody always telling me to shaddup?"

"Because you talk too much."

Frankie hated to be put down publicly. "Oh, yeah? Wait'll we get on dry land again. I'll show you who talks too much." Frankie looked around and sniffed disdainfully. "Boy I'd hate to be aboard one of these things underwater and get hit by a depth charge. What a way to go, huh?"

"Shaddup, Frankie," said Bannon again.

"Fuck you, Bannon."

It looks like I'm gonna have to kick the shit out of him again, Bannon thought. But Bannon didn't want to slug him in the submarine. There was barely room to do anything down there.

"Where's the shithouse on this sardine can?" Frankie asked.

The cook was about ready to throw a meat cleaver at Frankie. "You shoulda shit before you come aboard."

Frankie jumped to his feet and looked around frantically. "Who said that? I'll kick his fucking ass! Nobody can talk to me that way!"

"Frankie," said Bannon, his patience wearing thin, "sit down and shaddup."

"I gotta take a shit."

"You'll take a shit when you get ashore."

"Why can't I take a shit now?"

"Butsko will be here any minute now. You can talk to him about it."

Frankie sat down. He was feeling claustrophobic and chewed his gum viciously, snapping and cracking it, his eyes darting

54

around at the pipes and fittings on the ceiling.

"I wonder how many ships this sub's sank," Frankie said.

The men sat around and perspired into their uniforms. After a while Butsko appeared in the passageway, followed by the Third and Fourth squads. Butsko looked particularly cruel in the harsh shadows of the mess hall, and Frankie decided that he really didn't need to move his bowels. Butsko told the men from the Third and Fourth squads to sit down; then he leaned against a wall and took out his maps again, to go over the details of the mission one last time.

A group of spiffy young naval officers walked into the messroom.

"Hello," said one of them. "I'm Lieutenant Brown. Welcome to the *Silverfish*. We'll be shoving off soon, so sit here and make yourselves comfortable. We're only moving a few miles down the coast, so the trip won't take long. I'll have to ask you not to smoke while you're here. Chief Boatswain's Mate Murphy will stay with you, and if you have any questions, address them to him."

The officers left and Murphy stayed behind, a gnarled old salt with a big red whiskey nose. He put his hands in his pockets and tried to smile, but it came out gruesome.

"I wonder where they dug this guy up," Frankie muttered, and everybody heard him, including Chief Boatswain's Mate Murphy.

A few minutes later they felt motion on the ship.

"We're under way now," Murphy told them. "We'll be submerging soon."

The GIs could hear water splashing against the hull of the submarine. They could hear big diesel engines humming toward their rear, and the entire boat was trembling slightly.

"Clear the bridge!" yelled Lieutenant Brown in the control room.

A Klaxon went off, and Frankie La Barbara jumped three feet off the bench he'd been sitting on. Chief Boatswain's Mate Murphy moved nimbly around the messroom, checking valves and turning little wheels.

"Stand by to dive!" shouted Lieutenant Brown, and a few seconds later he called out, *"Hard dive!"*

Suddenly it became silent on the submarine as the diesel

engines cut out and electric motors took over. The GIs were aware that the front of the submarine was dipping down. Waves crashed against the hull of the submarine and rushed onto the deck. Frankie La Barbara broke out in a cold sweat because he was afraid something would go wrong and he'd drown like a rat.

"Pressure in the boat, sir!" somebody said.

"Open vents on main ballast tanks three and four," Lieutenant Brown replied.

Frankie looked nervously at Chief Boatswain's Mate Murphy. "Is everything okay, sir?"

Murphy nodded. "Yeah."

Butsko stepped away from the bulkhead and pointed his index finger at Frankie. "If something's wrong, *I'll* tell *you*. You don't have to ask, got it?"

"Hup, Sarge."

The commands of the officers drifted through the hatchways toward the soldiers, who sat still and tried not to think about how they were gliding along deep beneath the surface of Ironbottom Sound.

The stretch of beach looked like a tropical paradise in the moonlight. It was way behind enemy lines and thus far had escaped the ravages of war. An occasional shellburst or the chatter of machine guns could be heard in the distance, but except for routine patrol actions there was little fighting taking place on Guadalcanal.

The water between Guadalcanal and Florida Island was smooth and untroubled except for the gently rolling swells. Then suddenly a narrow rod of metal protruded from the water. It made a *V*-shaped ripple as it moved in the water, and a lens fitted into the metal was pointed to the shore.

Several seconds later the rod of metal rose into the air, and in a great swooshing sound the bridge of the submarine appeared. Then the conning tower broke the surface, and finally, in a roar like a waterfall, the deck and stanchions emerged.

Water poured in rivulets through slots on the deck as hatches were opened and sailors climbed out, pulling a deflated rubber raft with them. One of the sailors pulled the string on an air cylinder, and the raft twitched and buckled as it filled.

56

The First Squad crawled out of the hatch and crowded together. Their faces were darkened with camouflage and they were tense and jumpy.

Butsko and Lieutenant Brown came up with them.

Butsko looked Bannon in the eye. "All I can tell you, kid, is stay light on your feet and watch your ass. Stay close to your radio. Keep your eyes open and your head down. Don't take any chances."

Bannon nodded. "Hup, Sarge."

Butsko's eyes roved the faces of the others. "Good luck, boys. Remember your training, do what your squad leader tells you to do, and try not to fuck up too much."

"The boat's ready, Sergeant," Lieutenant Brown said.

"Hit it," Butsko said.

The boat bobbed up and down in the water next to the submarine. No sailors were aboard because it was an all-Army operation from then on. The men of the First Squad dropped down into the rubber boat, and Bannon designated the two biggest men in the platoon, Homer Gladley and Tommy Shaw, to pull the oars. Bannon was the last one in and he sat in the stern, laying his machine gun across his legs.

"Everybody okay?" Bannon asked.

Nobody said anything.

"Shove off," Bannon said.

The sailors kicked the raft away, and Gladley and Shaw began rowing. The boat was caught in a current and began spinning, and the two rowers struggled to put it on course, clattering oars and making a racket that echoed across the inlet.

"Settle down," Bannon said.

Shaw sat in the rear position and adjusted his strokes to Gladley's. They straightened the boat out and headed toward shore, their oars dipping in and out of the water smoothly. The others held their submachine guns tightly and scrutinized the shoreline, hoping the Japanese army wasn't waiting for them.

Bannon heard a rush of water behind him and turned to see the *Silverfish* sinking into the water. Waves raced across its deck and lapped at its conning tower.

"There she goes," said Frankie, a wistful tone in his voice.

Bannon felt the same desolation Frankie expressed in his voice. They were all alone now, behind enemy lines. None of them had done anything like this before. Each felt a little scared as they neared the beach.

Bannon's eyes scrutinized coconut palms leaning lazily toward the moon as he thought of the huge responsibility that had been thrust upon him. He was in charge of all these men. Their lives would depend on his judgment. He had no one to turn to now. The buck stopped with him.

He tried to give himself encouragment by reminding himself that he'd worked himself up to foreman of the old Double Bar C Ranch in Texas and that he'd bossed more men than this before he'd joined the Army. If he could handle a bunch of crazy cowboys, he surely could handle a bunch of crazy GIs. And besides, he didn't have any choice. This was one job he couldn't quit. His own life was on the line too.

The raft bucked and twisted as it hit the surf on the beach, and it was hard for the rowers to keep it under control.

"As soon as it touches down, everybody out and drag it ashore!" Bannon said. "Don't stop moving until we're under cover!"

The raft spun around as the white water boiled up all around it, and then it touched bottom. Everybody jumped out, grabbed the ropes that ringed the boat, and pulled it up on the beach.

Bannon ran in front of them in a crouch, his submachine gun ready, looking for a place to hide. Straight ahead were some bushes that he thought would do.

"Follow me!" he said. "Double-time!"

The men charged into the bushes, dragging the boat with them. Shaw pulled the plug on the raft and air swooshed out as the men formed a perimeter of defense around the boat and looked for trouble. All became silent except for the air leaving the boat and the squawking of birds in the trees above.

The men moved their heads from side to side and held their fingers on their triggers, their hearts beating wildly. But nothing was happening around them, and gradually they calmed down. Even the birds above them stopped making noise. They had made it ashore.

"Okay," Bannon said, "let's bury this boat and then get up on that hill over there to see if the radio's working all right."

The men took their entrenching tools off their packs and dug a huge hole in the ground. They rolled the rubber boat up, stomped the air out of it, threw it in the hole, and covered it with dirt, branches, and leaves.

They hoisted their packs on their backs and climbed the hill. It took two hours to get to the top, and another defense perimeter was established while Bannon stood behind Craig Delane and pulled the aerial out of Delane's backpack radio. Bannon turned on the radio, held the headset next to his face, and turned to the frequency designated for transmission.

"Red Dog One calling Hound Dog. Red Dog One calling Hound Dog. How do you read me? Over." He listened and heard only static. Looking around, he began to worry that maybe that hill was a poor transmission spot and they'd have to move. He hit the button and tried again. "Red Dog One calling Hound Dog. Red Dog One calling Hound Dog. How do you read me? Over."

On his fourth try he got the reply: "Hound Dog calling Red Dog One. I read you loud and clear. Over."

"This is Red Dog One calling Hound Dog. We've landed okay and just wanted to check transmission. Do you have anything for us?"

The Marine radio station at Henderson Field had no messages. It gave the correct time and signed off. Bannon returned the headset to Craig Delane, who put it on.

"All right, let's dig in and get some sleep," Bannon said.

He set up a rotating guard system of three shifts, with him and Delane working the first shift. The other men took off their packs and used them for pillows as they lay on the grassy top of the hill and closed their eyes.

Delane kept the headset on and listened to the airwaves while Bannon sat cross-legged with his submachine gun in his lap, looking around constantly, listening to the sounds of the night.

In the jungle a few miles away, Pfc. Shigaraki of the Japanese Imperial Army sat in a tent with his radio headset on, twiddling the dial in front of him, trying to pick up unusual American transmissions in the vicinity. Shigaraki spoke English fairly fluently, because he had worked as a houseboy in San Francisco before the war.

Shigaraki was part of Captain Mizushima's special jungle

patrol, and they'd arrived at this camp two hours earlier. Shigaraki had been listening to the radio ever since and was bored silly, certain that he'd never hear any Americans, because the odds were against it. He figured the Americans used their radios the same way the Japanese did: brief messages with frequent changes of frequencies. It would be a stroke of luck for him to move the dial to a frequency on which Americans were transmitting. The Americans, like the Japanese, used telephones for most of their communications and radios only in emergencies or other unusual situations.

"—Dog Two calling Hound Dog. Over."

Shigaraki nearly fell off the crate of ammunitions he was sitting on. His eyes bulging, he reached for his notepad and paper to write down the message. He was so happy, his pen shook as he wrote.

". . . This is Red Dog Two signing in and requesting if you've heard from Red Dog One yet."

"They checked in approximately one hour ago."

Pfc. Shigaraki ran out of his radio tent and sped toward the tent occupied by Captain Mizushima. Private Nagai stood guard in front of it."

"Ssshh," said Nagai, holding his finger to his mouth. "The captain is sleeping."

"Out of my way!"

Shigaraki pushed Nagai to the side and stuck his head into Captain Mizushima's tent. He saw Captain Mizushima sitting up and drawing his sword out of its scabbard, a fierce expression on his face.

Shigaraki saluted. "Sir," he said excitedly, "you told me to awaken you at once if anything unusual happened, and I just picked up an American transmission near here!"

Captain Mizushima's eyes glittered in the dark. "Are you sure?"

"Yes, sir. Absolutely sure."

"Were you able to get a fix on it."

"Yes, sir. A general fix, because the message was quite brief. It was northeast of here."

Captain Mizushima pushed his sword back into the scabbard. If the message was transmitted northeast of where he was sitting, that meant Americans were behind Japanese lines and located near the inlet where the supply ships came in.

"Send a message to Colonel Tsuji," Mizushima said. "Tell him you've intercepted the message and relay the contents. Tell him I'm leaving immediately to track down the signal. But before you do that, send Sergeant Jukichi to me at once."

"Yes, sir."

Shigaraki ran out of the tent to wake up the company's first sergeant while Captain Mizushima pulled on his pants.

SIX . . .

The sun rose like a ball of molten copper in the sky, and Bannon stood among the trees on the top of his hill, gazing at the inlet through his binoculars. No ships were out there, and the Japanese had landed no men or supplies in his area the night before. He thought that night would be different, because the Tokyo Express was operating with regularity, according to American intelligence. He'd decided that from now on his men would sleep during the day and stay up at night. Only a few guards would be posted during the day, and they would be on radio silence. At night the serious reconnaissance work would take place.

He lowered his binoculars and returned to the area where his men were having breakfast. They ate C rations cold out of the cans, because no fires were permitted on the mission. He took a can of franks and beans out of his pack and opened them up with his tiny can opener, then jabbed his spoon in and began eating.

On another hill a few miles away, Butsko was studying his maps while the men of the Second Squad also were having breakfast. During the night all the squads had reported to Butsko and had landed safely. The rubber boat belonging to the Fourth Squad had overturned in the surf and they were having problems with their radio, but they were able to receive and transmit messages through heavy static and weird noises.

Like Bannon, Butsko expected action before long. The Tokyo Express might have done its work the previous night before the recon platoon was deployed. But tonight should be a different matter.

Captain Mizushima's company made its way across the field of kunai grass that was taller than he was. Mizushima was at the head of his company, with Sergeant Jukichi to his left and Private Shigaraki at his right, carrying a field radio and listening to the airwaves as a man behind him twirled knobs and tried to pick up American transmissions.

They came to the edge of the jungle and Mizushima sent men with machetes forward to hack out a path. Mizushima took off his helmet and wiped sweat off his face as he watched his machete men whacking through trees and vines.

"The men are tired," Sergeant Jukichi said. "Perhaps they can have a rest?"

"There will be no rest until we locate the Americans," Captain Mizushima snapped.

The jungle was dense and dark. Monkeys screeched in the trees and lizards scurried along the ground. The machete men flailed at the vines and branches and slowly made a path into the jungle. The rest of the company followed them, lugging weapons and dragging their feet. Private Shigaraki had a headache from fatigue, but he bit his lips and listened to static and remote transmissions over the airwaves.

The day passed uneventfully for the soldiers of the recon platoon. They burrowed into bushes and tried to sleep in the intense heat. Insects buzzed around their ears and tried to eat them up alive. They crawled into the soldiers' ears and nostrils, and if the soldiers opened their mouths, the insects flew down their throats.

Frankie La Barbara sat near Bannon in the shade, both with their shirts off. Craig Delane slept fitfully nearby, his head on a pile of leaves.

"Jesus, I wish we had a breeze," Frankie said.

63

Bannon was too hot and irritated to reply.

"Does it get hot like this in Texas?" Frankie asked, anxious to get a conversation going so he could be distracted from his physical discomfort.

"It's not like this," Bannon said wearily. "We get a dry heat in Texas."

"I wish they would've sent me to Alaska. I can take the cold, but the heat just fucks me all up."

"If you were in Alaska, you'd complain about the cold."

Bannon stretched out on the grass and closed his eyes. He wished he could fall alseep. A bug bit him in the belly and he smashed it flat, flicking the mess away, although some of the gunk stuck to his fingers.

"Back in New York," Frankie said wistfully, "we used to go to Coney Island in the summer. Just lay around and eat ice cream, looking at the girls in their bathing suits. Sometimes we used to pick up girls and fuck them underneath the board-walk. You got any beaches in Texas, Bannon?"

"Not where I'm from."

"What do you do for fun, besides fucking."

"I used to go rodeoing."

"You mean watch the cowboys ride horses and all that shit?"

"I didn't watch them, Frankie. I was one of the cowboys myself."

"You used to ride wild horses?"

"I rode bulls mostly."

"Bulls!"

"Yeah. Brahma bulls. You haven't lived till you've rode a brahma bull."

"Jesus. You ever fall off?"

"All the time."

"You make any money at it?"

"Nah, there ain't much money in it. You do it for the fun and for trophies. I was the champion bullrider in my county in 1940. I was gonna enter some big rodeos. but then the war came."

"No shit?"

"No shit. But the problem with rodeos these days is that they're getting too organized. There are some cowboys who don't do nothing except ride rodeos. In the old days rodeos were just for ranch hands, but now it's getting big."

"Then there must be some money in it someplace, Bannon."

"There's money in the big rodeos, but shit, like I said, it's getting so organized and commercial, it ain't fun anymore."

"Your problem, Bannon, is that you don't realize that *money* is fun. Maybe you need a manager."

Bannon groaned and turned over. "Stop trying to be everybody's manager, Frankie. Shaddup and lemme go to sleep."

Butsko and the Second Squad were in the trees near the summit of a hill. He and his men lay on the ground, covering their eyes with their shirts and trying to sleep. Butsko was in a foul mood. He didn't like his special assignment. It was too hot to be hanging around on the tops of mountains. He wished he was back in the jungle with the men of the Twenty-third.

He was realizing that the transfer to Headquarters hadn't been such a good idea. The platoon had just been an ordinary platoon and nobody ever paid any attention to it before. It had been lost in the vast bureaucracy of the Army, receiving no special dangerous assignments. Now, at Headquarters, his platoon was going to get all the dangerous assignments. In a way it was nice to be away from all the ordinary chickenshit, but this duty was much more dangerous. He'd stand less of a chance of surviving the war, and his main goal was to stay alive.

"Shit!" he said, sitting up.

"What's the matter?" asked Sergeant McCabe.

Butsko stood and put on his helmet. He looked out into the inlet and saw the sun sparkling on the water. It would be nice to go down there and take a swim, but the inlet was full of sharks, or so they'd been told.

He heard something and perked up his ears. It was a faint hum and sounded like the engine of an airplane in the distance.

"Take cover!" Butsko yelled.

The men scrambled under bushes and into the shade of trees. Butsko dived into a ditch and looked up. He saw two spots in the sky, and gradually the spots became larger as the sound of airplane engines grew stronger. Finally Butsko could make out their configurations: They were two Japanese Zeros.

65

"Keep your heads down!" Butsko said.

The two planes soared low over the mountain and kept going. Butsko watched them and could see that they were following the coastline. *Are they looking for us,* he wondered, *or are they just a routine patrol?*

SEVEN . . .

The sun was setting on the west side of the island, and Captain Mizushima's company finally reached the edge of the jungle. Ahead of them was the range of mountains and hills that bordered the shoreline.

"Sir," said Sergeant Jukichi, "do you think the men can stop to eat now."

"We do not stop until we have reached our objective!" Captain Mizushima snapped.

Captain Mizushima moved his hand forward, and his exhausted company followed him toward the mountain straight ahead. Mizushima's plan was to get to the top of the mountain, where radio signals could be received more clearly, and listen for American transmissions.

The men trudged toward the base of the mountain. Captain Mizushima was as tired as the rest of them, but within him burned the fires of ambition and hatred.

"Keep moving!" he exhorted his men. "When we're on the mountain we'll take a rest!"

At Henderson Field, Colonel Stockton stood beside his radio, puffing his pipe. It was a few minutes before eight o'clock in the evening, and his recon platoon was supposed to start reporting in at eight, squad by squad, every five minutes. Colonel Stockton had been worrying about the recon platoon ever since it had left. He'd wondered if they had really been ready for such a complex and difficult mission behind enemy lines. Perhaps he'd been expecting too much of them. They were just an ordinary bunch of GIs, after all; maybe they couldn't handle a mission like this.

The minute hand of his wristwatch clicked toward eight o'clock, and the radio operator sat tensely, with his radio tuned to the frequency that would be used by the recon platoon that night. He had his microphone near his face, and the loudspeaker was spitting out static.

Suddenly the static stopped and Bannon's voice could be heard. "This is Red Dog calling Hound Dog. This is Red Dog One calling Hound Dog. Do you read me? Do you read me? Over."

The radio operator hit the button and replied, "This is Hound Dog calling Red Dog One. We read you loud and clear. Over."

Bannon kept his message brief. He said his squad was in position and watching the inlet. He asked if there were any messages for him, and when told there were none, he signed off. The static came on again.

Colonel Stockton breathed a little easier. At least one of his squads was doing okay. Corporal Bannon had sounded businesslike and in control of the situation. In a few minutes the Second Squad would check in; that was the squad Butsko was traveling with. Colonel Stockton took his pipe out of his mouth and waited for Butsko's transmission.

A cool sea breeze was blowing over the mountains, reviving Captain Mizushima's men. They'd eaten and had been resting for an hour. Private Shigaraki sat high in a tree with his radio, twiddling the dial back and forth, listening for American transmissions. If there were Americans around, their transmission would come in clearly. It took him ten seconds to make a complete revolution on the dial. Then he went back again. He hoped he wouldn't have to do that all night, because he was getting nutty from listening to static and muffled, broken transmissions.

Captain Mizushima sat on a branch beside him, thinking of the glory that would befall him if he could track down American spies. Colonel Tsuji was a famous officer, and surely he would show his gratitude. Captain Mizushima might win a medal and perhaps a promotion too.

"I hear them!" Private Shigaraki shouted, reaching for his aerial.

Captain Mizushima's eyes widened as Shigaraki tried to line up his aerial with the signal. Captain Mizushima looked in the direction in which the aerial was pointed.

"The transmission is finished, sir," Private Shigaraki said.

"What was its content?"

"It sounded like a routine contact. The person talking said that he'd seen nothing."

Captain Mizushima looked in the direction of the transmission. The aerial pointed to a mountain toward his right; if he were an American, he would consider it a good place to observe the comings and goings of ships in the inlet.

"Everybody up!" Captain Mizushima said. "Prepare to move out!"

"I hate this fucking Army," Frankie La Barbara said. "What the fuck am I doing here? Why me?"

"Shaddup, Frankie," said Bannon, scanning the inlet through his binoculars.

"I'm sick of you telling me to shaddup. Who the fuck do you think you are? I liked you better when you were an ordinary private."

"Keep your voice down. There might be Japs around here."

"My voice is down. You keep your own voice down."

Frankie felt like an animal in a cage. He rose to his knees and scratched his armpits and his balls while chomping gum furiously. The men of the first squad were formed into the circle on the ridge. Some gazed at the inlet; others watched the jungle around them.

"Who needs this fucking war?" Frankie said. "This war doesn't mean shit to me. I don't give a shit who owns this island. If the Japs want it, let 'em have it. You know who used to own this fucking island?"

"Get down, Frankie."

"Somebody told me that Lever Brothers used to own this island. That's the company that makes soap and shit. There's

69

something on this island that they use for soap. We're fighting for this island so that Lever Brothers can make soap."

Craig Delane hated the war even more than Frankie La Barbara, but he came from an old distinguished American family and thought he should defend his country's participation in the war. "Listen, Frankie," he said, "would you rather fight the Japs here or would you rather fight them in New York?"

"Don't give me that shit, you fucking fairy," Frankie replied. "The Japs don't want New York. There's no need to fight over it anyways. Where I come from, people know how to make deals. The Chinks are just like the Japs, and I used to live right next to a big Chink neighborhood. We do what we want to do in our neighborhood, and they do what they want to do in their neighborhood. Nobody messes with each other's territory. That's the way to handle things. If they put me in charge of this war, I'd settle it in a few hours."

Bannon turned to Frankie. "I'm not going to tell you again: Shut your fucking mouth!"

"Okay, okay," Frankie said. "You're the man with all the stripes, but when we get back, I'm gonna have to settle a few things with you, Bannon."

"It's a deal, Frankie. But shut up."

Frankie grumbled and chewed his gum. The last time he and Bannon had fought, Bannon had gotten the best of him, but next time Frankie was not going to play around. Next time he'd break Bannon in half.

Captain Mizushima's company was making its way through the trees and brush on the side of the hill from which the American radio transmission had come. He had divided the company into four platoons, and each was assaulting the summit from different sides. They were moving along silently, so as not to alert the Americans. The first platoon to make contact would open fire immediately. If the Americans tried to escape, they'd run into another platoon. Mizushima had told the platoon leaders to move as quickly as they could, and when they neared the top, they didn't have to worry about being quiet. He also ordered them to take as many prisoners as they could.

The Japanese soldiers crouched low to the ground as they

climbed the incline. They were halfway up and itching to close in on the Americans.

Butsko scanned the inlet with his binoculars from left to right and then back again, when suddenly he heard something. He spun around. The sound had been like a foot stepping on a twig and came from the woods below the summit.

"I heard something," he said.

"It's probably one of them land crabs," Sergeant McCabe said.

"There ain't no land crabs up this high."

Ka-pow! A shot crackled over their heads.

"Get down!" Butsko yelled.

The men of the Second Squad already were down, but they got down lower.

Ka-pow!

"Japs!" yelled one of the soldiers.

The air filled with the sound of rifle fire, and then a machine gun started up. Butsko looked around. The woods were flashing with muzzle blasts from all directions. The GIs raised their submachine guns to their shoulders, and the roar of their volleys echoed across the water. Butsko fired his submachine gun at the flashes in the woods, and it bucked and stuttered in his hands. He could tell from the volume of fire that he and his men were greatly outnumbered. And they were surrounded.

"Banzai!" screamed one of the Japs.

On Butsko's left, figures charged out of the woods, their bayonets flashing in the moonlight. Butsko swung his submachine gun around and opened fire, holding the barrel down because the explosions tended to push it up in the air. Japs tripped and fell to the ground, but hordes of Japs kept charging. The GIs in the Second Squad leveled their fire at them and the barrels of their submachine guns spit out death. More Japs fell, writhing and twisting on the ground. The surviving Japs continued their mad rush and the GIs continued to chop them down. Some Japs were only twenty yards away, and Butsko could see their bodies and faces clearly. The second squad maintained its murderous stream of fire until there was only one Jap left, and he ran toward the crest of the mountains as fast as his legs

71

would go. Butsko took aim and gave him a burst that shattered the Jap's stomach and stopped him cold. The Jap dropped to his knees and then fell on his face.

"Banzai!" shouted Japs straight ahead.

Another group of Japs rushed forward, and the Second Squad turned their submachine guns on them, raking them from side to side with fire. Some Japs caught the bullets in their stomachs and faces, but the rest shook their rifles in their hands and shouted as they rushed forward, led by a tall, lanky sergeant. Butsko aimed at him, pulled his trigger, and blew the sergeant down. The charge faltered, then another Jap took command and ran in front of his comrades, exhorting them to keep going. Butsko fired a burst at him and it ripped his head apart. The Jap fell onto his back, and the other Japs dropped down on their stomachs. A Jap somewhere in the woods shouted an order, and the Japs who'd charged stayed where they were, firing fusillades at the GIs.

Why aren't they throwing hand grenades, Butsko thought. *They could wipe us out with hand grenades.* *"Gonzales!"* he shouted.

"Hup, Sarge!"

"Get over here with that radio!"

Gonzales carried the backpack radio, and he raised himself off the ground to make a dash toward Butsko. But that was as far as he got. A Japanese bullet ripped through his chest and he fell down again.

"Keep firing!" Butsko yelled. *"Hold them off!"*

Terrified, aware they were surrounded and outnumbered, the GIs fed clips into their submachine guns and fired into the jungle all around them. Butsko held his submachine gun in his right hand and crawled over the rocks toward Gonzales as bullets whizzed over his head and ricocheted off the ground near him.

"I'm hit!" somebody shrieked.

"Keep firing!" Butsko hollered.

He continued crawling through the hail of Japanese fire and finally reached Gonzales, who lay unconscious on his stomach. Butsko took the headset from the radio and held it close to his face, hoping the apparatus was still working. A Japanese bullet hit Gonzales in the ass, and blood spurted into the air like a geyser. Butsko heard static through the headphone and was thankful that the radio was still working. He checked the dial to make sure it was turned to the correct frequency, then pressed the button and spoke.

"This is Red Dog Two calling Hound Dog! This is Red Dog Two calling Hound Dog! We're under attack and we can't hang on much longer!"

"This is Hound Dog. I'll pass the word along."

Having made his report, Butsko slammed the radio with the butt of his submachine gun, putting a huge dent in it because he didn't want it to fall into enemy hands. He whacked it again to make sure, then looked up. GIs writhed and shouted in pain all around him, and others were ominously still. Only two or three still were able to fire their submachine guns, and their shooting was pathetic against the massive volleys of the Japs. Butsko raised his submachine gun to his shoulder and prepared to take aim, when a bullet ricocheted off the rock in front of him, sending splinters into his face. He grimaced and opened his eyes; his vision wasn't impaired.

"Yaaahhh!" screamed Sergeant McCabe as he rolled onto his back, a bullet through his throat.

"Who's left out here!" Butsko demanded.

"I am, Sarge!" said the firm voice of Napoleon Denker.

"Hold your fire until they get closer."

Butsko pressed his chin to the ground and peered at the jungle. Bullets flew around him in all directions, and a machine gun kicked up stones directly in front of him. Butsko ground his teeth together and held his submachine gun tightly. *They're gonna charge any moment,* he thought, *and then it's gonna be all over for me.*

"Butsko's under attack!" Bannon said, looking in the direction of the sound of gunfire in the distance.

"Holy shit," Frankie said, his ears perked up. "Sounds like a whole lot of Japs from here."

"Yeah." Bannon tried to think of what to do. Should he ask for the P T boats to get him the hell out of there before the Japs found his squad too? he wondered. Or should he just wait for instructions?

"What're we gonna do next?" Frankie asked nervously.

73

"I don't know. Lemme think."

"I think we should get the fuck out of here!"

"I said shaddup and let me think."

Bannon looked in the direction of the gunfire. He knew from the briefing that Butsko's position was around two and a half miles away. It would take forever to get there through the jungle, but if they double-timed on the beach, they would make it in an hour. Would an hour be too late?

Longtree stepped forward, and the moonlight gleamed on his cheek. "I think we should get out of here. Japs might be on their way here too."

Bannon nodded. He hadn't thought of that. "You're right. Let's saddle up and move out."

The men ran to their packs and put them on. They looked around fearfully, because they thought the Japs might be closing in on them too.

"Headquarters is calling!" said Delane.

The men crowded around Delane and pushed their ears toward the headset so they could hear.

"This is Hound Dog calling Red Dog Two. This is Hound Dog calling Red Dog Two. Do you read me. Do you read me. Over." It was the voice of Colonel Stockton.

There was silence on the airwaves for several seconds, and then Colonel Stockton tried to raise Butsko again, with the same result.

Bannon closed his eyes. "The Japs must have got Butsko."

Frankie La Barbara was chewing gum a mile a minute. "They're gonna get us, too, if we don't get out of here!"

Colonel Stockton's voice came on the radio again. "This is Hound Dog calling Red Dog One. Do you read me? Over."

Bannon pressed the button. "I read you."

"What is your situation?"

"We hear gunfire in the distance, but we're all right here so far."

"Proceed to rendezvous point A and await further instructions."

Bannon returned the headset to Delane and looked in the direction of Butsko's position. The firing had stopped.

Frankie La Barbara moved from foot to foot as if he had to take a piss. "You know where rendezvous point A is?"

"Yeah, I know where it is."

"Then what the fuck are we waiting for?"

Bannon narrowed his eyes and gazed toward the hilltop where Butsko had been situated. He wondered if Butsko was all right. Maybe he'd got away and was hiding in the woods someplace. Maybe he was wounded and needed help. Or maybe he was dead.

Bannon turned and looked into the eyes of his men. "I think we should see if we can help Butsko," he said.

"What!" Frankie cried. "Are you kidding! Butsko's a fucking goner, and we will be, too, if we don't get a move on."

Bannon stared at Frankie. "Butsko would come back for you, you prick, and you fucking well know it!"

Frankie looked embarrassed, because he knew what Bannon said was true. "But Colonel Stockton said to proceed to rendezvous point A."

"We can do that later. I say we should go and see if we can do anything for Butsko and the Second Squad."

Frankie stomped his foot on the ground. "They're fucking dead!"

"Anybody coming with me?" Bannon asked.

Longtree nodded his head. "I'm with you."

"Me too," said Shilansky.

Homer Gladley shrugged. "I'll go if you go, Bannon."

"The way I see it," Tommy Shaw said, "we're fucked no matter which way we go, so we might as well save Butsko's ass if we can."

Delane adjusted the radio on his back. "I agree with Shaw."

Bannon began to like Delane for the first time since he met him. He turned to Frankie. "Are you coming or aren't you?"

"Lead the way," Frankie said.

EIGHT . . .

"Hold your fire!" yelled Captain Mizushima.

The Japanese fire dribbled off and stopped. Everybody's ears rang with the sudden silence.

"I think they're all dead, sir," Sergeant Jukichi said.

"They'd better not be." Captain Mizushima turned to Pfc. Shigaraki. "Tell them they're surrounded and don't have a chance. Tell them if they surrender, they'll receive good treatment."

Pfc. Shigaraki nodded, cupped his hands around his mouth, and shouted in English, *"You are surrounded and you do not have a chance. If you surrender, you will receive excellent treatment!"* He looked at Captain Mizushima. "Shouldn't I give them a time limit, sir?"

"Two minutes."

"You have two minutes to make up your mind!"

Butsko's face was covered with pinpricks of blood from tiny bits of stone embedded in his flesh. "You can surrender if you want to," he said to Denker, "but I was a prisoner of the Japs once and I can't go through it again. I'm gonna fight it out here."

Denker's hands were shaking and he had trouble making his tongue work. "He said he'd give us excellent treatment."

"You believe that?"

Denker closed his eyes. "No."

76

"Make up your mind, Denker. We ain't got much time."

Denker bit his lower lip. "I'd rather die clean than have them fuck over me."

"You sure?"

"I'm sure."

Butsko raised his head and screamed at the top of his lungs, *"Come and get us, you slant-eyed cocksuckers!"*

"What'd he say?" Captain Mizushima asked.

Pfc. Shigaraki thought for a few moments. "He says he doesn't want to surrender, sir."

Captain Mizushima cursed under his breath. The Americans were making it difficult for him to take prisoners alive, but at least they had courage. He wished they didn't have so much courage now. "Sergeant Jukichi!"

"Yes, sir?"

"Tell the men to attack in waves, platoon by platoon, but they must take those men alive. They must shoot over their heads or to their sides, but not directly at them. Is that clear?"

"Yes, sir."

Sergeant Jukichi moved away to pass the order along. Captain Mizushima narrowed his eyes at the moonlit top of the hill, wondering what kind of Americans were up there, willing to fight to the death.

"Here they come!" said Napoleon Denker, his teeth chattering.

"Take as many of them with you as you can," Butsko growled.

One platoon of Japanese soldiers attacked while the other three platoons covered them with harmless fire. The attackers ran as quickly as they could, holding their heads low, and Butsko and Denker poured hot lead into them. The Japs were spread out and moving quickly, and Butsko and Denker could only pick off a few of them before they flopped onto their stomachs.

Then the next wave charged, and Butsko whipped his submachine gun from side to side, raking them with fire, seeing three of them drop to the ground. Butsko's excitement was so great that he wasn't aware that the Japs weren't shooting to kill. He shot two more Japs and Denker also got two before the Japs dropped down to provide cover for the next wave of attackers.

They charged on signal and Butsko and Denker opened fire at them. Butsko's bolt went *click*—out of ammunition—and he ejected the empty clip, ramming in a fresh one. When he was ready to fire again, the third wave had hit the dirt and the fourth wave was attacking.

Butsko and Denker peppered them with fire, cutting down nearly half of them. Then Denker ran out of ammunition. He searched frantically in his ammo pouch and was shocked to realize he had only one clip left. That would give him a few more bursts of fire and then he'd be out. His lips trembled and his face was covered with sweat as he imagined Japs cutting him apart with their swords.

The Japs surrounded Butsko and Denker at a distance of less than twenty yards. Butsko and Denker realized the next series of charges would probably overrun them. A Jap farther back shouted an order, and then all the Japs jumped to their feet and attacked at the same time.

Butsko and Denker fired frantically, trying to kill as many of the Japs as they could, but the Japs kept coming. The American submachine-gun bullets cut many of them down, but Captain Mizushima had told them to take the Americans alive in this charge.

The Japs closed in on Butsko and Denker, who fought valiantly for their lives, spinning round and round, shooting down the stampeding Japs, who were so close their faces could be seen. Something snapped in Denker's mind because he was terrified of being captured alive. With a shriek of madness he turned his submachine gun around, bit the barrel, and pushed the trigger. He heard a short, sharp sound and felt nothing as his head blew away and he fell to the ground.

Butsko didn't even see him fall. Jumping to his feet, he held the butt of his submachine gun to his waist and pulled the trigger, spinning about and spreading a circle of death around him. One Jap dived at him, arms outstretched to tackle him, and Butsko gave him a burst in the head. Butsko dodged to the side and let the Jap's body sail by, spurting blood, then crouched and pulled the trigger again.

Click!

He was out of ammo and there was no time to reload. With a vicious snarl he threw his submachine gun at the nearest Jap, hitting him across the chest, then drew his bayonet, holding it blade up in his fist and charging the Jap in front of him.

The Jap tried to grab his wrist, but Butsko was too fast for him. Butsko punched the bayonet into the Jap's guts, spun around, slashed another Jap across the throat, turned again, and ripped a third Jap across the chest.

"Come on, you bastards!" Butsko screamed, his eyes ablaze with hate.

They all dived on him at once. Butsko thrust upward with his bayonet, burying it in a Jap's chest, and the blade tore across the Jap's ribs. Butsko tried to pull his bayonet back for another blow, but the weight of Japs was too much for him. They all piled on him and he fell to the ground at the bottom of the heap. Japs grabbed his legs, wrists, and throat. Butsko felt the life being choked out of him, but still he writhed and twisted.

"Lemme go!" he shrieked. *"Lemme go!"*

Colonel Stockton sat behind the desk in his office, puffing his pipe nervously and waiting for a call from General Vandegrift. Colonel Stockton had been awakened a half hour earlier with the news that the recon platoon was in trouble behind enemy lines, and now he was having misgivings about the whole operation. *I shouldn't have sent them,* he thought. *Maybe if they'd had an officer with them, things would have turned out differently.*

He couldn't imagine how things could have turned out differently, but maybe Butsko didn't have the good sense to take appropriate measures. Butsko was a good combat soldier, but maybe he was in over his head on a mission like the one the recon platoon had been sent on. Maybe seasoned Marine raiders would have done better. Maybe no one could have done better. It was hard to say.

The phone on his desk rang and he picked it up. "General Vandegrift speaking," said the voice on the other end.

"This is Colonel Stockton, and I have bad news. My recon platoon is in trouble and I have to get them out of there. May

I have permission to send P T boats to pick the survivors up?"

General Vandegrift was silent for a few seconds. "What happened?"

"I don't know exactly. The Second Squad of the platoon was attacked and evidently wiped out. The First Squad has fallen out of radio contact. The Third and Fourth squads have moved to their rendezvous points and I'd like to have them picked up before something happens to them too."

"I see," said General Vandegrift. "Call Commander Ames at the P T boat squadron and tell him to send two boats out. This is most unfortunate, but it was a chancy operation and we knew that from the onset. I'd like to be notified when you get the survivors out. Maybe they can give us a better idea of what happened. Keep trying to raise the squads that are out of contact. Maybe some of them are still alive."

"Yes, sir."

"This is Hound Dog calling Red Dog One. This is Hound Dog calling Red Dog One. Do you read me? Do you read me? Over."

"Bannon," said Craig Delane, "Headquarters is calling again."

"Don't answer."

The First Squad was moving along the beach, staying close to the shelter of the treeline. It was tough going, trudging through the sand. The firing in the distance had stopped, and the moonlight was dappled by the little waves in the inlet.

"Hey, Bannon," said Frankie La Barbara, breathing hard from exertion. "If we ever get out of here, we're gonna be in trouble for not answering those messages."

"He's right," Craig Delane agreed. "They'll probably court-martial all of us, and you especially."

Bannon stopped and the rest of the squad stopped with him. He'd been thinking about the radio, too, and knew they were right. "I guess the only thing to do," he said, "is to get rid of the fucking radio. That way we can say we never got the messages."

"But what if we need the radio?" Craig Delane asked.

"What do we need the radio for?"

"What if we need help?"

Frankie snorted. "Who's gonna help us out here? Who helped Butsko? Smarten up, asshole."

"If we need it," Bannon said, "we can always come back for it. We can hide it right here. Give it to me."

Delane removed the radio from his back and Bannon dropped his field pack to the ground. Bannon opened his pack and took out his poncho. "We can wrap it in my poncho in case it starts raining. Frankie, dig a hole for the radio."

"'Frankie, dig a hole for the radio,'" Frankie mimicked. "Why does it always have to be Frankie?"

"Jesus Christ!" Bannon said, taking out his entrenching tool. "I'll do it!"

Bannon looked around and picked two palm trees that would make a good reference point. He walked behind them and began digging. The other men took out their own entrenching tools and helped. Finally Frankie joined in. When they reached a depth of three feet, Bannon told them to stop and get out of the way. He wrapped the radio in his poncho and laid it in the hole.

"Cover it up."

The men shoveled dirt on the radio and Bannon sat down with his map and compass. He figured out where he was and made an X on the map with his pencil. Then he rose and tucked the map into his shirt. The men finished shoveling and stomped on the dirt so that it wouldn't be too high. Then they gathered branches and leaves and camouflaged the dirt.

"Let's move out," Bannon said.

The men put on their packs and slung their rifles over their shoulders, following Bannon toward the mountain where Butsko had been positioned.

The Japanese soldiers dragged Butsko to his feet as Captain Mizushima walked toward him. Butsko was bleeding from a split lip and his face was peppered with dots of blood. He was awake and struggling to get loose, but Japs held his arms, legs, waist, and head.

Captain Mizushima looked at him and smiled, pleased that he was alive. "My, isn't he ugly."

Butsko was in an insane rage, saliva frothing out of his mouth with the blood. He focused his eyes on Captain Mizushima and suddenly stopped struggling, his eyes bulging out of his sockets.

Captain Mizushima chuckled. *Even an ordinary American soldier is impressed by the sight of a Japanese officer,* he thought.

But Butsko wasn't impressed at all. He was shocked by his recognition of Captain Mizushima because he remembered Captain Mizushima from the Bataan Death March. Captain Mizushima had been one of the officers in charge of the march, and Butsko remembered him punching and kicking soldiers. One of Butsko's buddies, Sergeant Clyde Drake of Biloxi, Mississippi, had fallen exhausted by the road, and Captain Mizushima had shot him in the head with his Nambu pistol.

Butsko bellowed wildly and tried to attack Captain Mizushima, and the Japanese soldiers struggled to hold him back. Captain Mizushima was angered by the American soldier's sudden belligerence and wanted to punch him in the mouth, but remained motionless. Colonel Tsuji had ordered that the prisoners not be harmed.

"Tie him up like the dog he is," Captain Mizushima said, "and let's get out of here."

NINE . . .

Bannon set a fast pace for his squad, and they reached the base of the hill at four o'clock in the morning. Bannon told them to take a break while he figured out what to do next. It was silent at the base of the hill, although that didn't mean a battalion of Japs might not be at the top. Japs were quiet and sneaky. If they were at the top of the hill, they might have guards posted at the bottom.

Frankie spit out a wad of gum that was starting to taste like shit. "I'm tired," he said. "Why don't we sack out for a while, Bannon?"

"Keep your voice down." He turned to Longtree. "Chief, I'd like to scout the top of this hill. You feel up to it?"

Longtree nodded.

"Leave your pack here. Just take your gun with you and one clip of ammo. Hurry back."

Longtree took off his pack and helmet, laying them on the ground. He held his submachine gun in his right hand, bent low, and disappeared into the bushes.

"Okay, everybody get some sack time," Bannon said. "I'll stand guard."

The men were already on the ground, and they closed their eyes. Bannon sat on a log and laid his submachine gun on his lap, listening to the sounds of the forest. He couldn't hear anything coming from the direction in which Longtree had gone.

Butsko was bound hand and foot to a pole and hung from it like a monkey as the Japanese soldiers carried him into camp. The ends of the pole rested on the shoulders of two of his captors, and he swung from side to side, cursing noiselessly because the Japanese had gagged him.

Guards on duty looked at Butsko curiously as he was carried to Colonel Tsuji's tent. A soldier was on sentry duty and Captain Mizushima marched up to him.

"Awaken Colonel Tsuji and tell him I have returned with an American prisoner."

The sentry entered the tent and Captain Mizushima stood proudly beside Butsko, his hands on his hips. Seconds later Colonel Tsuji poked his head out and looked at Butsko.

"Only one?" Colonel Tsuji asked.

"The others were unfortunately killed, sir."

"I told you to take them alive!"

"But, sir," Captain Mizushima said, "they fought hard. We had to kill the rest to get this one."

"Nonsense. American soldiers don't fight that hard. But at least you have one. He's a sergeant, isn't he?"

"I believe so, sir."

"Very good. Awaken Major Yamai and tell him to report to my officer immediately. Bring the prisoner inside and have your men tie him to a chair."

The soldiers carried Butsko into the tent, and Butsko was so mad he was beyond fear. *If I ever get loose,* he swore to himself, *I'm gonna kill that little bowlegged Jap with my bare hands.*

Pfc. Longtree crept silently up the hill, pausing every ten feet to look and listen. Slowly he made his way around boulders and the trunks of trees, his feet touching down softly on leaves; he pulled branches aside in order to get along. His stomach strained and hurt, but the pain was easy for him to manage. He'd been put through far greater pain when he'd been initiated as an adult male in the Apaches.

He neared the crest of the hill, dropped down onto his knees, and glanced around. He pricked up his ears but could hear nothing ominous. It was becoming light, but the sun hadn't appeared on the horizon yet. He crept forward and looked ahead at the clearing on top of the hill.

He saw soldiers lying still, but couldn't tell if they were Americans or Japanese. He decided to wait until it got bright enough to see better. Lying on the ground, he felt an itch on the skin of his stomach. It was the stitches, and he figured they were ready to come out. The problem with American doctors, he thought, was that they made a mess. Apaches never worried about stitches when their witch doctors were finished with them. Either they were dead or they walked away. He'd have to take the stitches out himself before long; otherwise they might become infected.

Gradually it became lighter, and Longtree realized he was looking at the bodies of dead Americans from the Second Squad. He hoped they'd died fighting, because if they hadn't they wouldn't go to the Happy Hunting Ground.

He wondered if it was a trap. Maybe Japs were lurking in the bushes for someone like him to come along. He'd have to scout the perimeter of the clearing.

He rose and moved to the side, skirting the edge of the clearing carefully, not making a sound. It took him half an hour to cover the distance; then, to make sure, he threw a rock toward where the American soldiers were lying. Nothing moved or gave him cause for alarm.

Still not taking any chances, he pushed the bushes aside and inched his way into the clearing. He drew closer to the dead soldiers and saw the blood-spattered features of Private Tolliver looking straight at him, eyes wide open, horror on his face. Longtree passed another soldier lying on his stomach, his shirt soaked with blood. He crawled beside the dead soldier and looked into the face of Pfc. Stearns, the fisherman from Florida. Pausing, Longtree glanced around again, just in case. His comrades lay frozen in death all around, but he felt little sorrow, because they had all died fighting and gone on to a better place. He counted the bodies; there were eight of them. Creeping about, he searched for the body of Sergeant Butsko but couldn't find him. He found one soldier whose head had been blown apart, but he was too small to be Butsko. Where was Butsko?

Longtree stood and studied the ground. He could see that a great struggle had taken place on the hill. Crouching low, he walked around and saw where all the tracks came from. He knew the difference between American boots and Japanese boots and could see what had happened. The Japanese had surrounded the Second Squad and attacked. Blood on the ground indicated that the Japanese had carried their dead and wounded away. The Americans were left to feed the buzzards. Searching around, he found the trail the Japanese had taken when they left the hill.

Evidently they had taken Butsko with them. Longtree looked at the trail that led back down the mountain. *Follow that trail,* he thought, *and you find Sergeant Butsko.*

Butsko's arms, legs, and torso were lashed to a chair in Colonel Tsuji's office. His muscles flexed as he tried to break loose, and he glanced crazily at the two Japanese officers and two guards. Captain Mizushima had gone, now that his patrol was over.

Colonel Tsuji sat behind his desk, smoking a cigarette and examining Butsko as if he were an animal at the zoo. Lieutenant Yamai, the interpreter, sat on a chair beside the desk. The two guards stood at attention on either side of Butsko, who remained gagged.

"He appears to have lost his mind," Colonel Tsuji said. "Perhaps the fight on that hill was too much for him."

Lieutenant Yamai had studied engineering at UCLA and was more familiar with Americans. "I just think he's angry, sir."

"*That* angry?"

"Americans do not hide their emotions as we often do, sir."

"Barbarians, that's what they are. All they want to do is subjugate people who aren't as ugly as they are. Look at all the scars on him. I wonder if he got them fighting."

"Perhaps he was in an automobile accident, sir."

"He'll be in worse than an automobile accident if he doesn't answer our questions." Colonel Tsuji looked at one of the guards. "Take off the gag."

"Yes, sir."

The guard stepped behind Butsko and untied the gag, pulling it away."

"You fucking cocksuckers!" Butsko screamed. *"You dirty sons of bitches! You filthy skunks!"*

"What's he raving about?" Colonel Tsuji asked.

"He doesn't like us, sir."

"Well, I don't like him either. I think he's disgusting. Tell him to be quiet or we'll make him be quiet."

"Take it easy, soldier," Lieutenant Yamai said, having difficulty pronouncing his *r*'s.

Butsko was shocked to hear a Japanese officer speaking English so well. His mouth stopped in the middle of a word and he stared at Lieutenant Yamai for a few moments, then overcame his surprise. *"Fuck you, you bastard!"*

"I think you'd better calm down."

"Kiss my ass, you yellow runt!"

"If you don't calm down, we'll have to calm you down."

"Up your ass with a ten-inch meat hook!"

Colonel Tsuji looked at one of the guards. "Hold your bayonet to his throat and see what that does."

The soldier drew his bayonet and placed its point against Butsko's throat.

"Go ahead and kill me, you fish-eating prick!"

Colonel Tsuji sighed. "Stick it in a little."

The soldier pressed the point of his bayonet into Butsko's throat, and Butsko felt it cut his skin. A dot of blood appeared around the cold steel, and the pain brought Butsko to his senses. There was no point in getting killed yet. Maybe he could escape later, the way he did on Luzon.

Colonel Tsuji smiled. "That's much better. You may proceed with your questions, Lieutenant Yamai."

Lieutenant Yamai smiled at Butsko. Yamai had studied interrogation techniques and knew it was best to make friends with the person you were questioning. "Care for a cigarette, soldier?"

Butsko wanted a cigarette desperately, but he said, "Shove it up your yellow ass."

"Now, now, Sergeant. Why make things so difficult for yourself?" Lieutenant Yamai took a cigarette out of his pack

87

and placed it between Butsko's bloody lips.

Butsko spit it out. "I said shove it up your ass!"

Colonel Tsuji couldn't take Butsko's insolence anymore. He jumped up, sped toward Butsko, and slapped him in the face. *"Behave yourself!"* he screamed in Japanese.

Butsko's head spun around with the force of the blow. "Fuck your mother," he said.

"Sir," said Lieutenant Yamai, "perhaps you'd better let me handle this. I must say most respectfully, sir, that if you continue being rough with him, he'll get stubborn and never give us any information."

Colonel Tsuji looked down at Butsko. "I hate Americans," he hissed. Then he composed himself. "But you're right. Perhaps I'd better leave you here with him. I'll go and see if General Hyakutake is awake yet. He'll be interested to know that we've captured an American."

Colonel Tsuji put on his hat and marched out the door. Lieutenant Yamai looked at Butsko again and smiled.

"You must excuse the colonel," he said. "He is rather hot-headed."

"Fuck him."

"Are you sure you don't want a cigarette?"

"I told you what to do with your cigarettes." Butsko licked his busted lower lip with his tongue. He knew they wanted information from him. First they'd be nice, but when they didn't get their way, they'd put on the pressure.

"What is your name?" Lieutenant Yamai asked pleasantly.

"Sergeant John Butsko. Regular Army, one-one-two, eight-two-two, oh-three. According to the Geneva Convention, that's all I have to tell you."

"Butsko?" Lieutenant Yamai asked. "What kind of name is that?"

"An American name."

"I mean, where did your ancestors come from?"

"Fuck you."

"Isn't it a Polish name?"

"Fuck you again."

"Yes, I do believe it's a Polish name. I lived in America for a short while, you see."

"If I'd've seen you around, I would have kicked your fucking Jap teeth in."

Lieutenant Yamai leaned forward. "What is your unit?"

"The Two Hundred Fifteenth Mess-Kit Repair Battalion."

Lieutenant Yamai wrinkled his brow, trying to figure out why the Americans needed an entire battalion to repair mess kits, and then realized Butsko was joking with him. Lieutenant Yamai reared back his head and laughed. "Oh, that is a funny one, Sergeant Butsko. You are a very funny fellow, I can see that."

"I hope you choke, you cocksucker."

Lieutenant Yamai's smile froze on his face. "See here, Sergeant Butsko, I don't think you realize how serious things are for you here."

"Fuck Hirohito in his ass."

Lieutenant Yamai became stern. "You have a choice, Sergeant Butsko. You can answer my questions nicely now, or you can answer them later and it won't be so nicely, but one way or another you'll answer them."

"You wanna bet?"

"I'd love to bet with you, but you don't have anything worth betting. We have ways to make people answer questions. I promise you, when we finish with you, you'll answer any question I ask. But I'll be—how do you say in your country?—a *nice guy*. Yes, I'll be a nice guy. I'll give you one more chance. What is your unit?"

"The Rangoon Spitoon Platoon."

Lieutenant Yamai didn't laugh this time. "Sergeant, you're being a fool."

Butsko coughed some phlegm and blood into his mouth and spit a lunger at Lieutenant Yamai. It landed on his freshly laundered pale-green shirt. Lieutenant Yamai shot to his feet, rushed toward Butsko, and punched him in the mouth, cutting open his knuckles on Butsko's teeth.

Lieutenant Yamai screamed in pain and stepped back, looking at the blood oozing out of his wound. Butsko laughed at him.

"My fucking grandmother used to hit me harder than that," Butsko said.

Lieutenant Yamai sucked in air through his nose and tried to calm himself because he wanted to draw his sword and hack Butsko in two. "You'll pay for that."

"Suck my dick."

"Keep an eye on him," Lieutenant Yamai said to the guard, then marched out of the tent to tell Colonel Tsuji that harsher measures would be required with the American sergeant.

Bannon and his squad roamed among the dead men on the top of the hill, taking one dog tag from the chain around the neck of each soldier and leaving one to identify the body. Bannon put all the dog tags that were collected into his pack to give to G-1 if they ever made it back to their lines. The soldiers looked down at their dead friends solemnly, realizing the same thing could have happened to them.

They'd identified the corpse of Napoleon Denker, and Private Shaw kneeled next to him, feeling lousy because he'd punched Denker during the crap game the previous afternoon. "I'm sorry, buddy," Shaw whispered. "If I ever make it back to the States, I'll tell your kid what a great guy you were." His throat was clogged and his eyes burned. He patted the shoulder of Denker's corpse and stood up.

All the men were angry about the way the Second Squad had been wiped out. The Japs even had emptied their pockets and taken their weapons and ammunition away. Bannon's jaw was set as he hiked his pack onto his back.

"Let's get moving," he said.

Longtree took the point and they moved out in a column of twos. Bannon was thinking about Butsko and hoped he still was alive. *I'm gonna bring you back, Sarge*, he vowed to himself. *Just hang on a little while longer.*

Lieutenant Yamai waited in the clerical section of General Hyakutake's headquarters tent, wiping the spit off his shirt with a handkerchief. A tent flap was pushed to the side and Colonel Tsuji appeared. "Well?"

"The American insists on being uncooperative," Lieutenant Yamai told him. "We'll use more extreme methods."

Colonel Tsuji frowned. "I knew it would turn out this way. I knew your fancy interrogation methods wouldn't work with

that one. Tell Sergeant Kaburagi to report to my tent immediately."

"Yes, sir."

The First Squad moved through the hot green jungle. Birds
crackled overhead and monkeys sat on branches, eating berries
and watching the men curiously. Longtree was twenty yards
in front of the others, bending low to the ground, following
tracks. Farther back Bannon walked through the swelter, thinking about Butsko, wondering what the Japanese were doing
with him.

"I'm hungry," said Homer Gladley. "When do we eat?"

"Yeah, let's take a break," Frankie La Barbara added.

"Keep going," Bannon said. "We can take a break later."

"When?" asked Frankie La Barbara.

"Another hour. We just got started, for Chrissakes."

Carrying his torture implements, Sergeant Kaburagi approached Colonel Tsuji's desk and saluted.

Colonel Tsuji nodded toward Butsko. "Go to work on him.
Make him talk."

"Yes, sir."

Lieutenant Yamai stood to the side of the desk. Butsko
watched as Sergeant Kaburagi emptied his leather bag onto the
desktop. Butsko saw pins and screws spill out and knew what
was going to happen. It was going to be a long, hard day, and
he pulled himself together to face it.

"Untie one of his hands and put it on the desk," Sergeant
Kaburagi said.

The soldiers loosened the rope on one of Butsko's hands,
and Sergeant Kaburagi affixed a vise to the edge of Colonel
Tsuji's desk. Colonel Tsuji smoked a cigarette and smiled faintly.
The soldiers lifted Butsko's chair and carried him closer to the
desk, then placed his wrist within the jaws of the vice. Sergeant
Kaburagi twirled the lever and the jaws tightened around Butsko's wrist. Butsko tried to send his mind someplace else so
that he wouldn't feel the pain as much. He knew what was
coming, and it was going to be terrible. He hoped he could
hold out.

When Butsko's hand was secured, Sergeant Kaburagi took

a long pin and held it up to the light, where it gleamed evilly. He smiled, because basically he was a sadist, and turned to Colonel Tsuji for the order to begin. Colonel Tsuji looked at Lieutenant Yamai.

"This is your last chance," Lieutenant Yamai said to Butsko.

"Fuck you."

Colonel Tsuji didn't need a translation to know that Butsko had again refused to speak. "Begin," he told Sergeant Kabragi.

Sergeant Kaburagi inserted the pin under the nail of Butsko's forefinger, and Butsko tensed in the chair. Sergeant Kaburagi pushed the pin in an eighth of an inch, and Butsko gritted his teeth at the vicious pain. The pin was pushed in another eighth of an inch, and Butsko bellowed like a wild elephant.

"Speak!" said Lieutenant Yamai. "What is your unit!"

Sweat poured down Butsko's face and hate welled up in his heart. He shook his head. Sergeant Kaburagi wiggled the pin under Butsko's nail, and Butsko screamed again, his voice carrying across the Japanese encampment. Soldiers stopped what they were doing and looked toward Colonel Tsuji's tent. They knew a captured American soldier was in there and they shrugged, continuing with their duties.

When the men from the Third and Fourth squads returned to the American lines, they were taken immediately to Colonel Stockton's headquarters. The men waited outside while Sergeant Slattery and Corporal De Pietro were sent into Colonel Stockton's office.

"Have a seat, men," he told them, his eyes heavy-lidded from lack of sleep. "I guess you know by now that the First and Second squads are still out there someplace. Do you have any idea of what happened to them?"

"No, sir," said Corporal Di Pietro.

"We heard some gunfire," Sergeant Slattery added. "A lot of it was submachine-gun fire, so I guess Butsko and the Second Squad got into a fight."

Colonel Stockton nodded. "Anything else?"

"No, sir."

"You may return to your platoon area. Sergeant Slattery, you'll be in charge of the platoon until further notice."

"Yes, sir."

The two men rose, saluted, and marched out of Colonel Stockton's office.

Colonel Stockton leaned back in his chair and looked out the window at the green leaves and the blue sky. He felt sick over the loss of the First and Second Squads of his recon platoon and believed it was all his fault. He shouldn't have sent them out on such a hazardous mission. They'd fought well in battle, but the mission had been too much for them. They had been good men, but not that good. He hated to lose them.

He wondered if things would have turned out differently if an officer had been in charge of them.

The First Squad pushed through the jungle, sweat pouring from their bodies. The sun was rising in the sky and the jungle was steaming. All their canteens were nearly empty, and Bannon debated whether to stop following the Japanese tracks and head for a stream to get some water.

They left the jungle and entered a field of kunai grass through which passed the beaten-down trail of the Japanese force that had taken Butsko away. They didn't know it, but they were very close to the Japanese encampment. Suddenly Sam Longtree stopped and furrowed his brow.

"I hear something," he said.

Bannon listened, and above the faint wind and sounds of creatures in the jungle, Bannon heard a new sound. It sounded like a man screaming not too far away.

"Jesus," he said, "that sounds like Butsko."

Sam Longtree nodded. "It's Butsko all right."

"Let's see if we can move a little faster," Bannon said.

Butsko had needles under all his fingernails, and the pain was unbearable. He and his chair bounced up and down as he shrieked and swore.

"Hold him down," Colonel Tsuji said.

The soldiers pressed down on Butsko's shoulders, whose face was wrenched in pain. He strained against the ropes that tied him, and blood oozed out from beneath his fingernails. Also his wrist was bleeding from pulling against the jaws of the vise.

Lieutenant Yamai looked at him, wondering how he could

93

tolerate the pain. "What was the nature of your mission?"

Butsko couldn't stop his lips from trembling. "Kiss my ass!"

Colonel Tsuji turned to Lieutenant Yamai. "He still refuses to cooperate, does he?"

"Yes, sir."

Colonel Tsuji was losing patience. He drew his cigarette out of his mouth, stood, and walked in front of Butsko. "You miserable stupid pig," he uttered. Holding the lit cigarette in his fingers, he put it out on Butsko's forehead.

The end of the cigarette burned into Butsko's flesh, and he hollered louder than he'd ever hollered before. The tent filled with the odor of singed flesh, and Colonel Tsuji held his cigarette against Butsko's skin until it went out. Then he reared back his fist and punched Butsko in the mouth.

"I'm sick of all his noise," Colonel Tsuji said. "Put him in the box for a while. That may break down his will to resist."

"Yes, sir," Sergeant Kaburagi said. He turned to the guards and told them to untie Butsko.

Butsko felt as if somebody had stuck a knife in his head. His hand was on fire and he was so disoriented he couldn't even yell. *I'm losing control of myself,* he thought. *I've got to hang on somehow.*

The guards released him from the chair and picked him up. His hands, arms, and feet were bound, and they carried him outside, with Sergeant Kaburagi following.

Colonel Tsuji returned to the chair behind his desk. "He's a tough one," he said.

"He can't hold out much longer," Lieutenant Yamai replied. "After a few hours in the box he'll tell us anything we want to know."

"I'm not so sure," Colonel Tsuji said. "Some men never talk, and he might be one of them. But that'll be his funeral. I shall behead him with my own sword."

TEN . . .

At noon Bannon told his men to break for lunch. The first thing Frankie did was take off his pack and move away from the rest of them so he could take a shit. He didn't want to get too far away, because he knew Japs were nearby, so he found a secluded little spot, pulled down his pants, and squatted, thinking of how wonderful modern bathrooms were, with toilets that flushed and sinks for washing your hands afterward. As he squatted there, surrounded by smelly vapors, he wondered who the man was who invented the toilet. *They should build a statue of him in every town in the world,* Frankie thought.

A twisted black branch lay a few feet in front of Frankie, and all of a sudden he realized it was moving! It was a big black snake, and Frankie could see it heading straight for him.

He opened his mouth to scream, but stopped himself when he realized that Japs were nearby. He was afraid to move, because that might cause the snake to lunge at him. All he could do was sit still and watch the snake. He thought of drawing his bayonet for protection, but the snake was watching him too closely. The snake moved closer, and Frankie stared into his eyes, hoping to hypnotize him. It didn't work. His stare didn't faze the snake at all.

Oh, shit, Frankie thought. *This fucking snake's going to bite my dick.* Then his bowels broke loose and he dropped a huge amount of excrement onto the ground. There was a horrible stink, and the snake cringed. Turning around, it slithered away quickly and disappeared into the underbrush.

Frankie pulled up his pants and ran back to where the others were. They became alarmed and dropped their cans of C rations, reaching for their submachine guns.

"It was a snake," Frankie said, his face ashen, buckling his belt. "He almost bit me."

Shaw grinned. "What'd you do, bite him first?"

"Ha ha. Very funny."

Frankie sat next to his pack and took out a can of sausage patties. He wished he could wash his hands, but he only had a swallow of water left in his canteen and he wanted to save it for an emergency. He opened his can and stuck his fork into the sausage patty on top.

"I almost got killed and you guys don't even give a fuck," he muttered.

At the Japanese encampment General Hyakutake was also having lunch, fresh raw fish caught that morning and flavored with soy sauce. Colonel Tsuji entered the office quietly.

"I apologize for disturbing you," Colonel Tsuji said, "but I thought I should report on our interrogation of the American."

"What have you learned?" General Hyakutake asked.

"Nothing. He's very stubborn."

"Really? Well, keep at it. He'll break sooner or later."

"We're putting him into the box, sir. That ought to do it."

General Hyakutake picked up a piece of fish with his chopsticks. "Indeed it should," he said.

The box was in the middle of a clearing, in the hot afternoon sun. Actually it was more of a cage than a box, made out of bamboo and so small that Butsko couldn't stretch his legs or straighten his back. He was bent over like a pretzel, his ankles and hands bound, and the sun baked him unmercifully as sweat poured off his body. Two Japanese soldiers guarded him.

His back and legs ached and he felt extreme claustrophobia. The hand that had been tortured with pins had become swollen and infected. He was bound so tightly that he was numb in his hands and feet, and he thought gangrene would set in very soon.

The pain and hot sun were making him delirious, and he muttered to himself, trying to keep sane. "I'm not going to tell them anything," he kept saying over and over. He was confident he could hold out to the bitter end, but he thought that after a while he might go crazy and babble anything they wanted to know.

Japanese soldiers passed by and looked at him, some feeling pity. Butsko cursed them, the war, and everything else he could think of. He entertained himself with fantasies of disemboweling Japs, stomping on their faces, gouging out their eyes, shooting them to pieces. They gave him nothing to eat or drink and he became dehydrated. After two hours he fainted dead away.

At three o'clock in the afternoon Captain Mizushima approached Butsko. Mizushima was curious about his prisoner and wanted to take a look at him. He stood beside the cage and noticed that Butsko had passed out. Picking up a stick, he prodded its end into Butsko's ribs.

Butsko felt the new pain and turned his head to see his tormentor. His eyes burned with perspiration and the sun seared his brain, but he saw the bandy-legged Japanese officer from the Bataan Death March standing there with a grin on his face, and he flew into a rage.

"You fucking cocksucker!" Butsko growled. "If I ever get my hands on you, I'll take you apart!"

Captain Mizushima couldn't speak English, but he had a good idea of what Butsko was saying. A stern, cruel man, he responded by jabbing the stick harder into Butsko's ribs. Butsko couldn't move much; he just had to take it.

"I'll cut your fucking throat someday!" Butsko said, his mouth dry and his lips cracking.

Captain Mizushima prodded Butsko a few more times, then dropped the stick and walked away. The American still had some fight in him, but he wouldn't have it for long. The sun had a way of sapping men's strength.

Butsko watched him go, and his brain was so hot that Captain Mizushima seemed to be walking on air, aureoled with light as bright as the sun.

"Someday I'll get you," Butsko muttered. "Someday."

Pfc. Longtree had seen it all.

When the First Squad had neared the Japanese encampment,

Bannon sent Longtree ahead to scout the area. Longtree crept forward slowly and carefully, parting the leaves in front of him and looking directly into the encampment. His eyes fell immediately on the cage in the center of the clearing, and he recognized the bulky form of Butsko bent inside. Then the Japanese officer had come by and poked Butsko with a stick. Longtree had been tempted to raise his submachine gun and cut him down, but that would have doomed Butsko and him. So he'd just watched, raging inside at the Japanese officer and proud of Butsko for his defiance.

Longtree took his notepad and pencil out of his pocket and sketched the Japanese encampment the way Bannon had ordered him to, making special note of the guards throughout the area.

"Just be patient, Sarge," Longtree whispered. "We'll get you out of there before long."

In the late afternoon, as the sun was dropping toward the horizon, Colonel Tsuji and Lieutenant Yamai came to see how Butsko was doing. Butsko was out cold from lack of food and dehydration, his body covered with welts and insect bites.

"Hmmm," said Colonel Tsuji, cocking his head to the side and examining Butsko, "you don't think he's dead, do you?"

"I don't know, sir."

Lieutenant Yamai picked up the same stick Captain Mizushima had dropped and stuck the end into Butsko's neck. "Wake up, Sergeant!"

Butsko opened his eyes and turned in the direction of the voice. His mind was turbid and his eyes weren't focusing properly, but he saw two figures standing beside him and knew they weren't friendly.

Lieutenant Yamai knelt beside Butsko. "Make it easy on yourself, Sergeant. Just say the word and we'll let you out of here."

"No," Butsko whispered, his tongue and throat parched.

"You're being very foolish," Lieutenant Yamai said suavely. "We'll let you out of there and you can stretch your arms and legs. Think of how nice that would feel. And we'd give you food and water. Wouldn't you like to drink water right now, Sergeant? Don't be a fool. Don't die for a lost cause. Just

98

answer a few questions and we'll give you anything you want."

"No," Butsko said. "Never."

The sun set on the horizon and the First Squad huddled in a dense part of the jungle a mile from the Japanese encampment. They ate another meal and then tried to get some sleep, because at two in the morning they were going to launch a quick surprise attack against the Japanese and try to rescue Butsko.

In the last rays of the setting sun Bannon put the final touches to his battle plan. He had six men and each would have a specific job. They'd have to move in fast and get out fast, and he didn't want anybody else to get hurt. It wouldn't be easy, but they'd all agreed to make the try because each one knew in his heart that Butsko would do it for them under the same circumstances.

Bannon knew that the odds were against them. It was a large Japanese encampment; Longtree had estimated that a regiment of Japs was bivouacked there. But they wouldn't be expecting anything. The plan had a good chance of working. It would be dark and the Japs wouldn't dare send up flares, because it would attract American planes and artillery.

The main problem was reaching the edge of the Japanese encampment without being detected. They'd have to be silent, and it would be difficult for six men to be silent in the woods at night. The only way to be silent was to move slowly and carefully. Bannon intended to leave where they were at midnight, so they'd have two hours to cover the distance to the Japanese encampment. Then they'd strike like tigers in the night.

Bannon finished his can of beans and wanted to smoke a cigarette, but he didn't dare smoke so close to the Japanese encampment. He took a swig of water; they'd found a stream and filled their canteens, dropping in chlorine pills to kill any microorganisms. Getting Butsko back to safety would be only half the problem. The other problem would be the explanation he'd have to make to Colonel Stockton, if they ever made it back. Bannon knew he'd disobeyed orders by going after Butsko. If the Japs didn't get him, Colonel Stockton would. And all the shit would fall on him, because he was in charge. But Bannon thought he could handle it. They wouldn't give him the firing squad or anything like that. Probably they'd just bust him back to private, but that wouldn't be so bad. It was better than stopping a Jap bullet or knowing that he'd left Butsko behind.

He thought about Butsko, tied hand and foot in a cage in the hot sun. Longtree had described what he'd seen, and it sounded awful. No one knew for sure that Butsko would live through it. But he was a tough old son of a bitch. It would be hard to kill him. Surely he'd be alive. How horrible it would be if they got him out of there and found out they'd liberated a dead man.

Butsko wasn't dead yet, but he wasn't very much alive either. He had become so delirious that he couldn't feel pain anymore, and he was hallucinating wildly, seeing people he hadn't seen in years. His former wife, Dolly Crane, danced naked in front of him, holding her big breasts in her two hands and shaking her ass.

"Dolly," he whispered. "Dolly, come here."

But she only stuck her tongue out at him. Butsko ordinarily tried not to think of her, because she'd broken his heart, sleeping around with other men and finally leaving him altogether. Before he could divorce her he was shipped overseas, and then the Japs had attacked the Philippines. She was still his legal wife and still received an allotment from him, living high on the hog and screwing other guys.

"Jesus, Dolly," he said, "why did you do it?"

She laughed and kept dancing, blowing him a kiss. She'd always insisted that she'd loved him, even when she was screwing other guys, but he didn't believe her. He'd beaten her up once, and shortly thereafter she'd left him. That had been in Hawaii, and he'd moved back into the Scofield Barracks. It had tormented him to know that she was sleeping with other guys only a short distance away in Honolulu, so he put in for a transfer and wound up in the Philippines. A few months later the Japs attacked Pearl Harbor, and then they'd landed on Luzon.

He couldn't bear to think of her sleeping with other men, doing the same tender and wonderful things to them that she'd done to him, so he'd ruthlessly blocked her out of his mind, but now his mind was weak and she was back again, dancing obscenely in front of him the way she used to do sometimes when they got drunk together.

She'd been great in bed, but in other ways she was awful. Her cooking was lousy, she always had their apartment full of stinking cats, and she was usually in a bad mood. But when she was in a good mood, she was marvelous. She laughed and teased, tossing her hair around, and then she'd start tugging at his clothes, undoing his buttons, rubbing up against him, and driving him out of his mind.

She'd do anything and everything in bed. Never had he known such a wanton, uninhibited woman. Most of the other women he'd screwed were prostitutes, who were businesslike and mechanical, or the kind of women who kept you away until the wee hours of the morning, when you were drunk and half asleep, and then let you screw them once, while you struggled to stay awake.

Dolly liked to fuck any time of the day, and she liked to fuck for long periods of time. They'd do it, smoke cigarettes, do it again, eat a sandwich, do it again, talk for a while, and do it again. She was strong and supple and could tie you up in knots, all the while moving that sweet caboose of hers, making little animal sounds. Butsko had thought he was the only one who turned her on that way, but found out to his great sorrow that evidently she was like that with all men. It nearly drove him insane when he found out she did those same things with lots of other guys. So he'd punched her out and she'd left him. Afterward he never talked about her and even said he'd never been married. He'd almost convinced himself that she never existed, but now here she was, back again, slithering around his cage.

"You're the best I ever had, Johnny boy," she said. "There's never been anybody like you."

"You're a fucking liar," Butsko mumbled. "You're no good and you've never been any good, Dolly."

Captain Mizushima rushed across the clearing, buttoning his shirt. It was night, with a full moon that cast an eerie, bowlegged shadow in front of him. He entered Colonel Tsuji's tent and saw Sergeant Kaburagi sitting behind the desk.

"Colonel Tsuji wishes to see me," Captain Mizushima said.

Sergeant Kaburagi nodded toward the tent flap that led to Colonel Tsuji's office, and Captain Mizushima pushed the flap aside and entered.

Colonel Tsuji was drinking a cup of green tea and examining a map. "How soon can you and your men move out?" he asked.

"A half hour, sir."

"Good. A convoy is arriving tomorrow night with the Forty-eighth Division, and they'll disembark here." Colonel Tsuji pointed to a spot on the map. "I'm concerned that there still may be spies or American patrols in the vicinity, so I want you to sweep through the area with your men and clear it out. Is that clear?"

"Yes, sir."

Colonel Tsuji narrowed his eyes. "Captain Mizushima, I want you to understand the gravity of the situation. The Forty-eighth Division will give us the strength we need to defeat the Americans on this godforsaken island. Nothing must occur that will impede their landing. Therefore I'm counting on you to keep that area free from enemy observation."

Captain Mizushima nodded. "You can rely on me, sir. What time will the convoy arrive?"

"We don't know for sure. In the early hours of the morning, I suppose. It depends on the tides and the disposition of American naval forces. The sooner you start clearing that area, the better."

"Yes, sir. Before I leave, sir, I was wondering if any information was obtained from that American yet."

Colonel Tsuji frowned. "No, but I don't think he'll be able to resist much longer. He's babbling to himself out there. The poor fellow is probably losing his mind."

ELEVEN . . .

Spread out across the jungle, the men of the First Squad crawled toward the Japanese encampment. They moved slowly, clearing twigs and dead leaves out of their paths, trying to be as quiet as possible.

Bannon had given them two hours to cover the distance. When they reached their assigned positions they were to remain still and wait for the signal to move into action. The signal would be Bannon standing and running toward Butsko. Each man had been given a particular job, and Bannon had questioned each of them to be sure he understood. Homer Gladley had been given the simplest job, one that wouldn't confuse him, and would move in with Bannon, so that Bannon could keep an eye on him.

The moon was full and filled the jungle with phantoms. Every shadow seemed to conceal a Jap with rifle and bayonet. The American soldiers could hear random activity in the Japanese bivouac, the doors of vehicles being opened or closed, the snick of rifle bolts being closed, the sound of boxes being moved around.

The GIs were twenty yards apart, so that if one of them drew fire, the others could get away. They were edgy but determined to get Butsko out of there if he still was alive. Even Frankie had gotten into the mood. He thought he might get a medal if they rescued Butsko, and maybe then they'd send him home for a furlough, so he could go AWOL.

Finally, one by one, they came to the edge of the encampment and lay in the bushes, waiting for the signal to move in. Bannon peered through the leaves and saw the cage about fifty yards away in the middle of the clearing, with Butsko folded nearly in half inside and guards standing on either side of him. Other guards were posted in front of tents, but this encampment was far behind the enemy lines, and they weren't expecting any trouble. They probably believed the Americans didn't know it existed.

Bannon looked at his watch. It was ten minutes before two o'clock. He heard a soul-rending groan; it had come from Butsko. Bannon couldn't believe that such a mournful sound ever would escape Butsko's lips. They must have done terrible things to him. Bannon wondered how he himself would make out if the Japs ever got their hands on him.

The minute hand of his watch moved closer to two o'clock. Bannon gripped his submachine gun and got ready to charge. He'd loaded the gun with a fresh clip before leaving their hiding spot in the jungle, and all of them had slept and eaten. They were in good shape, and if they moved fast, they should be able to get Butsko out of there. He wished there was no moonlight, but you couldn't have everything. You had to make the best of what you had.

The minute hand touched twelve, and Bannon took a deep breath, jumping to his feet. He charged through the bush in front of him and ran into the clearing, heading straight for Butsko.

The other men in the squad were watching the spot where he'd been hiding, and they came out of the jungle, too, running as fast as they could and aiming their submachine guns straight ahead. The sound of their boots on the ground made the two Japanese guards spin around.

Bannon opened fire on one of them, and the Japanese soldier was thrown back by the impact of the bullets. The other Jap squeezed his trigger, but before his rifle could fire, he was cut down by a burst from Sam Longtree's submachine gun. The GIs charged into the clearing, shooting from the hip and throwing hand grenades. Homer Gladley headed for the crate that held Butsko, because his job was to carry Butsko away. Bannon was a few feet from him, to provide cover, and the others formed a defensive line to protect Gladley and Bannon.

The other Japanese soldiers heard the commotion and poked their heads out of their tents, but it was night and hard to see what was going on. The first shot had awakened Butsko, who twisted in his cage, half insane and trying to make sense of what was going on.

Japanese soldiers ran toward the sound of the gunfire, and the First Squad was waiting for them. The GIs fired their submachine guns in great rolling volleys. General Hyakutake jumped out of bed and fumbled around for his glasses. Colonel Tsuji grabbed his Nambu pistol and ran naked out of his tent. The GIs swung their submachine guns back and forth, spraying tents with bullets and ripping apart every Jap they could see.

Homer Gladley reached down and scooped up the cage that held Butsko. He hoisted it onto his shoulder and ran back toward the jungle, taking huge strides with his thick, muscular legs and size-twelve combat boots, and Butsko bounced up and down painfully in his cage. The other men in the First Squad continued their stream of submachine gun fire and backed toward the jungle.

The submachine guns made a huge racket and the Japanese soldiers thought they were under serious attack. Orders were shouted and men were sent to General Hyakutake's tent to form a defensive perimeter. The Japanese soldiers fired at moving shadows and imagined sounds in the jungle. Only those nearest the spot where Butsko had been kept had any idea of what was happening, but they couldn't make their voices heard over the general confusion. In minutes the GIs had rescued Butsko and disappeared into the jungle.

They ran as fast as they could, not worried about making noise, just trying to put as much distance between them and the Japs as they could. They heard shouts and gunfire behind them as the Japanese soldiers fought off an imagined attack. Sam Longtree led the long file through the jungle, slapping branches and leaves out of the way, fleet-footed and hawk-eyed, his wounded stomach protesting against the intense exertion.

One hundred yards into the jungle, Bannon ordered a halt. Homer Gladley lowered the bamboo crate to the ground, and Shilansky slashed the ropes that bound the door. Butsko was still bent over grotesquely inside, his hands and legs tied, trying to come to his senses, wondering if he was dead or alive.

The last fiber of rope was sliced through, and Shilansky opened the top of the crate. Bannon and Shaw grabbed Butsko under his arms and pulled him out of the crate. Butsko's spine straightened out and he opened his eyes. Shilansky cut the twine that bound Butsko's hands and feet.

"Whaz goin' on?" he asked dreamily.

"Give him a drink of water," Bannon said.

Shilansky opened his canteen and held it to Butsko's lips. Butsko felt the cool water on his tongue; it was like ambrosia. Feebly he moved his tongue and swallowed some down, trying to make sense of what was happening. In the distance the commotion in the Japanese encampment could be heard.

"We'd better get going," Bannon said.

Shilansky took his canteen back and dropped it into its case on his belt.

"Let's go, Sarge," Gladley said, lowering his mountainous shoulder to Butsko's middle. Butsko leaned forward and Gladley picked him up again.

Bannon, Gladley, and Butsko went in one direction, Frankie La Barbara and Sam Longtree in another, Shilansky and Shaw to the left, and O'Rourke and Craig Delane to the right. In minutes they had all vanished into the jungle, while behind them the Japanese were still trying to figure our what had happened.

General Hyakutake sat behind the desk in his headquarters tent, his helmet strapped to his head, his sword lying across his desk, sipping a cup of green tea and waiting for someone to tell him what was going on. He heard sporadic bursts of fire around his encampment, and orders being shouted, but it did not appear to him that much serious had happened. He suspected some of his guards had gotten trigger-happy and perhaps fired upon a returning patrol. He wished everything would settle down so that he could go back to sleep.

The flap to his office was pushed aside and Colonel Tsuji entered, tall and lean, dressed in his baggy jodhpurs and boots, his Nambu pistol in his hand. The kerosene lamp atop General Hyakutake's desk cast a sheen on Tsuji's hairless chest.

"It was an American raiding party, sir," Colonel Tsuji said. "They came for their comrade and got him out."

General Hyakutake's eyes widened. "How many Americans were there?"

"Anywhere from ten to a hundred, depending on who you talk with."

"How could they get so close without our guards seeing them? We'll have to review our security procedures here. I take it you've sent troops after them."

"Yes, sir. And we have numerous military units patrolling the area, who can prevent the Americans from either returning to their lines or reaching the sea. The Americans will not get away."

The jungle near the Japanese encampment was crisscrossed with trails, and Bannon and Gladley moved quickly along one of them, Gladley carrying Butsko over his shoulders. Gladley charged like an elephant over the ground, while Bannon lagged a few feet behind, glancing back toward the Japanese encampment, listening for the sounds of pursuit.

Meanwhile, Butsko was coming back to his senses. Although weak and woozy still, he was aware that men from his platoon had rescued him from the Japanese. His back ached sharply with every step Gladley took, and finally he cleared out his throat and murmured, "Lemme down."

Gladley stopped and turned to Bannon. "He wants me to let him down."

"Then let him down."

Gladley bent and let Butsko's feet touch the ground. Butsko tried to stand but his knees caved in and he fell down. Gladley lifted him as if he were a feather.

"Hey there, old Sarge," Gladley said. "Whatsa matter?"

"I don' know," Butsko murmured, trying to pull himself together.

"Get down!" Bannon said.

The three of them dropped to the ground and listened. They heard footsteps coming from the direction of the Japanese headquarters area.

"Into these bushes here," Bannon said.

Bannon and Gladley crawled into the bushes, dragging Butsko with them. The jungle was dense, and soon they were out of sight. Bannon crawled out again to cover their tracks, then returned to Butsko and Gladley.

"I think we should stay here until he gets some of his strength back," Bannon said.

"I can carry him okay," Gladley replied. "He don't weigh that much."

Butsko weighed two hundred pounds and was five feet ten inches tall. He had a powerful constitution and moved his limbs on the ground, trying to make himself normal again. Bannon took off his pack and picked out a can of fruit cocktail that had been part of a C ration box. He opened the can and handed it to Butsko with his spoon. "Have some of this, Sarge."

Butsko had gone without food for so long that his stomach was cramped, but he accepted the food and utensil with trembling hands. Bannon and Gladley noticed the tips of his fingers swollen and caked with blood.

"Jeez," said Gladley, "what'd they do to you, Sarge?"

Butsko chewed and swallowed some of the slippery fruit mixture. "They stuck me with pins," he said hoarsely.

Bannon looked at the bruises on Butsko's face and body and knew he'd been through a terrible ordeal. The food loosened up Butsko's stomach and he felt normal pangs of hunger amidst aching.

"Gimme some more water," he said.

Bannon handed him the canteen. A shot was fired in the distance, and Japanese voices shouted orders.

"Where're the others?" Butsko asked.

"I split up the squad," Bannon replied. "Thought we'd have a better chance of getting away if we split up."

"Maybe and maybe not," Butsko said. "We're still pretty close to the Jap camp, ain't we?"

"It's about three hundred yards away."

Butsko looked up at the full moon. "We'd have a better chance if it was darker. When'll it be morning?"

Bannon looked at his watch. "It's a little after two in the morning."

Butsko finished the can of fruit salad and chucked it deep into the jungle. He took another drink of water and wiped his mouth with the back of his hand. Then he worked his shoulders and leaned backward and forward, trying to make his spine feel right again.

"Those fucking Japs." Butsko murmured.

"Feel any better, Sarge?" Bannon asked.

"A little. Lemme lie down for a few minutes."

Butsko stretched out on his back, closed his eyes, and dropped off to sleep. Homer Gladley was puzzled, because he thought they shouldn't stay so close to the Japanese encampment.

"How long we gonna stay here?" he asked Bannon.

Bannon looked at his watch. "We'll let him sleep an hour, and then we'll get going again."

Bannon moved his head around and listened to the sounds of the forest. He could still hear an uproar in the encampment; Japanese troops moved into the jungle in pursuit of the other members of his squad. Butsko began to snore, and Bannon muffled the sound with his dirty handkerchief. Japanese soldiers approached on the trail that passed by their hiding place, and Bannon and Gladley got low to the ground. Bannon pressed the handkerchief against Butsko's nose and mouth, but the passing Japanese soldiers made a racket that overwhelmed any noise Butsko made.

The Japanese soldiers ran by and their sounds receded into the jungle. Bannon lay down and closed his eyes, to get a little rest before resuming the trek to the sea.

Sam Longtree and Frankie La Barbara galloped through the jungle like two wild stallions, stretching out their long legs, trying to put as much distance between them and the Japs as they could.

Sam Longtree led and Frankie followed on the same trail they'd used to approach the Japanese camp. It was wide and spacious and offered no impediment to their progress as they ran along, their packs bouncing up and down on their backs, their shirts soaked with sweat, and panic in Frankie La Barbara's heart.

Sam Longtree wasn't in any panic, because he knew what he was doing. Longtree had picked out landmarks on the trail and now knew exactly where he was. Frankie knew nothing and followed Longtree blindly.

Longtree came to a point where the main trail intersected a narrower trail, and he veered onto it, branches and leaves scratching at his face. Frankie clawed at the air to protect his eyes and stumbled along after Longtree, who had to slow down for Frankie. Longtree knew Frankie was impeding his progress and making life more dangerous, but he couldn't leave him behind, because Frankie was a warrior-brother.

They continued for two hundred yards on the narrow trail, then Longtree jumped into the thick of the jungle and crawled on his stomach underneath the branches and vines. The ground was covered with moist, rotting vegetation and then a long stretch of mud. Again, Longtree knew he could move faster if it weren't for Frankie. He stopped and turned around, waiting for Frankie to catch up.

"You're going too slow," Longtree said.

Frankie was wheezing. "I'm moving as fast as I can, Chief. Whataya want from me?"

"Frankie, look at me."

"Whataya mean, look at you?"

"I said look at me."

Frankie gazed up into Longtree's face and saw his eyes glowing like hot coals in the night. Frankie almost could feel the strength and power of Longtree's being.

"Do you want to live or die?" Longtree asked.

"What do you think?" Frankie replied.

"Then you'll have to do two things: You'll have to leave your pack behind, so you can move faster, and then you'll have to stop thinking so much and just follow me as quickly as you can."

"Leave my pack behind?" Frankie asked. "But all my chow and stuff is in there."

"Take a couple cans of chow and put them in your pockets, but leave the rest behind. We can live off the land. It's better to be alive and not have much stuff than be dead and have a lot of stuff."

Frankie thought about it for a moment and realized Longtree made sense. "Okay, Chief," he said. He slipped off his shoulder straps and laid his pack on the ground, taking out two cans of C rations and stuffing them in each of his back pockets.

Longtree also removed his pack and took out some C rations.

He checked his map and his compass. His stomach itched from the stitches, and he told himself he'd remove them first chance he got. He took off his helmet and laid it on the ground. "Leave your helmet behind too," he said.

Frankie removed his helmet, took his cloth fatigue cap out of his pack, and put it on. Longtree also put on his fatigue cap. Now they just wore their cartridge belts, canteens, first-aid pouches, and extra ammo clips for the Thompson submachine guns.

"Ready?" Longtree asked.

"Yeah."

"Let's go, and don't slow me down anymore, because if you do, I'll leave you behind."

"Okay, Chief."

Longtree crawled through the jungle again, and Frankie stayed close behind him. Longtree wouldn't have left Frankie behind, but the threat worked. They slid rapidly across the floor of the jungle like two giant lizards and in a half hour came to a field of kunai grass. Longtree examined his map in the moonlight, checked his compass, and looked at the moon. He saw a dark mass on the horizon and hoped it was clouds.

"We're gonna cross that field," Longtree said. "Follow me and don't stop for nothing."

Frankie was all hepped up. "Go ahead, Chief. I'll be right behind you."

Longtree sprang to his feet and ran swiftly into the tall kunai grass. Frankie was right on his tail, his legs kicking out under him, holding his submachine gun in his right hand and punching the air with his left. They sped across the field, zigzagging and twisting so the razor-sharp leaves of grass wouldn't cut them. The full moon shone down upon them, two fleet creatures of the night.

Colonel Tsuji stormed into the radio tent, his samurai sword strapped to his waist and his helmet low over his eyes. The radio operators looked fearfully at him but didn't get up and salute, because that would interfere with their transmission and reception of messages.

"Get me Captain Mizushima," Colonel Tsuji barked, then sat on a chair and took out a cigarette.

111

One of the radio operators hunched over his microphone and tried to raise Captain Mizushima, as Colonel Tsuji crossed his legs and smoked, his hands trembling with anger.

It infuriated Tsuji to think that Americans had actually attacked General Hyakutake's headquarters so far behind the front lines. Colonel Tsuji could hear tents being taken down and crates loaded onto trucks, because the camp would have to be moved now that the Americans knew where it was. The Americans might have had a radio with them and notified their airplanes where the camp was. Airplanes might be on the way at that very moment.

"I have Captain Mizushima, sir," said one of the radio operators.

Colonel Tsuji stood and walked to the radio. The operator gave him his chair and Tsuji sat down. "Is that you, Captain Mizushima?" he said into the radio.

"Yes, sir."

"Listen to me carefully. An American raiding party has attacked this camp and taken away our prisoner. They're probably headed in your direction or toward their own lines. Deploy your company so as to cut them off. We estimate that there are twenty or thirty of them. Do you understand my message?"

"Yes, sir."

"Very good. Over and out."

Pfc. Shaw and Private Shilansky were running through the jungle and could hear Japanese soldiers not far behind them. Shaw and Shilansky switched directions and doubled back a few times, but still the Japanese kept coming. The two GIs had made so many twists and turns that they didn't know where they were headed anymore, so Shaw stopped to look at his compass and Shilansky crashed right into him. Both lost their balance and fell to the ground.

Shaw grunted something nasty as he looked at his compass. The Japanese soldiers were coming up quickly behind them. Shaw tried to figure out which way to go, but he'd taken a lot of punches to the head in his life and he wasn't the fastest thinker in the world.

"Jesus Christ, they're almost here!" Shilansky said, ripping a hand grenade off his lapel.

He pulled the pin as Shaw also removed a hand grenade from his lapel. The Japs crashed through the jungle behind them and their figures became visible through the leaves and branches. The two GIs hurled the grenades and flopped forward onto their faces. The grenades sailed through the air and the Japs didn't even see them coming. One grenade bounced off a Jap's helmet and in the next second exploded, taking off the Jap's head and the head of the Jap beside him. The other grenade hit the ground and exploded, blowing away feet and legs. The Japanese soldiers had been bunched together closely on the narrow trail, and there had only been ten of them. The two hand grenades killed or disabled them all.

"Let's get out of here!" Shaw said.

"I'm getting rid of my fucking pack first!"

Shilansky dropped his pack to the ground and so did Shaw. They didn't waste any time taking food; they just turned and fled down the trail, running as quickly as they could, and then rounded a corner and ran into another Japanese patrol.

The Japanese and GIs were both surprised at first, but then went for their weapons. The Japs carried long Arisaka rifles with bolt actions, but the GIs had submachine guns and opened fire first, spraying the Japanese patrol with lead. A few of the Japanese soldiers managed to fire some wild shots before the submachine-gun bullets bit into them and tore away their lives. The Japanese soldiers stumbled and spun, falling backward and twisting in the air, finally dropping to the ground.

Shilansky and Shaw jumped over their dead bodies and kept going like running backs heading for a touchdown.

High in a tree, Jimmy O'Rourke and Craig Delane sat on branches, looking down at Japanese patrols running back and forth over jungle trails. O'Rourke, the former movie stuntman, had gotten the idea to climb the tree and had dragged Delane up with him. They had a good view and could even see Japanese soldiers striking their tents and loading equipment onto trucks in their headquarters compound.

Delane watched the turmoil in the Japanese camp and had to admit to himself that O'Rourke had probably saved his life. The Japs had been swarming all around them before they'd climbed the tree, and would have gotten them before long.

Delane realized he'd probably be indebted to O'Rourke for the rest of his life, and he wondered whether or not it might be better to be dead.

O'Rourke was so overjoyed by his cleverness that he couldn't stop giggling and wiggling on the branch, jabbing Delane with his elbow, snorting and guffawing. "Stupid fucking Japs," he said. "I guess they can't see so good with them slant eyes they got."

"Keep still," Delane said. "They might hear you."

O'Rourke tried to settle himself down. He respected Delane immensely, because Delane was rich and had good manners. O'Rourke tried to behave like Delane but usually was unsuccessful and quickly lapsed back into truculence or submissiveness, depending on who was around.

"Well," O'Rourke said, "at least we got old Butsko out of there. I hope he remembers who saved his ass when we get back to our lines."

"*If* we get back to our lines."

"We'll get back," O'Rourke said confidently. "You just stick with me and I'll get us there."

Delane frowned in the darkness. He knew that if O'Rourke got him back to safety, he'd be further in debt to him. He'd probably have to give him a job after the war if they both survived. O'Rourke would hang around him forever. Once again Delane cursed himself for joining the Army. After all, his father could have bribed his way out of the draft. He could be sitting in the Metropolitan Club in New York City right now, drinking fine old sherry and reading *The Wall Street Journal* instead of sitting in a tree on Guadalcanal. He looked at his watch.

"It'll get light pretty soon," he said. "We can't stay here much longer."

"Just leave everything to old Jimmy. I told you I'd get us out of here, and I'll get us out of here."

Delane looked back at the Japanese trucks driving away down the makeshift road and wondered how Butsko was making out.

"Hey, Sarge, get up!" Bannon said, slapping Butsko lightly on the cheek.

114

Butsko opened his eyes and tensed. He rolled his eyes around, checking everything out. "What's going on?" he asked hoarsely.

"Time to move out."

Butsko pressed his hands against the ground and sat up. He took a deep breath and felt almost like his old self again. His right hand ached but it wasn't so bad.

"How're you feeling?" Bannon asked.

"Better. What time is it?"

"Oh, four hundred hours."

"I'm hungry," Butsko said. "You got something to eat?"

Bannon opened his pack and took out a can of pork and beans. He opened it and handed them to Butsko along with his spoon. "Your back any better, Sarge?"

Butsko wiggled his hips. "Yeah, I think so." He dug the spoon deep into the can of beans and shoveled the food into his mouth.

Gladley got hungry looking at Butsko, so he took out a can of C rations, too, opening it up. He wound up with sausage patties and picked up one of the patties with his thumb and forefinger, pushing it into his mouth.

Butsko felt his strength coming back. He wasn't normal yet, but normal for him was almost superhuman, compared to most people. He ate the food quickly; the cramps in his stomach nearly were gone. Finishing the can of beans, he tossed it into the jungle and held out his hand.

"Water," he said.

Bannon passed his canteen and Butsko took a long swig. Butsko said "Aaaahhhhh" and handed the canteen back.

"Well," he said, his voice stronger but still hoarse, "anything happen while I was asleep?"

"There was a lot of activity back where the Japs were. Sounded as if they've been pulling out."

"Figures," Butsko said, and punctuated the word with a burp. "We know where they are now and they're afraid they might be in for an attack. I'd like to attack the cocksuckers— oh, boy, would I like to rip the bastards up." He remembered the Japanese officer from the Bataan Death March and thought of telling Bannon about him, but decided to keep it to himself. "Still a lot of Jap patrols out?"

"No," Bannon replied. "It's been pretty quiet for the last

ten minutes or so. I heard some submachine guns firing, so I guess some of our boys got into a jam. Hope they got away."

"Let's hope *we* get away." Butsko looked at Gladley, folding a sausage patty into his mouth. Under other circumstances he would have hollered at Gladley and told him to hurry up, but Gladley had carried him out of the Japanese camp, and he couldn't get mad at him now.

Butsko felt embarrassed. He realized the entire squad had risked their lives to get him out of there. He wanted to say thank you but didn't know how.

"We'd better get moving," he said. "You know where we're going, Bannon?"

"We'll head for the coast, Sarge. We buried our radio there and can ask headquarters what to do next."

"Why didn't you bring it with you?"

"Headquarters told us to go to the rendezvous point, but we wanted to come here, so we got rid of the radio and thought if anybody asked us about it afterward, we could say it broke down."

"How're you gonna say it was broke down if you call headquarters with it when we reach the shore."

"We thought we'd worry about that when the time came."

Butsko shrugged. "We can always say we fixed it."

The three men stood up. Bannon and Gladley put on their packs, and Butsko felt strong enough to travel. He wouldn't be able to use his right hand for a while, and he might have to stop and rest more than usual, but he thought he could keep up with the others.

"Move out," Butsko said, "and keep quiet."

Deep in the jungle Captain Mizushima was leading a squad of men through a thick tangle of cut vines. Ten feet ahead of him, a soldier with a machete was hacking a path. Captain Mizushima carried his samurai sword in his hand as he moved forward on his short, bandy legs. He'd been astonished when he received the message that his prisoner had been released by American soldiers. He knew the American soldiers had to be somewhere between him and the main Japanese camp. His men were spread into a line a half mile long in the jungle and were sweeping through it in a net. Captain Mizushima's detachment

116

was moving in a direction that led through a particularly thick part of the jungle.

Captain Mizushima could see the man with the machete tiring, so he ordered another soldier to step forward and take his place. The fresh soldier took the machete from his comrade's hand and proceeded to attack the jungle with all his might.

Captain Mizushima was confident his men would make contact with the Americans soon. The Americans would have to come this way if they wanted to reach the sea, and they would have to come to the sea, because it would be far more hazardous for them to infiltrate the main Japanese lines.

Captain Mizushima's beady little eyes searched the jungle for signs of the Americans. His men held their rifles ready to shoot American soldiers as soon as they appeared.

TWELVE . . .

The clouds on the horizon moved across the sky and erupted into a heavy downpour, but it didn't stop Pfc. Longtree and Private Frankie La Barbara, who spent most of the night running across Guadalcanal. Near daybreak they sat in a ravine and ate cold C rations as the rain fell on them and plastered their uniforms against their bodies. They estimated they were only a mile or two from the sea.

"Shit," said Frankie, his mouth full of ham and peas, "we've been making real good time. I'll bet we're the first ones there."

Longtree grunted something, because he didn't like small talk.

"I got to hand it to you, Chief," Frankie said, "you really know how to travel through the fucking woods. I guess if a man has to be in the woods, the best person for him to be there with is a fucking Indian just like you."

Sam Longtree grunted again. White men were always chattering about something. Longtree couldn't understand it. He felt pretty good, because the rain had cooled him off and made him feel more energetic. He was certain that if he'd stayed in the hospital, he'd still be sick.

He'd removed the stitches from his stomach during the breaks he'd taken during the night, and now his stomach barely bothered him at all. Sometimes hardship was a better cure than comfort, he believed. It strengthened the bodies and minds of warriors. Comfort was for women and dogs.

118

He jerked his head around and twitched his nose. "I smell something," he said.

Frankie raised his nose and sniffed. "I can't smell anything."

"Smoke," Longtree said.

"Probably Japs," Frankie told him. "Which way's it coming from."

Longtree pointed in the direction that the wind was blowing from. "That way."

"Maybe we'd better go the other way."

"Maybe we should look to make sure. It might be somebody from the squad."

"They'd have more brains than to light a fire."

Longtree didn't believe that at all. "Let's go see to make sure."

Frankie looked exasperated. "Aw, come on, Chief. Let's not fuck around. We're almost to the shore. Let's go there and sit tight until the others show up."

"Do that if you want to," Longtree replied, "but I want to see where the fire's coming from."

Longtree cleaned his spoon with dirt and washed the dirt away with water from his canteen. He took a drink from his canteen, dropped the canteen into its case, readjusted his cartridge belt, and picked up his Thompson submachine gun. Positioning the bill of his cap low over his eyes, he walked into the wind. Frankie followed reluctantly, because he didn't want to wander around Guadalcanal alone.

Longtree climbed the side of the ravine and came to the ridge at its top. He squinted his eyes at the gray drizzling morning and spotted a faint trail of smoke curling out of the forest below. Frankie, panting like a dog, drew beside him.

"I don't see nothing," Frankie said.

"I do," Longtree replied.

They descended the incline and entered the forest, whose trees were spaced several feet apart, unlike the usual jungle on Guadalcanal. Many of the trees were coconut palms, and green fruit the size of footballs lay on the ground. The smell of smoke was stronger in Longtree's nostrils, and he swiveled his head around, trying to define its source.

"Gee, it's kinda nice in here," Frankie said.

"Ssshhh."

119

Longtree looked down and saw the shell of a coconut cracked open. Kneeling, he examined the edges of the shell and could perceive that it had been cut with a sharp instrument, like a machete, not long before. That meant whoever was using the fire had been in the area for a while. Longtree motioned with his hand and Frankie followed him forward. After another twenty yards they heard a *clunk*, such as a machete or an ax would make against wood. Then they heard a voice that sounded like an old woman's.

Frankie's face lit up. "Pussy!"

"Quiet."

They got low and moved through the forest, holding their submachine guns ready. The outlines of a little shack came into view, and Longtree pointed toward the ground. He and Frankie dropped to their stomachs and crawled forward. The shack was on stilts and was made of vines and leaves entwined around poles that had been driven into the ground. In the front yard a native man wearing a skirt was hacking wood with a machete. He was around five feet tall, had gray hair, and was muscular. Nearby, a fire was smoldering and some pots hung over it, suspended by a metal rod.

Longtree stared at the man, and the scene reminded him of the reservation in Arizona. He felt a spiritual link with the man chopping wood, as if they were both from the same tribe. The experience was so sudden and strange that for a moment he thought he was back in Arizona, but then his mind clicked into its GI mode and he was on Guadalcanal.

The door to the hut opened and a stout lady in a wraparound sarong came down the steps. She said something to her husband in a strange native tongue unfamiliar to Frankie and Sam Longtree.

Frankie hadn't seen a woman since the Twenty-third left Australia, and he was always horny. He preferred beautiful showgirls but would fuck anything in a pinch, so he wouldn't have minded getting his hands on that old lady out there. Any old port in a storm.

"I wonder whose side they're on," Frankie said.

"In the orientation lecture the officer said the natives of these islands don't like the Japs much."

"You wanna go talk to them?" Frankie asked. "Maybe they've seen some of the guys in our squad."

The native man and woman straightened suddenly and pricked up their ears, because they heard Frankie's last utterance. All Longtree and Frankie could do now was get up and advance into the clearing, holding their submachine guns ready, looking around furtively.

The old man and woman stared at them in astonishment, and then the old man smiled and pointed at them. "You American soldiers?" he asked in a thick gutteral accent.

Longtree nodded. "Yes." He looked around. "Anybody else around here?"

The native man and woman glanced at each other and became nervous. "No," said the man, "nobody else here."

Frankie nudged Longtree. "What're they so nervous about?"

"Maybe they think we're going to shoot them." Longtree smiled at the man. "You see any Japanese soldiers around here?"

The native man nodded vigorously. "Some pass by in the night. Go that way." He pointed to the interior of the island. "We never see Amelican soldiers before. Lotsa Amelican soldiers come soon?"

"Pretty soon," Longtree said.

The old man shook his head. "Japanee soldier velly bad. Beat people up. Steal food. Velly bad people, Japanee soldier."

Something moved in the hut, and Frankie and Longtree pointed their submachine guns up there. The native woman hugged her man and both became terrified.

"Who's up there!" Frankie demanded.

"Nobody there, sir," the man replied.

Longtree turned to Frankie. "You cover them. I'll see what's going on."

Longtree held his submachine gun tightly in his hands and waved its barrel back and forth across the front of the hut as he walked toward the ladder. He couldn't see anybody moving behind the windows, but a few Japs might be hiding up there, maybe snipers who'd stopped by to steal chow from the natives and fuck the old lady. Longtree considered tossing a hand grenade through one of the windows, but he might be wrong,

121

and he didn't want to ruin the natives' home. That had happened too many times to the Apaches, and he didn't want to do it to somebody else if he didn't have to.

He climbed the ladder, grabbing the rungs with one hand and holding the pistol grip of his submachine gun with the other. He reached the little patio outside the hut's entrance and saw bamboo baskets and a stack of green coconuts. The drizzle had stopped and he listened to the silence of the forest while trying to perceive a human figure in the darkness inside the hut. Aiming the submachine gun straight ahead, he entered the hut and dropped to a crouch.

It was a small one-room structure with mats on the floor and bedclothes piled in the corner. Pottery and clay plates were on a bamboo table, and there was a cast-iron wood stove with a chimney that exited through a rear window. The shelves held clothes, and there was no place a person could hide that he could see.

Then his sharp eyes noticed a quiver of the bedclothes in the corner. Longtree aimed his submachine gun at the bedclothes and focused his complete attention on them. They moved again, and he wasn't imagining things. The safest thing to do would be to fire a burst into the bedclothes, and he knew he should do that right away, but decided to take a chance and see what was there, because a submachine gun burst might attract the attention of Japs.

"Come out of there!" he demanded.

The bedclothes quivered again. Longtree thought the natives might be hiding a pig or a few chickens underneath the bedclothes so he wouldn't steal them. He advanced toward the bedclothes and saw them tremble again. Holding his submachine gun in his right hand, he bent down, grabbed a corner of the material in his left hand, and pulled it away.

He sucked wind and took a step backward, astonished by the sight of a beautiful young girl shivering and hugging herself in the corner. She looked Japanese, and also Apache, with similar eyes and cheekbones and nearly the same coloring.

"You speak English?" Longtree asked.

She stared at him and trembled, obviously terrified.

Longtree smiled and motioned with his hand for her to get up. She stood, wearing a sarong like the native woman downstairs, and Longtree guessed that she was no more than twenty years old. He pointed to the door and indicated that she should go outside. She bowed to him and then did as he said, walking toward the door.

Meanwhile, standing outside, Frankie had been guarding the natives, his eyes roving over the native hut from time to time. It was too quiet up there, and it seemed as though Longtree had been gone for an eternity, when suddenly the Japanese girl appeared on the veranda. Frankie's eyes bulged out at the sight of her, because she had long black hair and was gorgeous. She descended the ladder and Sam Longtree followed her down.

The native man and woman became extremely agitated. "Please no shoot her, sirs!" the native man exclaimed, rubbing his hands together and jumping up and down. "She not harm anybody. She good girl."

The Japanese girl bowed her head dejectedly as if she knew she was going to die, and the gesture touched Sam Longtree's heart. Frankie La Barbara, however, had fastened his eyes on her breasts, which were somewhere between oranges and grapefruits in size, and then he checked out her rear end, which had a voluptuous curve to it. He began to get a hard-on.

Sam Longtree looked at the native man. "Where'd she come from?"

"She Japanee comfort girl and she escape. She no like to be comfort girl for Japanee soldier. She nice girl and they make her be comfort girl. They kill her if they find her here."

Sam Longtree and Frankie knew from their orientation lectures what functions comfort girls performed in the Japanese Army. They were young women recruited to travel with the Imperial Army and fuck the troops. Some were professionals and others were simple working girls or farm girls forced to become comfort girls for the glory of the Emperor.

"No hurt her, sir," said the native. "She good girl. She very scared. She need help."

"We won't hurt her," Sam Longtree said.

"Hell no," Frankie added, "we won't lay a hand on her."

The native man smiled. "You take her with you? You help her out?"

Frankie grinned. "Sure we'll help her out, won't we, Chief?"

"If she wants to come with us," Longtree said.

123

The native man turned to the girl and spoke to her in halting Japanese. She looked shyly at Longtree and Frankie, then back at Longtree. She bowed her head to him and said, *"Hai."*

"She said yes," the native man told Longtree.

Longtree moved toward her and placed his big hand on her tiny shoulder, gazing into her eyes. "I will take care of you," he said.

She nodded as if she understood.

Frankie was getting jealous already. He thought the Japanese girl went for Longtree instead of him, and that pissed him off. In civilian life Frankie had been a Don Juan, fucking anything in a skirt. He never took it well when a woman rejected him.

"Tell her to get her things," Longtree said.

"She no have no things except what she got on."

"Say good-bye to her, because we're leaving right now."

The native man and woman embraced the girl, and tears came to her eyes. *"Arigato,"* she said over and over, kissing them.

The native man looked at Longtree. "She a very good girl, sir. Please be on good lookout for her."

"I give you my word," Longtree said.

The girl separated from the native man and woman and looked at Longtree, her chin close to her chest, holding one hand in the other in front of her.

"Let's go," Longtree said.

He and Frankie moved toward the forest, with the Japanese girl walking between them.

In a denser part of the jungle Craig Delane and Jimmy O'Rourke were moving along a narrow trail. The rain had stopped but the sun still hadn't come out, and they could hear a roaring in the distance that sounded like a huge river.

They'd stopped for a couple of hours during the night to sleep, but had been on the move the rest of the time, checking their compasses regularly, hoping to reach the sea before nightfall.

"How're you doing, Delane?" O'Rourke asked over his shoulder.

"Okay—how about you?"

"Shit, I could do this forever."

Delane grit his teeth, because O'Rourke was always bragging about something. Delane didn't thing he could take much more of O'Rourke. And O'Rourke was always so condescending, asking how he was. Although Delane wasn't as tall and husky as most of the other men in the platoon, he'd represented the New York Athletic Club at amateur track meets on the East Coast and had always been in excellent physical condition. He'd never smoked a cigarette in his life until he joined the Army.

Hating O'Rourke, but also glad he wasn't alone in the jungle, Delane followed the former movie stuntman over the winding trail. The foliage was so thick around and above them that it was like night, damp and cool, with green slime covering the ground and the vines that hung around them like snakes.

The roaring became louder, and through the jungle they saw white water. Continuing another several paces and turning a bend, they came to the muddy banks of a river. The river was thirty yards wide and overflowing its banks due to the rain the night before. The current was fast and ferocious, sending up whitecaps and rooster tails where it flowed over boulders.

Delane looked to his left and right and couldn't see any narrow spots in the river. "How're we gonna get across that?" he asked.

"I don't know," O'Rourke replied. "We can either try to swim across it, or we can move along the banks and see if we can find a narrow spot to cross."

"Do you think we can make it across?"

"I don't know if you can," O'Rourke said, "but I'm sure I can."

"Well, if you can, I can."

O'Rourke raised an eyebrow. "Think so?"

"I know so."

"I'm not so sure. Maybe we ought look for a narrow place."

"We might be looking all day, and we don't have the time. I think we should just try to get across as best we can."

O'Rourke took off his pack and lowered it onto a log. "I've got some rope in here. I'll tie you to me so nothing'll happen to you."

"Forget it. I can make it on my own."

O'Rourke smiled superciliously. "C'mon, don't bite off more than you can chew."

"If you can get across, I can get across."

"Yeah, but I'm tougher than you."

"No, you're not."

"You don't think so?"

"No."

Delane took off his pack and dropped it into the mud. He took out one can of C rations for lunch and would worry about dinner when the time came. Stuffing the can into his back pocket, he pondered whether he should leave anything else behind, because he didn't want to carry a lot of weight when he tried to cross the river. He decided to empty his canteen and fill it up on the other side of the river, using chlorine pills to purify the water. That made him realize he'd better take his chlorine pills with him, so he took them out of a side pocket of his pack and buttoned them into his shirt pocket. He took off his helmet and laid it on his pack. "I'm ready," he said, strapping his submachine gun crossways on his back.

O'Rourke was also packless, bareheaded, and with his submachine gun strapped across his back. "You sure you don't want to tie yourself to me."

"I'm sure."

"You go first and I'll keep an eye on you. That way I won't have to go looking for you on the other side."

O'Rourke's remark infuriated Delane, although he knew O'Rourke was probably right. Delane moved into the swiftly-moving current, which thundered and howled as it ran to the ocean. He could see logs and branches floating by and knew the white water was caused by huge boulders beneath the surface. It wasn't going to be easy, but somehow he'd have to get across. Wading deeper into the cool current, he wished he hadn't started smoking, because he'd need all the wind he could get to reach the other side.

He was up to his knees now, and the current pulled him to the side. He slipped on a stone and fell sideways into the river, banging his left arm and shoulder on the sharp rocks.

"Watch out!" said O'Rourke.

Delane kicked his feet and tried to breaststroke away from

the shore, but the river did that for him, picking him up and carrying him off. It happened so suddenly that Delane panicked. The current dragged him under and spun him around. He kicked back to the surface, glimpsed the opposite shore, and swam toward it with long, firm strokes, the river pulling him downstream at an alarming rate. He saw white water in the middle of the channel and something told him his trajectory would take him right into it, but all he could do was swim with all his strength and hope for the best.

A big log came out of nowhere and whacked him in the shoulder, scaring the shit out of him. At first he thought it was a crocodile, but it rolled and scraped across his back. Delane kept power-stroking for the far side. The river roared like an angry monster, and he felt himself being drawn toward the white water in the middle of the channel. He swam furiously in an effort to escape it, although deep down he knew there was no escape. Frightened that he'd be broken to bits on the rocks, he swam more vigorously, but the white water came closer and he braced himself for the shock of collision. The river hollered at him and his elbows and knees hit the rocks. The rapids caught him and tossed him into the air like a pancake. He landed on his back on top of a boulder and cried out in pain, then the river swept him away again. He fell six feet in white foam and dropped beneath the surface, his cheeks puffed out with air as water pounded over him.

Breaststroking and kicking his feet, Delane rose to the surface and thought he must have broken his back, so great was the pain. He raised his arms out of the water and swam toward shore again, taking long, powerful strokes, each one aggravating the pain in his back. Something caught his eye and he glanced toward his right to see the top half of a tree bearing down on him. He put on a burst of speed, but the current was too fast for him and the tree crashed into him, its branches scratching and tangling him up, threatening to hold him and carry him out to sea.

Delane tried to climb up on the tree so that he could jump off, but the branches cut into his skin, threatening to poke out his eyes. Frightened, he wrestled and fought frantically with the branches, trying to break loose, but when a foot came free in one spot it immediately became entangled in another, and the same thing happened with his hands. Finally he made a desperate leap to break loose, but even that didn't work, and he landed in more branches and twigs.

His motion brought him to the edge of the tree, unbalancing it, and Delane screamed in terror as he saw himself toppling into the water. The tree rolled over, plunging Delane beneath the surface. He dived downward, kicking his feet and stroking with his arms, breaking away from the entanglement. The tree continued downstream while Delane continued swimming underwater toward shore. Looking beneath him, he could see smooth water-worn pebbles shimmering in the swift current. When his lungs were ready to burst, he kicked toward the surface, broke through, took a deep gulp of air, and was promptly sucked again into white water. He tried to get away but once more was dragged across a cluster of boulders and then pulled down into a whirlpool. Nearly exhausted, gasping for air, he flailed against the swirling currents and finally worked himself loose into a rush of water that carried him into a pool formed by the widening of the river at that point.

Delane was amazed by his sudden good fortune. The river shrieked for his blood and he dog-paddled to shore, knowing full well that the torrent would have claimed him in another five or ten minutes of hard going. His fingers scraped bottom and he stood up, teetering from side to side, gulping air with his mouth wide open, and then staggering to shore, where he collapsed onto the mud, his chest heaving, afraid his heart and lungs would burst from his exertion. The arteries in his neck pounded and he uttered a prayer of silent thanks to God.

Then he remembered Jimmy O'Rourke. Getting up and turning around, he blinked his eyes and looked back at the roaring water, but he couldn't see O'Rourke. Standing, he shielded his face from the glare of the sun and swept the surface of the water with his eyes. No one was swimming out there. Then he spotted something that he thought was O'Rourke, but it only turned out to be another log.

Good grief, Craig Delane thought, *didn't he make it?*

The river was fed by numerous streams and tributaries, and one of these sources was a swamp that collected rainwater rolling off nearby hills and mountains. Morris Shilansky and

128

Tommy Shaw were approaching the edge of this swamp, which stank horribly and sweltered in a green haze.

"Holy fuck," said Shilansky, taking off his helmet and wiping his forehead with his sleeve, "what're we gonna do about this swamp."

Shaw looked to the left and right. "Damned if I know. Maybe we should go right through it."

"Go through it? Are you crazy? There's quicksand all over this island. I'm not going through this fucking swamp."

"Then we'll have to go around it. Let's take a break first."

Shilansky sat on a rotting log and Shaw leaned against a tree covered with damp green moss. They took out their cigarettes and lit them up, filling their lungs with the fragrant smoke. Shilansky held up his compass and took an azimuth.

"Shit," he said, "we were doing all right until we hit this fucking swamp."

"I still think we should go right through it."

"You wanna go through it, go through it. I ain't going through it. I'll just sit here and watch you sink into the quicksand."

"What quicksand?" Shaw asked. "I don't see no quicksand. I only see water. We can probably swim across the fucking swamp."

"Go ahead—you show me."

"When I finish this cigarette."

They puffed in silence for a few moments. Both were famished, because they'd thrown their packs away last night.

"I wonder," Shilansky said, "if there's any frogs in this swamp. They serve frog legs in fancy restaurants, you know."

"You think you're the only one who's ever ate in fancy restaurants, you cheap small-time cook?"

"Go fuck yourself."

Shilansky took another drag on his cigarette and looked at the shoreline of the swamp. He couldn't hear or see frogs or anything else to eat. He was so hungry he thought he was ready to pass out.

Shaw smoked his cigarette to a butt and threw it in the water. Then he waded into the muck, to show Shilansky there was no quicksand.

Suddenly Shaw and Shilansky heard furtive, rustling movements in the underbrush that lined the swamp. Jumping up and reaching for their submachine guns, they heard splashes all around them, and Shilansky saw a long green form slip into the swamp.

"Crocodiles!" Shilansky screamed.

Shaw ran out of the swamp as crocodiles slithered through the underbrush and swam toward them. The two GIs caught glimpses of the long sharp teeth and the cruel eyes of the crocodiles as the creatures glided rapidly in their direction.

"Holy Christ!" Shaw yelled.

They both opened fire at the same time, standing back to back, their submachine guns bucking and twisting in their hands as the air filled with gunsmoke and the jungle around them was raked with lead. The bullets hit the crocodiles and blood spurted out of their thick hides. The crocodiles rolled over onto their backs, exposing their white bellies, and the two soldiers kept peppering them with bullets, ripping open their stomachs and sending red guts spattering into the air.

The whole world seemed to be full of crocodiles swarming toward them in motions so quick they were long green blurrs. The GIs bent low and gritted their teeth as they swept their submachine guns from left to right, spraying the jungle with death. Shilansky heard the snap of jaws to his left and turned to see a crocodile bearing down on him in the water of the swamp. He aimed at the crocodile's head and fired a quick burst, shattering the crocodile's skull and sending blood spouting into the air like a geyser.

The crocodiles crawled over each other's dead bodies and became smeared with blood, which made them go beserk. They snapped their gigantic jaws at each other and chewed each other's guts. One made a pass at Shaw's ankles, but Shaw aimed his submachine gun down and blew the giant reptile's snout away. Then he aimed at another crocodile heading in his direction, and his submachine gun went *click*.

"Help!" Shaw yelled, ejecting his empty clip.

Shilansky spun around and fired a wild burst that stitched across a sea of squirming crocodiles and finally tore into the one heading for Shaw, who meanwhile loaded a fresh clip into his submachine gun and ripped apart the torso of a fat crocodile who'd come perilously close to Shilansky.

By now the crocodiles were awash with each other's gore and had forgotten about the two GIs, so overcome were they by bloodlust and feeding frenzy. They turned on each other, chomping down on each other's heads and tails, sinking their huge fangs into each other's bellies. Shilansky and Shaw retreated toward drier ground, still firing at the crocodiles, and the water at the edge of the swamp turned red with blood. The crocodiles chewed each other and thrashed their powerful tails, making horrendous trumpetlike sounds as Shilansky and Shaw fled into the jungle.

A few miles away Captain Mizushima stopped cold. Behind him he could hear the faint sounds of American submachine guns. He knitted his brows together and turned around. "Somehow the Americans have gotten behind us," he said to Sergeant Jukichi. "They must have run into one of our other platoons."

"Yes, sir. Perhaps we should go back?"

Captain Mizushima looked at his watch; it was nearly ten o'clock in the morning. He realized then that he should have stayed where he was by the ocean and let the Americans come to him, but he'd been eager to fight them and bring a few live prisoners back to Colonel Tsuji.

"Yes," Captain Mizushima said. "Tell the men to turn around and head back. It should be easier going, because the trail has already been cut."

Sergeant Jukichi passed the word along, and the men turned around, moving backward in the direction from which they'd come.

"Double-time!" Captain Mizushima shouted. "We must reach the ocean before the Americans!"

Butsko, Bannon, and Homer Gladley also heard the submachine-gun fire in the distance.

"Somebody's in trouble," Butsko said, squinting his eyes and looking in the direction of the fire.

"Some of our guys must have run into some Japs," Gladley said.

"No," Bannon told them, "I don't hear anything except submachine guns. Our guys are firing at something that's not firing back."

Gladley's eyes brightened. "Maybe they're shooting at something to eat."

"They wouldn't do that, because the noise would give away their positions to the Japs."

Butsko reached for his canteen full of water. "If there are any Japs in the area, they'll probably head straight for that shooting. We'd better steer clear of it."

Butsko took a drink while Bannon looked at his map and estimated where the firing was coming from. The map indicated a swampy region, which they'd want to keep away from anyway. He pointed the blade of his hand toward the jungle.

"We should keep going in that direction," he said.

Butsko put away his canteen. "Let's go."

The three soldiers moved out again, Bannon and Gladley holding their submachine guns ready in case of trouble, and Butsko a few paces behind them, his health and strength returning, feeling naked without a gun of his own.

THIRTEEN . . .

Sam Longtree, the Japanese comfort girl, and Frankie La Barbara were climbing a hill. Longtree held the girl's hand, helping her along, and Frankie walked behind them, looking up at the round haunches of the girl, wanting to reach under her skirt and grab some of her goodies. Each of her steps caused the skirt to rise and reveal part of her thigh, and her skin was smooth and honey-colored, with a nice flowing shape to her leg.

Frankie wanted to screw her so badly he could scream. If Longtree weren't around he'd rip off her clothes, throw her to the ground, and fuck her silly. Then he'd roll her onto her stomach and do it again. Then he'd stuff his cock down her . . .

Frankie became so entwined in the fantasy that he lost his footing, slipped on a rock, and dropped to his hands and knees.

Longtree turned around. "You all right?"

From his low position Frankie could look right up the girl's dress. "Yeah, I'm all right."

Frankie raised himself and continued to follow Longtree and the girl up the hill. Weird thoughts were going through his mind. He could shoot Longtree down with his submachine gun and have the girl all to himself, and he actually toyed with this idea, weighing the pros and cons, although deep in his heart he knew he never could kill Longtree, because they'd been

133

together since Fort Ord, California, and had usually gotten along well together.

Then a new possibility entered Frankie's mind. Maybe he could convince Longtree to join him in a little gang bang. Longtree, after all, was a man, too, although he was an Indian, and he probably liked a little poontang once in a while himself. But it looked like Longtree was going to be selfish about it. Longtree was behaving as if the girl were his, as though Frankie were just along for the ride.

They came to the top of the wooded hill and caught a strong whiff of the ocean. They could see it sparkling in the distance, for the sun had come out again, although there were large, puffy white clouds in the sky. All they'd have to do to reach the ocean would be to descend the other side of the hill and pass through a half-mile of jungle. Then they could move east along the shore to the spot where the radio had been hidden.

"Let's take a break," Sam Longtree said.

They sat in the woods near the top of the hill, and in the distance they could hear the faint sounds of a battle. Artillery was fired and bombs were bursting and they could hear the pepper of machine guns and small-arms fire. Sam Longtree took out his last can of C rations, opened it with his can opener, and passed it and his spoon to the girl. He made eating motions with his hands and mouth. "Eat," he told her.

She bowed her head and said: *"Arigato."*

Then, with dainty fingers and a pert expression, she spooned the cold beef stew into her mouth. Frankie took out his last can of C rations and opened them up.

"You want half of these, Chief?" he asked.

"That's okay, Frankie. You have them all."

"But you must be hungry, Chief."

"No, not that much."

Frankie glanced at the girl. "She's a real looker, isn't she?"

"Yes, very pretty."

"Why don't we fuck her?"

Longtree gazed stone-faced at Frankie for a few moments. "I don't think that would be a good idea."

"Why not?"

"You should not take what is not given."

134

Frankie laughed, his mouth full of beans. "Cut out all that Indian shit, Chief. You want her as bad as I do. Admit it."

Longtree maintained his stone face. "Forget about her, Frankie. Think about something else."

"How can I think of anything else? I ain't had no pussy since we left Australia."

"A little longer won't hurt you."

"What's the matter with you, Chief? She'd probably love to fuck the both of us, but she's too afraid to ask. She ain't no virgin, you know. I bet if I went over there and kissed her neck a few times, she'd spread her legs for you and me both."

Sam Longtree didn't reply, and his face showed no expression. The girl's eyes were downcast and she was eating hungrily, like a little girl, while trying to show good table manners.

Frankie finished his can of beans and threw them over his shoulder. He took a drink of water from his canteen and gargled before swallowing it. "I guess it's okay to have a smoke."

Sam Longtree nodded and took out a cigarette of his own. Both of them lit up. The girl finished her can of food and set it down near her feet, then licked the spoon clean and handed it to Longtree.

"Arigato," she said, bowing her head again.

"You're welcome," he replied.

She sat on her knees, with her hands folded in her lap, very still, gazing into the distance while Frankie stared at the outline of her nipples, which showed through the thin cloth of the sarong she was wearing.

"Hey, Chief," Frankie said, "why don't we fuck her and get it over with?"

"I told you to think about something else, Frankie."

"Hey, nobody tells me nothing—I do what I fucking please." Frankie stood, hitched up his belt, and looked at the girl, grinning like Rudolph Valentino. She noticed his attention and turned her eyes downward, her cheeks flushing red.

"Listen, Chief," Frankie said, "I found her at the same time you did, and the way I look at it, she's as much mine as yours."

Longtree looked up at him. "Be a man, Frankie. Don't shame yourself."

"Hell, I am a man, and all I wanna do is what men do."

135

He moved toward the girl. "I'm gonna get me some of this slant-eyed little bitch."

Frankie reached down and grabbed the girl by the arm. "Let's go, sweetheart. It's poontang time."

Longtree shot to his feet. "Let her go, Frankie," he said in a low, deadly voice.

Frankie was so horny and crazy he felt as if high voltage were surging through his veins. "Stay out of this, Chief. Like I said, it's poontang time."

Frankie pulled the girl to her feet and brought his face close to hers. "I'm gonna fuck the jelly out of your beans, kiddo, and you're gonna love it."

"This is the last time I'm gonna tell you, Frankie," Longtree said. "Let her go."

"I do what I fucking please," Frankie said, and dragged the girl toward the bushes.

Suddenly the world went black in front of Frankie's eyes, and he felt as if a Mack truck had hit him in the throat. When the world became light again, he found himself suspended in the air by Longtree, who gripped his throat with one hand. Longtree drew back his arm and threw Frankie as if he were a rag doll. Frankie hit a tree and slid down to the ground, unconscious.

Craig Delane crouched low as he made his way across a field of kunai grass. His body was covered with cuts and welts, and he was sure he had some sprained muscles in his back, but he was following his compass and moving as quickly as he could toward the ocean.

His mind was turbulent with conflicting emotions. He felt vulnerable and scared, being all alone behind enemy lines, but he also felt powerful, in control of his destiny, without that odious O'Rourke and his nonstop condescension.

Delane felt bad because O'Rourke had evidently drowned in the river, but he also was relieved that he didn't have O'Rourke around anymore. He'd reached the point where he couldn't bear O'Rourke's blustering, exaggerating manner, his ignorant political beliefs, and his inability to evaluate information without prejudice. O'Rourke was a good man to have around in a tight situation, but Delane's self-confidence was growing and he was sure he could take care of himself.

He thought he'd stop to check his compass and take a drink of water. Kneeling in the kunai grass, he took out his compass and sighted the azimuth that would bring him to the ocean sometime that night. He was right on course and felt proud of himself. Then he reached for his canteen, but his hand froze in midair.

He'd heard something in front of him. Pointing his nose in the air like a hunting dog, he moved his head from side to side and tried to pick up the sounds. He heard birds chirping overhead and monkeys chattering in the jungle, but underlying that was the sound of men's footsteps and voices headed his way, and he knew they had to be Japanese soldiers.

Delane dropped to his stomach and unslung his Thompson submachine gun. Then he crawled off the trail into a denser patch of kunai grass. Lying still, he tried to plot the direction of the Japanese patrol. He didn't want to admit to himself that they appeared to be headed straight for him.

Soon he no longer could fool himself. He could hear the Japanese soldiers talking, and their equipment clanked and rattled. One of them laughed and another said something in response. They were headed directly toward Delane, who began to feel stark terror. He recalled seeing Sergeant Butsko twisted into knots inside the little bamboo cage and thought he'd go insane if the Japs ever did that to him. If the Japs captured him, he was afraid he'd break down under torture and give away information that would get Americans killed. He remembered the pictures he'd seen of Japanese officers hacking off the heads and limbs of captured British officers in Singapore, and he knew all about the Bataan Death March.

The Japanese patrol came closer and Delane tensed up. He decided the only thing to do would be to kill as many of them as he could with his submachine gun and then turn the gun on himself and blow his own head off. That way they couldn't torture him and he wouldn't give away any secrets. *I made it across the river to get killed over here,* he thought. He should have known that he would never make it back alive.

The Japanese soldiers marched closer, and Delane's heart

pounded like an old jeep engine. They were only ten or twenty feet away, but he couldn't see them in the thick kunai grass. He could hear them, though. They were talking and grunting, and he could even hear some of them wheezing. They drew closer to him and he knew that in a few moments they'd be on top of him and he'd have to rise and fire.

His muscles tensed and he prepared to charge them, to take them by surprise and kill as many of them as he could before they got him. Looking ahead in the kunai grass, he saw the pale green trousers of a Japanese uniform. They were about to collide with him, and Delane ground his teeth together, hoping a miracle would occur and they wouldn't see him.

"Beikoku!" shouted the Japanese point man when he saw an American lying in the grass in front of him.

Delane leaped to his feet and opened fire, the plain of kunai grass echoing with the explosions of his submachine gun. He cut down the point man and the two Japs behind him before the other three Japanese soldiers knew what was happening. Shocked, they reached for their rifles, but Delane kept his trigger depressed and charged into them, swinging his submachine gun from side to side as the gun spat out hot lead.

It was over in a few seconds. Astonished, Delane looked down through the cloud of gunsmoke and saw six dead and bleeding Japanese soldiers sprawled over the flattened kunai grass. Delane blinked, unable to believe what he'd done. The firepower of a Thompson submachine gun and the element of surprise had wiped out the Japanese patrol before they knew what had hit them.

Delane thought he should go through their packs and see if they had any food, but a little voice told him to get the hell out of there while he had the chance. Holding his hot smoking submachine gun in both hands, he ran through the kunai grass, heading for the safety of the jungle.

Longtree kneeled before Frankie and slapped his cheeks lightly. "You okay, Frankie?"

Frankie opened his eyes halfway. Out of the blur came Longtree, with the Japanese girl standing behind him. Frankie remembered what had happened, but he didn't get mad. He generally admired people who stood up to him. He rubbed his throat and grinned. "Well, Chief," he said, "I guess when you say something, you really mean it."

Longtree winked. "Let's get going."

Frankie stood and brushed himself off. He picked up his submachine gun and looked at the Japanese girl, who continued to regard him with horror.

"Sorry if I scared you, kiddo," he said, "but you know the way things are."

She glanced from Frankie to Longtree and back to Frankie again and was obviously very confused.

Frankie looked at Longtree. "We got time for another cigarette?"

"Afraid not," Longtree said. "I just heard some more gunfire, and I think it'd be best to keep moving right now."

"You know what's best, Chief," Frankie said. "Lead the way."

They descended the hill, with Longtree going first, the Japanese girl behind him, and Frankie bringing up the rear. Frankie looked at the back of the Japanese girl and resented her. If she wouldn't fuck him, what good was she? She was only slowing them down and getting in the way. Frankie wasn't mad at Longtree, because it was normal for men to fight and horse around, but he disliked the Japanese girl because she hadn't gone off peacefully to the bushes with him. *Goddamn sneaky little slanty-eyed bitch,* Frankie thought. *It was people like her who'd bombed Pearl Harbor.*

Captain Mizushima heard the submachine-gun fire, and it didn't sound far off. *"Forward!"* he yelled. *"Don't let them get away!"*

He and his men ran across the trail they'd previously made in the jungle and after several minutes came to the field of kunai grass. They waded into it in a long skirmish line, hacking grass out of their way with their machetes.

"Be careful!" Captain Mizushima shouted. *"The Americans may be hiding in here!"*

The men put their machetes away and held their rifles ready, peering into the thick grass, looking for American soldiers.

They heard a groan.

"What was that?" Captain Mizushima asked. He jerked his

head around. "Keep a sharp eye out and be ready to fire at anything that moves!"

They advanced through the kunai grass and heard the groaning again. Captain Mizushima told them to move in that direction. *"Who's there!"* he shouted. *"Stand up and identify yourself!"*

The groaning and moaning continued. Finally one of his men stumbled upon the soldiers shot by Craig Delane. *"Sir!"* the soldier yelled. *"Look!"*

Captain Mizushima ran toward him and looked down at the slaughtered red soldiers in the kunai grass. He recognized the men as members of his company.

"Ambushed," he said. "The Americans must have caught them unawares. Always be on your guard, men. The Americans are a very treacherous people." He knelt beside the soldier who was moaning. "How many were there?" Captain Mizushima asked.

But the soldier was unconscious and couldn't reply. Captain Mizushima shook him a few times and realized he'd obtain no information. He turned to Sergeant Jukichi. "Call headquarters and tell them to send somebody to pick these men up. Also tell them we're proceeding to the ocean as quickly as we can."

"Yes, sir."

Captain Jukichi tried to raise headquarters on his radio while Captain Mizushima led his men toward the jungle ahead.

Long columns of Japanese soldiers lined the piers in the port of Rabaul on New Britain Island, northwest of Guadalcanal in the Solomon Islands. Tied to the piers were transport ships, and officers and NCOs hollered at the soldiers, exhorting them to move quickly and get on board.

The soldiers made up the Forty-eighth Division, which had seen action on Borneo and was commanded by Major General Michio Ooka, a professional military officer who'd served as an observer with the German army in the attack on Poland and who considered himself a more advanced military thinker than most other generals in the Japanese army.

Ooka was husky and tall, with a pencil-thin mustache and a stern expression on his face. He stood on the bridge of the battleship *Aoba* with elderly Admiral Yukio Tamaki, who studied the boarding soldiers through his binoculars. The sun was shining in Rabaul and the weather reports were favorable. Admiral Tamaki would command the fleet of transport ships, destroyers, and the battleship *Aoba*, which would carry the Forty-eighth Division to Guadalcanal.

Ooka looked at his wristwatch. "How soon do you think we can leave?" he asked.

"When your men are all on board," Admiral Tamaki said dryly.

"That should take no more than another hour."

"If you're correct, then we shall be under way within two hours."

General Ooka gripped the rail and looked down at his men boarding the ships. Trucks were lined up on the dock, carrying more soldiers, and farther back were artillery and tanks. General Ooka knew that the Seventeenth Army on Guadalcanal had been disgracefully ineffective against the American force that had landed there in August, and he was anxious to get ashore with his men and tanks and apply the blitzkrieg techniques he'd learned from the Germans. He felt certain the blitzkrieg would furnish impressive results and enable him to push the Americans off Guadalcanal, and then perhaps he'd be given command of the Seventeenth Army, while General Hyakutake could be transferred to Imperial Headquarters in Tokyo, where he could push papers and pencil around all day long, which was all he was good for, as far as General Ooka was concerned.

General Ooka expected that by daybreak he and his Forty-eighth Division would be ready to wage war against the Americans on Guadalcanal, and he could hardly wait.

Shaw and Shilansky sat in a coconut grove, eating coconut meat and drinking coconut milk. They said nothing to each other, so intent were they on filling their empty stomachs. Empty coconut shells lay all around them, and their uniforms and boots were stained with coconut milk. Gnats and flies buzzed around them, and they swatted the insects away as they continued to eat.

"Hiya, guys," said a voice behind a bush.

Shaw and Shilansky dropped their coconuts and reached for their submachine guns as Jimmy O'Rourke came out from behind the bush and sauntered toward them as if they were on a street someplace in Los Angeles.

"I heard somebody chopping something," O'Rourke said with a grin, "so I thought I'd come over and take a look. Thought it might be somebody from the squad."

Shaw looked at Shilansky. "I told you we shouldn't have cut open these coconuts. Every Jap within ten miles probably heard us."

"Well," replied Shilansky, "you were doing it too. Don't blame it all on me."

"Maybe we'd better get the fuck out of here before some Japs come snooping around."

"Which way?" asked Shilansky.

Shaw pointed. "That way."

"Not according to my compass," said O'Rourke. "My compass says that way." He pointed in a different direction.

"It doesn't matter," Shaw said. "Either way we'll hit the ocean."

"But my way will bring us closer to the radio we buried."

Shilansky looked at O'Rourke and wondered why he was alone. "Where's Delane?" he asked.

"Dead," said O'Rourke, looking down at the ground, his face becoming serious.

"Japs get him?"

"No, a fucking river got him. I told him he wouldn't be able to make it across, but he said he could and he was wrong. I saw him go under in some white water and he never came up again."

Shilansky blew out the corner of his mouth. "Better than the Japs getting him, I guess."

"He wasn't a very tough person," O'Rourke said. "I told him we should look for a narrow place to cross, but he wouldn't listen."

"Yeah, well, he was always trying to prove something," Shilansky said. "Tough break, because he wasn't a bad guy."

"Just kind of a sissy, that's all."

Shaw cleared his throat and spat at the ground. "Let's get out of here."

142

Shilansky chewed coconut meat as he followed Shaw across the grove, and O'Rourke walked next to Shilansky, thinking of Craig Delane, whom he'd always hoped would get him a good job someday when they'd gotten out of the Army, but now Delane was fish food somewhere in the river, and another dream was shattered for Jimmy O'Rourke. He was always looking for opportunities to advance his station in life, but somehow nothing ever worked.

FOURTEEN . . .

Longtree, the Japanese girl, and Frankie La Barbara reached the shoreline in midafternoon and determined the radio was buried somewhere to the east of them. They moved in that direction, staying close to the treeline so that they could take cover quickly if a squadron of Japanese planes appeared suddenly overhead.

Their strategy was well chosen, because Japanese airplanes did zoom past later in the afternoon, following the shoreline and heading toward the front lines, probably for another bombing run on Henderson Field. The two GIs and the Japanese girl dived into the jungle and stayed there until the planes were gone, then returned to the sand and continued walking west.

The sun twinkled on the choppy waves of the sea, and it was a glorious afternoon. Longtree kept his eyes peeled for the landmarks that would indicate the location of the radio, while Frankie walked a little farther back, where he could watch the Japanese girl's buttocks dance around underneath her sarong. The Japanese girl was aware of his presence and still afraid of him; she stayed close to Longtree, her protector.

Longtree saw many geographical configurations that resembled the area surrounding the spot where the radio had been buried, but when he got closer he saw different details, and the radio wasn't there.

"You sure we're going in the right direction?" Frankie asked.

"Yes, I'm sure."

"This beach all looks the same to me," Frankie said. "I think I'm gonna come back here after the war is over. It's a real nice spot for a hotel and a casino. I bet I could turn this island into another Hawaii."

Longtree chuckled. Frankie always was scheming up ways to earn money, but he seemed to have no idea of what happiness was. He was never content, and Longtree didn't think Frankie would ever be content no matter how much money he had.

At five o'clock in the afternoon Longtree thought he saw the two leaning palm trees that marked the spot where the radio had been buried. As he drew closer he picked out many familiar details, and he realized this time he'd really found it.

"The radio's over there," he said, pointing.

"Yeah?" Frankie said. "How do you know?"

Longtree walked by the trees and entered the bushes. After a few feet he found the spot where the radio had been buried. "It's down there."

"You're right!" Frankie told him. "I recognize this place now. Should we dig it up?"

"No. We'll dig it up when we have to transmit a message."

"Aren't we gonna transmit a message right now, so's we can get the fuck out of here?"

Longtree looked at the sun dropping toward the horizon. "Let's wait awhile and see if any of the others turn up. They should get here tonight, and then we can all leave together."

"Okay," Frankie said. "What the fuck." He looked around and saw some coconut palms. "I'll get us something to eat."

Frankie moved into the woods to look for coconuts lying on the ground, and Longtree looked at the Japanese girl. Every time he saw her, she reminded him of an Apache squaw. She could almost be a member of his tribe. Longtree had often reflected on the resemblance between Japanese people and Apaches, but he didn't like to think about it too much, because he didn't like to think he was warring on the side of the white eyes against his own people.

He sat on the ground and she sat a few feet away. He could perceive something happening between them, that she felt an affinity for him just as he did for her. Shyly she turned her gaze to her hands resting in her lap, and he took out a cigarette, lighting it up and blowing a column of smoke into the air.

As the sun was setting on the horizon, Captain Mizushima and his squad of men reached the beach. He was annoyed, because visibility would be poor in the darkness, but Americans usually made a lot of noise and maybe he could track them down anyway. But there was so much beach to cover, and the Americans could come out anywhere. They might even have beaten him to the ocean and might be hiding in the bushes watching him right now.

"Sergeant Jukichi!"

"Yes, sir!"

"Contact the other platoons and find out where they are."

"Yes, sir."

Sergeant Jukichi knelt with the radio and called Captain Mizushima's other platoons, while Captain Mizushima took out a pencil and paper and worked out a plan so that his company could cover as wide an area of the beach as possible and yet still be effective.

Longtree threw a coconut shell on the ground and looked at his watch. "Well," he said, "we might as well sack out."

"That's okay with me," Frankie replied. "I don't even remember the last time I slept. I think it was back on Henderson Field."

Longtree turned to the Japanese girl and made motions with his hands to indicate they were going to sleep. She nodded and waited to see where he would lie down, because she wanted to stay close to him, since he was her protection against Frankie La Barbara.

Longtree knew she'd follow him, so he walked twenty paces into the woods, found a little clearing covered with leaves, and lay down. Meekly she entered the clearing behind him, pointed to the ground, and asked a question in Japanese, which he guessed was a request that she be permitted to lie in the same area. He nodded and said yes. She bowed again and lay several feet away from him. She turned her back toward him and curled up, and in the moonlight he could see the fine curve of her rump.

He wanted to go over and grab her but thought it would be dishonorable to do so. He had promised to protect her, and you don't protect somebody by making sexual advances. If that's what she wanted, she'd have to come to him, and if she didn't, he could endure it. All his life he'd been trained to endure hardship, and this would be nothing compared to other tribulations that he'd been through. He rolled over so that his back was to her and dropped off to sleep.

The Japanese girl's name was Reiko, and she was the daughter of a farmer on Japan's northernmost island, Hokkaido. Only nineteen years old, she'd been a comfort girl for six months, four of them on Guadalcanal. The army representatives had come to her little village and told all the young girls it was their duty to entertain the men who were fighting so valiantly for the Emperor. Her father put up no argument because he was poor and she'd be one less mouth to feed. So she went away and became a comfort girl.

She had been horrified when she found out what the "entertainment" really was. She'd felt betrayed and abused by her country and the Emperor and had cried and suffered. The soldiers treated her roughly, and she was a delicate child with a poetic nature. Miserable, she'd contemplated suicide many times, but then one day, during an American bombardment, she saw a chance to escape and fled into the jungle. The old native couple had taken care of her. Now she had a new protector.

Lying with her head on her hands, she gazed at his broad back. Men had treated her cruelly for a long time. Even her father had been mean to her, but that strange soldier had been kind and saved her from rape. He looked vaguely Japanese and reminded her of stories she'd heard about the samurai warriors who'd roamed Japan in the old days. She could see his strength and sense his inner power. She was a frightened, simple young woman, and he had been good to her. She wanted to curl up in his arms and feel sheltered and loved, and in turn she wanted to love him, because she knew soldiers were lonely and that death faced them at every turn.

She wondered what he'd do if she reached over and touched him. Would he become angry? Perhaps he would think she was a bad girl. Perhaps he would push her away. But she'd seen that gleam in his eyes when they'd said good night, and she didn't think he'd push her away. She knew there was something between them already, and she knew he knew. People do things in wars that they'd never dream of doing in civilian life.

She rolled over and, like a cat, crept over the leaves toward the big American soldier.

Longtree awoke with a snap when he heard the sound of someone moving behind him. His instincts refined, his senses attuned to the forest, he could pick out the unusual sound from all the other sounds of the jungle and the waves of the ocean crashing on the beach.

He knew it was she. She was coming for him and he'd suspected she might. She'd looked at him earlier as if he was her man. He knew that look, and he'd told her with his eyes that she was his woman. They both knew that under the circumstances she would have to make the first move, and she was making it.

He lay still on his side, his arms crossed over his chest, and heard her crawl closer. He hadn't been with a woman since the whorehouses in Australia, and every fiber of his body called out to her and tried to draw her closer to him. Leaves crackled behind him and then he felt her tiny hands on his shoulders, and her breasts against his back. Her abdomen and legs fastened against his and she touched her lips to the back of his neck, sending shivering ripples all over his body.

She wrapped her arms around his waist and pressed the side of her face against his back, twining her smooth, supple legs in his. He placed his hands over hers and let her kiss his back for a while, then he let her hands go and rolled over to face her.

She moved a few inches back to give him room, and then they looked at each other. The moon cast a sheen over their features, and their eyes glittered like diamonds. The wind rustled the leaves on the trees and she held his face in her tiny hands and kissed his lips, making him dizzy, and Longtree thought of how strange it was that a young woman's kiss could debilitate him more than the mightiest blow from an enemy.

Their lips parted and their tongues touched. Longtree hugged

148

her tightly against him, while her fingers made a slow, sensual dance on his cheeks and their tongues did soft combat. She ran her fingers through his thick, straight hair and he reached down and cupped her buttocks in his hands, drawing her pelvis against him, his manhood like a steel rod between them.

They kissed and hugged, rolling over on the leaves, sinking into the whirlpool of ecstasy. She lay on her back and he bent over her, unfastening her sarong and gazing down at her supple body, the lovely alluring curves, and her breasts like two fruits on a field of gold.

He lowered his head and kissed the hollow between her breasts, then moved to the side and took her left breast into his mouth. It was soft and sweet, and he twiddled the nipple with his tongue until it became a hard little cone. She grabbed fistfuls of his hair and pulled him more tightly against her, and he opened his mouth wide, trying to suck her entire breast inside, but it was too big. He licked the top of her breast and kissed her throat while she arched her neck backward and spread her legs. He kissed her chin, touched his lips to hers again, and thrust his tongue deeply into her mouth, wanting to eat her alive.

She tore at his clothes, trying to unfasten the buttons, squirming and undulating beneath him. Summoning all her strength, she pushed him off her, and he rolled onto his back. She leaped on him like a wild animal, unbuttoning his shirt and nuzzling against his chest. She kissed his neck and ears, bit his nose playfully, licked his lips tantalizingly, and then moved her head down again, kissing his chest and the scars on his stomach while her hands groped down and unfastened his belt and unbuttoned his fatigue pants.

She kissed his lower abdomen as her hand snaked inside the front of his shorts and pulled out his long, throbbing warrior's spear. Squeezing it tightly, a drop of dew appeared at its point, and she lowered her head over it, licking it away. Then she kissed the hard, hot muscle, running her tongue around its head, and with a sigh opened her mouth and sucked it into her throat.

Longtree's toes curled and his fingernails dug into the ground. He looked up at the moon as her head bobbed up and down and his body was covered with tickles. She made tiny animal sounds, pulling her hair out of her way and then grasping his fleshy tower in her fists and slavering it with her tongue. Longtree wanted it to last forever, but he was a vigorous young man and couldn't control himself. His balls exploded and the cream shot out of him, filling her mouth and dripping down her chin, but still she kept sucking him, moving her head up and down, dizzy and reeling with lust, trying to slurp up every drop. She had to pause to catch her breath, and he reached up and grasped her shoulders, easing her to the ground and lying on top of her.

She reached for his sopping-wet cock and guided it toward her burning desire as he pushed his hips forward. It slid in smoothly past the delicate petals and the scattered pearls, the nooks and crannies and silken passageways, down and farther down into that secret magnificent place that is the source of life and pleasure for men.

She sighed and dug her fingernails into his back, closing her eyes and opening her mouth. One of his arms was wrapped around her back and the other held her sweet little ass. He drew out and glided in again, taking it slow, afraid he'd hurt her because he was so big and she so small. But she didn't react as if he was hurting her, she wrapped her legs around his waist and wiggled her hips from side to side lasciviously, trying to pull his entire body into her quivering, dripping vagina.

Longtree held her tightly and pumped her, working his hips up and around, trying to touch all those special places, especially the one on top that made her twitch whenever he rubbed his dong against it. She thrashed around like a wild woman underneath him, her hair like a black fire around her face, and she reached up in a paroxysm of passion and bit his throat, nearly drawing blood, but it felt like just another kiss to him as he swiveled his hips and pushed in and out, scooping and lunging and skittering across her soul.

Frankie La Barbara figured they'd start fucking before long, and he wasn't surprised when he started to hear the oohs and ahs on the other side of the bushes. He closed his eyes and tried to fall asleep but couldn't, knowing that an orgy was going on only a few feet away. He imgained what the Japanese girl would look like naked and thought of how nice it would be to chew on her boobs for a while and then stick his dick into her little coozie. Maybe he could even convince her to give him a blowjob. Maybe she'd let him put it up her ass.

He ground his teeth together and rolled over when he realized that Longtree, not he, was fucking her brains out. Frankie could hear her little sighs and Longtree's grunts and wanted to scream in rage and jealousy. *Why did she pick him instead of me?* he wondered. *What's the matter with me? I'm better-looking than he is. What's he got that I don't?*

Periodically in his life women had preferred ugly men to him, and he never could figure it out, but it hadn't been much of a problem, because there always had been plenty of woman who did think he was terrific and would fuck him at the drop of a hat. But he hadn't had a woman since Australia, and sexual frustration was setting his mind on fire. He lusted for the Japanese girl, and he even thought for a moment of going on the other side of the bushes and shooting Longtree in the back, or cutting his fucking throat, so that he could have the Japanese girl for himself. But he couldn't do that to Longtree. Any man who fought over a woman was an asshole, because no woman was worth it.

Frankie had a big hard-on and he was going out of his mind. He thought that maybe he should jerk off and calm himself down, but somehow it seemed perverted and sick to do that while Longtree was fucking only a few feet away. He thought of Cindy, his girl friend back in New York, and figured she was probably fucking somebody else just then too. Frankie thought he would explode with unfulfilled lust. He wanted to run on the beach and scream, but a Jap probably would see him and shoot him dead. He couldn't even smoke a cigarette, because it was dark and a Jap might see him.

He heard Longtree and the Japanese girl rolling and thrashing about and wondered what they were doing. It sounded really wild. Maybe Japanese people and Indians did it differently from Americans and he could learn something. It was perverse to peek at people who were screwing, but Frankie managed to convince himself that the experience would be educational, so

151

he drew himself silently to his knees and crept toward the bushes, where he could take a look.

He knew Longtree had sensitive ears, so he moved slowly and carefully, placing his knees and hands down easily, feeling foolish, but he was only human. Finally he reached the bushes and parted them silently with his hands. The moon cast an eerie glow on the clearing in front of him, and in the middle of the clearing were Longtree and the Japanese girl, fucking each other like wild animals.

Her legs were wrapped around his waist and his ass bounded up and down like a machine. She squirmed like a snake and he kept ramming it in to the hilt, the lucky son of a bitch. Some women were crazy, and once they started fucking, they couldn't stop. Maybe the Japanese girl would fuck Frankie after she was finished with Longtree. Now Frankie had something to hope for as his tongue hung out of his mouth and he watched the two of them humping away.

He heard a sound behind him and then another sound: footsteps! Spinning around, he dashed back to where he'd been sleeping and picked up his submachine gun. Raising his head, he spotted a solitary figure entering the treeline from the beach. The figure was hatless and Frankie couldn't see his face, but there was something familiar about him.

"Don't move!" Frankie said.

"It's me!" said Craig Delane.

Frankie stood up. "Hey, Delane, how're you doing?"

Delane walked toward the spot where Frankie was, his submachine gun in his right hand. "I'm starved," Delane said. "Any chow around here?"

"Lots of coconuts. You alone?"

"Yes. O'Rourke and I had to cross a river, and he didn't make it."

"No shit."

"I guess the current was too much for him. I barely made it across myself. Where're the coconuts? You alone too?"

"Naw," Frankie said, pointing his thumb over his shoulder, "the Chief is back there, getting greased."

"Getting what?"

"Fucking."

Delane wrinkled his nose. "Fucking who?"

"Some little Japanese girl we picked up along the way."

"Japanese girl?"

In the darkness Japanese soldiers and engineers chopped down trees and cleared land for General Hyakutake's new headquarters. His tent stood tautly on a flat area, glowing faintly from the kerosene lamp inside. Camouflage netting had been stretched from tree to tree overhead so that American night bombers couldn't see the encampment under construction.

General Hyakutake and Colonel Tsuji were inside the tent, drinking sake and discussing the events of the day, because it was impossible to sleep with all the work going on.

"Bad luck is hounding us here on this accursed island," General Hyakutake muttered. "Nothing we do ever turns out right. It is as if the gods and the elements themselves are against us."

Colonel Tsuji knew that he and General Hyakutake had made many wrong decisions and bad moves on Guadalcanal and that the gods and elements had little to do with it, but he only nodded and said, "Yes, sir, unquestionably you're right," because he was a toady, like most officers before their superiors.

The tent flap was thrown aside and Sergeant Kaburagi marched into the office, throwing a salute. "You asked to be notified immediately, sir, if any word came in on the convoy, and we've just received a message that it is under way and proceeding about an hour behind schedule."

"Hmm," said General Hyakutake, "that means it should arrive around three o'clock in the morning. They'll only have a few hours to unload before daylight. Colonel Tsuji, see that we have an adequate number of men at the beach to make sure the unloading goes smoothly. In fact perhaps you ought to take personal charge of the unloading operation yourself."

Colonel Tsuji stood and saluted General Hyakutake. "Yes, sir."

FIFTEEN . . .

Shaw, Shilansky, and O'Rourke were passing through a large coconut grove that bordered the beach, which they could see fifty yards ahead. The breeze wafted the salty ocean air past their nostrils, and the moonlight danced on the tops of the waves, while bats flapped their wings overhead, looking for tiny creatures to eat.

"Wow, looka there," Shilansky said. "What a sight. Jesus, this island can be beautiful at times, can't it?"

"The only problem with this island," Shaw said, "is that there ain't any fucking cunt around. They ain't even got any nurses or Red Cross girls."

"Maybe you should've tried to fuck one of those crocodiles while you had the chance."

O'Rourke was walking to the right of them, the barrel of his submachine gun pointed downward. "I remember this red-head I met in Melbourne," he said. "I met her in this department store, where I was trying to find something to buy for my mother. She was working behind the counter and..."

Beeeaaannngggggggg!

A bullet ricocheted off a palm tree a few inches from his head, and he dived to the ground. Shilansky and Shaw also hit the dirt as a volley of rifle fire opened up in front of them and to their right, sending bullets whizzing over their heads. The three GIs looked around and saw the yellow flashes of the muzzle blasts in the woods. They realized they had walked into a trap.

"Looks like a couple of squads of Japs," Shilansky said, his chin so low that it touched the ground.

Shaw glanced around. "Let's get the fuck out of here."

"Which way?"

Shaw pointed to their rear. "Back that way."

O'Rourke raised his submachine gun to fire a burst at the Japanese patrol that had found them, but Shilansky knocked it down. "Don't shoot—you'll only tell them where we are!"

"They know where we are!" O'Rourke replied.

"Keep your voice down, asshole."

They crawled around on the ground and crept back in the direction they'd come from, when suddenly rifle fire erupted in front of them, forcing them to stop and hug the ground.

"Malines, you sullounded!" shouted a Japanese soldier. *"Give it up!"*

The Japanese gunfire stopped for a moment, and the three GIs looked at each other in the light of the moon.

"Whataya say?" asked Shaw.

"I don't want them to put me in a box like they put Butsko in," Shilansky said.

"Me neither," said O'Rourke.

"How's your ammo situation?" Shaw asked.

"I got two clips, plus the one in my gun," Shilansky answered.

"I got one plus the one in my gun," O'Rourke said.

"I only got the one in my gun." Shaw bared his teeth. "Fuck 'em. Let 'em come for us. Maybe when they get close, we can wipe them out."

None of them believed that, although they wanted to.

"Maline, if you no sullender, we kill you all!"

"Don't say nothing," Shaw said.

There were a few moments of silence. The three GIs changed positions so each of them faced in opposite directions.

"Maline, you had you chance! We come for you now!"

The Japanese soldiers opened fire, and the coconut grove was filled with whizzing bullets. The GIs could see the Japanese soldiers moving from tree to tree in the moonlight, but they were heading to the left, because they didn't know exactly where the GIs were. Shaw, Shilansky, and O'Rourke knew the Japs would locate them sooner or later. It was only a matter of time. And then it'd be down and dirty to the bitter end.

Butsko spun around at the first volley of gunfire. "What the fuck's that?"

"Sounds close," Bannon said.

Homer Gladley pointed with his submachine gun. "Sound's like it's coming from right over yonder."

Butsko wiped his mouth with his hand. "Sounds like a lot of Japs, maybe two squads of them. They must have run into a few of our boys."

"I don't hear them firing back," Bannon said.

"Evidently the Japs don't know exactly where they are, and they're keeping quiet." Butsko tried to think of what to do. From the sound of the gunfire, there were more Japs than he, Bannon, and Gladley could handle, but those GIs out there had helped to rescue him, and he couldn't turn his back on them.

"Let's see if we can get them out of there," Butsko said. "Come on."

Captain Mizushima also heard the firing in the distance and raised his hand to stop the column he was leading. He and his men were on the beach, heading west, and the shooting was coming from his rear. He turned around and estimated the distance, figuring the gunfight was at least a half-mile or maybe even a mile away. One of his patrols must have found Americans. If he and his men ran, they could get there in fifteen minutes, maybe less.

"Double-time!" he shouted, running on his short bandy legs toward the sound of firing.

The Japanese girl was on her hands and knees and Longtree was behind her, holding her hips in his hands and humping like a dog. She wagged her butt from side to side and he pushed in and out of her, looking down at the curve of her waist and her nice round bottom. This was Longtree's favorite position; he thought he could get in deeper this way, and he liked the feel of women's asses against his thighs, plus he found the basic lewdness of the position most stimulating.

156

In fact he was so stimulated that he felt himself coming again. He opend his eyes and gulped for air as the mad itch began in his testicles and spread up and down his spine. He saw lights flashing in front of his eyes and his hip motions became erratic as the orgasm struck him like a bolt of lightning. He lurched like a bucking bronco, lifting the Japanese girl's rear end into the air as the hot cream gushed out of him and dribbled down her legs. He heard firecrackers and huge gongs and felt as if his whole life were spurting out of his cock. Losing his balance, he toppled to the side, taking her with him, and they fell to the ground, his cock still deep inside her; he hugged her close, still screwing away. Gradually his movements became weaker and then he was still, gasping for air, trying to summon the strength for another good fuck.

The delicious sensations, flashing lights, and sound of gongs all went away, but he still could hear the firecrackers.

"Hey, Longtree!" said Frankie, on the other side of the bush, "there's some shooting going on. Can't you hear it?"

"I can hear it. I'll be right there."

Longtree came to his senses. Jumping up, he found his clothes and put them on. The girl was aware of the gunfire, too, and wrapped herself in her sarong.

Longtree grabbed his submachine gun and walked through the bush, where he saw Frankie squatting on the ground with Craig Delane.

"When did you get here?" Longtree asked.

"About an hour ago."

"Where's O'Rourke?"

"Dead."

Frankie winked at Longtree. "I hope you gave her a few good shoves for me, Chief."

Longtree raised his face and listened. The firing couldn't have been much more than five hundred yards away. "Some of our guys must be in trouble," he said. "We'd better go see if we can do something."

The girl came out from behind the bush, looking very shy, because she knew the other American soldiers must have heard what she and Longtree were doing.

"What about the radio?" Delane asked. "Should we leave it here or take it with us?"

157

Longtree thought about that for a few moments. "If we take it with us, something might happen to it. We'd better leave it here." He turned to the girl, pointed to the ground, and said in a stern voice, "Stay!"

She didn't speak any English, but she got the message. She sat cross-legged on the ground and folded her hands in her lap.

"Let's go!" Longtree said, running toward the sound of the gunfire.

Frankie La Barbara and Craig Delane followed him. The girl watched them dash through the coconut grove and disappear into the darkness.

Shaw, the ex-prizefighter; O'Rourke, the ex–movie stunt-man; and Shilansky, the ex-thief, lay on the ground like a three-pointed star and watched the Japanese soldiers closing in like a tightening noose. The Japs had stopped firing and were searching the area for the GIs, and one group of four Japs, walking slowly in a low crouch, was drawing perilously close to Shilansky.

The three GIs knew they had to make every shot count, so they couldn't fire until they had to. The Japs walked closer to Shilansky, muttering to each other and jerking their heads around, advancing cautiously to each tree and looking behind it.

Shaw and O'Rourke moved around to face the Japs along-side Shilansky. They knew that the moment they fired, their position would be given away and the end would come pretty soon after that. They gritted their teeth and held their subma-chine guns tightly, waiting for the shit to hit the fan.

The Jap in front stopped suddenly, looking directly down at Shaw, Shilansky, and O'Rourke. He didn't want to believe his eyes, because he saw three submachine guns pointed di-rectly at him, and at that moment the three GIs opened fire.

The sound of their submachine guns roared through the woods, and the four Japs were blown away, their bodies riddled with bullets and blood spurting out of the holes. They dropped to the ground and lay still as the grove echoed with the sound of Japanese orders being shouted, followed by a fusillade of rifle fire.

The Japanese soldiers intended to use the same tactics on

158

the three GIs that they'd used on the Second Squad, because they were still under orders to take prisoners. Keeping the Americans pinned down with intense fire, the Japanese advanced in waves, and the GIs fired wildly, trying to keep them away.

The Japanese soldiers ran forward like furtive forest animals, and the GIs tried to aim their submachine guns and cut them down, but it was difficult to aim because Japanese bullets whizzed around their ears and kicked up dirt in front of them.

The Japanese soldiers tightened their ring around the GIs and prepared to make their final charge. The GIs rocked from side to side on the ground, firing their submachine guns in short bursts and trying to conserve ammunition. Each was on his last clip, and they knew it was just a matter of time before the end came. Their faces were covered with sweat, and O'Rourke had bitten his lips so hard they were bleeding. Shaw thought it tragic that he'd never have a shot at the heavyweight title, and Shilansky figured he was going to be shot down like his idol, John Dillinger, in front of that movie theatre in Chicago.

Suddenly the Japanese gunfire stopped.

"This is your last chance, Malines!" the Japanese soldier said. *"Give up now while you can!"*

The three GIs looked at each other. They'd seen what had happened to Butsko and didn't want any part of it.

"Fuck 'em—don't say anything," Shaw muttered.

The GIs remained silent, waiting for the final Japanese charge.

"You clazy Malines!" the Japanese soldier shouted. *"We come for you now! Banzai!"*

The Japanese soldiers jumped to their feet and charged the Americans, who held their submachine guns tightly against their shoulders and opened fire. Again the coconut grove filled with the roar of their gunfire, and the lead Japs were cut down, but the rest kept coming. When the Japanese were ten yards away, the GIs scrambled to their feet and kept firing, but in seconds they all were out of ammunition. They turned their submachine guns around and grasped them by their barrels, preparing to use them like baseball bats and bash a few Japanese heads before the end came.

159

Three Japanese soldiers charged Shilansky and he swung downward, busting open the middle Jap's head. The other two Japanese soldiers dived on him, and he kicked one in the face, then fell to the ground with the other, rolling over on the ground with him and trying to rip out his windpipe with his bare hands.

Then suddenly the coconut grove filled with the sound of submachine-gun fire, and Shilansky wondered if he was hearing things that weren't there. The noise came from his left and took the Japanese soldiers by surprise. They stopped their charge and looked around, wondering what was going on, and then one of their sergeants shouted an order and they fell back to reorganize and try to gauge the seriousness of the attack.

As they retreated, more submachine-gun fire erupted to their right, throwing the Japanese into total confusion. More orders were shouted, and the Japanese fled deeper into the coconut grove, thinking they were surrounded by a large American force, because the submachine guns made a terrific racket.

Shilansky got up on his hands and knees, unable to believe his eyes. Shaw's nose was bleeding and his lower lip was split open, but there was a big smile on his face. "Lookit the bastards run!"

O'Rourke couldn't say anything, because a Japanese soldier had kicked him in the stomach and he was trying to catch his wind. Gasping for air, he hugged his stomach and rolled around on the ground, in severe pain.

"Who's there?" shouted the inimitable voice of Butsko.

"It's us!" replied Shaw. *"Over here!"*

"Us too!" yelled Longtree from the left.

Shilansky and Shaw jumped for joy as the two groups of American soldiers joined them. Everybody was smiling and patting each other on the back, and a few even hugged each other out of sheer joy.

"Jesus," said Shilansky, "you guys showed up in the nick of time."

Butsko, nearly returned to normal, was charging back and forth like a wild man. "What the fuck's going on here!" he said. "What the fuck's going on!"

Shaw brought him up-to-date on the activities of his group, while Craig Delane looked down at the ground to see Jimmy

160

O'Rourke writhing in pain. At that same moment Jimmy O'Rourke glanced up and saw Craig Delane.

"*I thought you were dead!*" they said in unison.

"Shaddup, you two!" Butsko said. "I'm trying to think."

Butsko wrinkled his brow, and his face was more hideous than ever with all the cuts and bruises. He turned to Bannon. "We'd better call for help on the radio. Where the hell is it?"

"That way." He pointed in the direction of the spot where the radio had been buried.

"Let's go." Butsko looked at O'Rourke. "Are you okay?"

"I think so."

"Delane, help him up."

Delane bent and grabbed O'Rourke underneath his armpits, pulling him up. "You okay, old man?"

"Yeah, I think so."

"Just put your arm around my shoulder and lean on me and you'll be all right."

"Let's go," Butsko said.

Butsko led the First Squad toward the beach, and Craig Delane brought up the rear, half carrying Jimmy O'Rourke.

The Japanese convoy continued in a southeasterly direction through New Georgia Sound. Admiral Tamaki stood on the bridge of the *Aoba,* looking through his binoculars at a huge landmass to his left.

"What island is that?" asked General Ooka, gazing in the same direction through his own binoculars.

"Santa Isabel. It has no strategic significance whatever."

"I hope there are no spies there to report our position."

"If there are spies there, they won't see much. It's night, you know. The only reason we make these runs at night is so that we won't be seen."

There was a supercilious tone in Admiral Tamaki's voice, and it grated on General Ooka's ears. Naval officers always thought they were better than army officers, for reasons that escaped General Ooka. The Japanese Navy had been battered in two major sea battles with the Americans, and General Ooka felt they should walk around with their heads hung low in shame, but instead they were as arrogant as ever.

161

"Do you anticipate we'll land the troops on schedule?" General Ooka asked.

"I do," Admiral Tamaki replied.

The First Squad came to the area where the radio had been hidden, and the Japanese girl trembled behind the bushes, because she thought they might be Japanese soldiers, but when she saw Longtree among the men, she stood and showed herself.

Butsko stopped cold in his tracks. "Who the hell's *that*?"

"A Japanese girl," Longtree said. "She ran away from the Japs and we brought her here. She was one of them comfort girls. You know what comfort girls are, don't you, Sarge?"

"Yeah." Butsko glowered at her, because the Bataan Death March had taught him to hate everything Japanese.

Frankie chortled. "Longtree's been fucking her brains out," he said.

Longree wanted to beat Frankie to a pulp, but he remained still, his face expressionless. The Japanese girl tiptoed to his side and stood quietly.

"Where's the fucking radio?" Butsko asked.

Bannon pointed to he ground. "In there."

None of the men had packs and equipment anymore, so they got down on their hands and knees and dug out the earth with their bare hands. The Japanese girl sat beside a coconut tree, watching them, and Butsko looked at her out of the corner of his eye, expecting her to pull out a pistol and start shooting at him, because it was impossible for him to trust a Jap.

The soldiers clawed deeper and came to the poncho that covered the radio. They lifted out the radio and removed the poncho. Craig Delane put on the headset and turned it on.

"It's working," he said.

"Call Headquarters," Butsko said, "and tell them to get us the fuck out of here."

Delane waited until the set warmed up, dialed the emergency frequency, and pressed the button for a transmission. "This is Red Dog One calling Hound Dog. This is Red Dog One calling Hound Dog. Do you read me. Do you read me. Over."

Butsko snatched the headset away from him. "I'll talk to

them," he growled. "You'll probably fuck it up."

The men of the squad looked at each other philosphically, because they realized that Butsko was his horrible old self again.

Butsko listened to the static on the airwaves, then pressed the button for transmission and called Headquarters again, asking if they were reading him. He waited again and turned down the corners of his mouth. "Cocksuckers are probably asleep at their radios," he grumbled.

Then, a few seconds later, a voice came through to him. "This is Hound Dog calling Red Dog One. This is Hound Dog calling Red Dog One. I read you loud and clear. What is your position?"

Butsko gave him the coordinates of the position where Bannon and the first squad had landed and requested that all of them be evacuated as soon as possible.

"Stand by," said the radio operator at Henderson Field and signed off.

Butsko spat into the dirt.

"What'd he say?" Bannon asked.

"He said to stand by. I guess he's trying to find out what to tell us."

Colonel Stockton was sound asleep in his hut, when he heard a knock on his door. "Who is it?" he asked sleepily.

"Sergeant Jorgenson from the radio shack, sir. We've just received a transmission from the recon platoon."

Colonel Stockton sat bolt upright in his bed. "The recon platoon!"

"Yes, sir. It was Sergeant Butsko himself, sir. He requested evacuation for himself and eight other men, sir."

Colonel Stockton fumbled for the light and turned it on. "I'll be right there."

"Yes, sir."

Colonel Stockton pulled on his clothes, amazed to learn that Butsko and some of his men were still alive. He tried to figure out how to evacuate the recon platoon as expeditiously as possible. A submarine wouldn't be good enough, because it was too slow. He'd have to call the PT boat squadron on Guadalcanal and see if they could send a boat out. Those PT boats could go sixty miles an hour over the water; there was nothing faster afloat in any navy.

Colonel Stockton put on his helmet and left his hut, walking quickly through the regimental area toward his headquarters. He opened the door and the officer of the day, Lieutenant Alvin Coombs, jumped to his feet and saluted. Colonel Stockton walked past him, threw open the door to his office, flicked on the light on the desk, and sat down, reaching for his telephone. "Get me Commander Ames at the PT squadron," he told the operator.

The phone buzzed in his ear and after several seconds a young Ensign, who was the OD in the P T squadron, came on the phone. Colonel Stockton identified himself and said he had to speak with Lieutenant Commander Ames immediately about a matter of great importance. The ensign said he would awaken Lieutenant Commander Ames without delay.

Colonel Stockton held the phone to his ear with his shoulder as he stuffed his pipe with fine Virginia burley. He tamped it down and lit it up, and his head disappeared in a cloud of blue smoke.

"This is Ames speaking," said the voice in his ear.

"This is Stockton of the Twenty-third Regiment. I have a problem and I'll get right to the point. Nine of my men are behind enemy lines and I need to have them picked up. Can you give me a PT boat?"

"Sure thing. Where do you want it to go?"

"I'll have that information for you in a few minutes, but first I wanted to know how long it would take to get a PT boat under way."

"We've got one under way right now on patrol duty offshore. It can turn around and go wherever you want it to go at a moment's notice."

"Good. I'll get back to you in a few moments. Stay close to your phone."

"Will do."

Colonel Stockton hung up and bounded out of his chair, encouraged by the cooperative manner of Lieutenant Commander Ames. The PT squadron on Guadalcanal had the reputation of being a bunch of madmen and daredevil hotshots, but at least they were ready to pitch in if you needed them.

Colonel Stockton entered the radio shack, and everybody looked at him expectantly, because the news about the recon platoon had electrified them.

"Where's Butsko's message?" Colonel Stockton asked.

Sergeant Jorgenson handed it to him. Colonel Stockton saw the coordinates of Butsko's position and recognized them as the drop-off point of the First Squad when the mission behind enemy lines had first begun. He might as well have them picked up right where they were.

"Get Butsko for me on the radio," Colonel Stockton told the operator sitting in front of the console.

The Japanese soldier stopped suddenly and pointed to the sand. "Look!"

Captain Mizushima ran forward to see what the soldier was pointing at. He looked down and saw two sets of footprints. Dropping to his knees, Captain Mizushima held out his hand and Sergeant Jukichi dropped a flashlight into it. Captain Mizushima shined the light on the footprints and could see that they were made by American combat boots.

Captain Mizushima stood and looked at the trail the footprints had made. It headed east, and Captain Mizushima salivated like a bloodhound who'd just picked up his quarry's scent. He motioned with his arm and the men followed him as he walked with his face to the ground, on the trail of two American soldiers.

Butsko and the First Squad sat around the radio, waiting for the reply from regimental headquarters. They could hear waves lapping on the shore and the tide coming closer.

Frankie La Barbara had no gum to chew, so he was biting a twig. "What's taking them so fucking long?" he said.

Butsko ignored him and flexed his right hand, trying to get it back to normal. The tips of his fingers still were swollen and infected, and the joints ached worse than ever. He knew he had a fairly serious infection and needed to have it looked at quickly.

165

"Fucking Japs," he muttered, glaring at the Japanese girl.

She knew he didn't like her and moved closer to Longtree. Butsko was amazed at how alike they looked.

"This is Hound Dog calling Red Dog One."

It was the voice of Colonel Stockton coming over the radio, asking if they read him.

"We read you loud and clear."

"Are you still at the First Squad drop-off point?"

"Yes, sir."

"Sit tight. I'm sending a PT boat to pick you up. When you hear them coming, give them three short flashes with a flashlight. Do you have a flashlight?"

Butsko looked up. "Anybody here remember to keep a flashlight?"

"I got mine," Bannon said.

"We got a flashlight," Butsko said into the mike.

"Good. We'll have you out of there before you know it. Over and out."

Butsko handed the headset to Craig Delane. "They're sending a P T boat to pick us up," he said. "Go get your rubber boat and blow the fucking thing up. And keep your eyes peeled because you never know when more Japs might show up."

SIXTEEN . . .

Eighty feet long and fifteen feet wide, shuddering before the push of its three Packard engines, *PT–114* rumbled through the waters off Guadalcanal. A thin fleecy cloud was sweeping across the face of the moon, and the crew of the PT boat sat at their stations, looking for seaborne Japanese raiding parties trying to sneak behind the American lines.

Lieutenant (jg.) Bobby Woodward from Boston, Massachusetts, sat behind the wheel of *PT–114*. He was a tall extremely thin young man wearing a Boston Red Sox baseball cap that his younger brother had sent him. He was unshaven and bleary-eyed, because he'd spent the day drinking jungle juice brewed by some renegade Marines and purchased for the crew of *PT–114* by its chief boatswain's mate, Alvin Trask from San Diego, California.

Lieutenant Woodward wore no shirt, and neither did any of the ten crewmembers on his boat. Like him, they were unshaven and tended to be rowdy because they operated far from the Navy brass most of the time.

The boat was filthy and cluttered inside and out, but its crew kept it in good running condition and its firing systems were always ready to go. They were a bunch of speed demons, always hoping for the opportunity to open up *P T–114*, because it was basically a speedboat with guns and torpedoes, powered by three twelve-cylinder Packard supermarine engines of the same design used in the famous Gold Cup–winning speedboat *Miss America*.

Chief Boatswain's Mate Trask climbed the steps to the bridge, his big belly hanging over his belt and an unlit cigar in the corner of his mouth. "The old man wants you on the radio, Bobby," he said. "I'll take the wheel."

Lieutenant Woodward got out of his seat, stretched his legs and arms, and descended the ladder to the main deck. Kicking an empty can of fruit salad out of his way, he turned the corner and pushed open the door to the radio shack, sitting next to the radio operator, who pushed the mike toward him.

"Lieutenant Woodward speaking, sir."

"Woodward," said Lieutenant Commander Ames, "how's your fuel situation?"

"We've got plenty of fuel, sir. We just filled our tanks about two hours ago and haven't done much since."

"Good. I've got something special for you to do. I want you to pick up nine American soldiers stranded behind enemy lines."

Lieutenant Woodward felt himself rising out of his lethargy. "Where are they, sir?"

Lieutenant Commander Ames told him the coordinates. "They're waiting for you right now, and they'll flash a light three times to let you know exactly where they are. Move in and out quickly, and don't get in any trouble, understand?"

"Yes, sir."

"Are you sure?"

"Yes, sir."

"Good. Report back to me if you have any trouble. When you pick up the men, let me know. Any questions?"

"No, sir."

"Over and out."

With a big grin on his face, Lieutenant Woodward walked out of the radio shack and onto the deck. He cupped his hands around his mouth and shouted, *"Meeting up on the bridge! Let's go, on the double!"*

He climbed the stairs to the bridge and his grungy crew followed him. Chief Boatswain's Mate Trask still sat at the controls, keeping *PT–114* on a steady course.

Lieutenant Woodward rested his ass against the instrument panel. "Just spoke with the old man on the radio," he said. "We're going behind Jap lines to pick up some doggies who're stranded there. He said to go in fast and get out fast, so we're going to open this son of a bitch up. We might run into some Jap interference, so man your battle stations and be ready for anything. Got it?"

His crew was happy about the chance to do something exciting for a change. They grinned and jabbed each other with their elbows like a bunch of playful children.

"Okay, battle stations!" Woodward yelled. "Chief, lemme behind the fucking wheel!"

Chief Boatswain's Mate Trask stood and Lieutenant Woodward slipped into the chair. He rammed forward the throttle levers for the three engines all the way and cut the wheel sharply to the right.

The three Packard engines roared mightily and the boat spun around in the ocean, leaving a huge spiraling wake behind it. Lieutenant Woodward straightened the wheel and licked his lips as the P T boat zoomed through the water and slowly lifted itself to planing speed. The wind whistled around his ears and he pulled his Red Sox cap tight on his head, sucking salt air through his clenched teeth and feeling alive again.

"Hang on, you doggies!" he shouted into the wind. "PT One-fourteen *is on the way!"*

He stood up and flexed his legs each time the speeding boat bucked and kicked over the waves, and *PT–114* streaked across New Georgia sound toward the Japanese side of the island.

The footprints veered to the right and entered a huge coconut grove. Captain Mizushima held up his hand, and his men stopped behind him. He dropped to one knee and peered into the coconut grove, trying to spot American soldiers moving about, but he saw only the trunks of trees leaning in all directions.

He motioned with his hands for his men to spread out and then motioned again to send them forward. They entered the pine grove, moving slowly and cautiously, not wanting to fall into an American trap. Captain Mizushima walked in front of them, trying to follow the footprints, but they were difficult to

169

see in the firm ground of the coconut grove.

Captain Mizushima gnashed his teeth nervously and wondered why the Americans had turned into the grove. Were they going to bed down for the night or did they have some sinister purpose in mind? All he knew was that the footprints on the beach had looked fresh, and the Americans couldn't be too far away.

"Look!" said Sergeant Jukichi, pointing straight ahead.

Captain Mizushima squinted and saw in the distance something that looked like bodies lying on the ground. He motioned with his arm and moved forward on his short, bandy legs. His men followed him, and he soon realized that the bodies were no illusion caused by the moonlight.

He drew his samurai sword and his men held their rifles ready. They drew closer to the bodies, and Captain Mizushima noticed the cut of Japanese uniforms and the shape of Japanese helmets. "They're ours," he whispered, his heart sinking in his chest.

He and his men knelt down and he recognized the dead soldiers. Blood had coagulated on their bodies and their faces were wrenched in pain. Flies and bugs crawled over the corpses, which had stiffened from rigor mortis.

Ambushed, Captain Mizushima thought. *Those sneaky Americans*. He glanced around and counted his men. There were thirty of them. He wondered how many Americans had been involved in the ambush. Getting onto his hands and knees, he tried to estimate the size of the American force from their footprints. It was difficult to be accurate, but he was sure there weren't too many of them. After the raid that had liberated the captured American sergeant, the final estimate of the number of Americans participating had been around twenty. The footprints he saw could have been made by that number of men. At any rate he would have to follow the tracks and see where they led. Colonel Tsuji would have him court-martialed if he didn't at least do that.

"Sergeant Jukichi!" Captain Mizushima said. "Can you see which way the Americans went?"

"I believe this way, sir," Sergeant Jukichi said, pointing toward the sea in an easterly direction.

Captain Mizushima examined the tracks and decided that Sergeant Jukichi was probably right.

"Follow me, men," he said, "but keep quiet, because the Americans may be very near."

The convoy plowed through the moonlit waters of New Georgia Sound, heading for the debarkation area hacked out of the jungle by Japanese military engineers. General Ooka looked through his binoculars at Guadalcanal, lying like a big black slug on the twinkling water. Admiral Tamaki turned to his navigator and asked for an estimate of the convoy's position. In seconds the navigator gave him the coordinates.

"Ensign Totsuka!" said Admiral Tamaki.

"Yes, sir."

"Transmit a message to the other ships in the convoy. Tell them to steer right twenty degrees."

"Yes, sir."

Ensign Totsuka scurried off to carry out his orders. Admiral Tamaki looked at General Ooka. "We shall reach our debarkation point within the hour," he said.

Colonel Tsuji leaned against a sidecar attached to a motorcycle and looked at his watch. It was a few minutes after one o'clock in the morning, and he expected the convoy to appear soon. It would blink its lights as it approached, and he had lookouts posted to watch for those signs.

Colonel Tsuji looked up at the sky and didn't like what he saw. The moon was three quarters full, and only a few clouds were floating by. He would have felt better if there were no moon at all, but there was no indication that the American fleet was aware of the approaching Japanese convoy, which would unload soon.

Colonel Tsuji was eager for the Forty-eighth Division to come ashore and move up on the line. It would make an important difference in the balance of forces on Guadalcanal, and he'd be able to mount large-scale operations again. General Ooka, the commander of the Forty-eighth, was said to be a progressive military man like himself, and he was coming with tanks and more artillery. Perhaps with General Ooka and the

171

Forty-eighth the humiliations of Guadalcanal could be turned to victory.

The prospects for a change in the situation on Guadalcanal made him excited, and he held his hands behind his back, pacing back and forth.

P T–114 shot like a rocket over the waves of New Georgia Sound, leaving a long white wake behind it. Lieutenant Woodward held the wheel tightly in his bony hands, his Red Sox cap on backward, his eyes glittering with excitement.

"Chief!" he yelled. *"Where the fuck are we?"*

Chief Boatswain's Mate Trask carried a chart to the bridge and flattened it with his hands on the instrument panel. The ends of the map fluttered in the wind and he pointed to a section of the ocean. *"Right around here!"*

Lieutenant Woodward bent low and looked at the map. He was nearing the pickup point and thought it was time to steer toward shore.

"I'm taking her in right now!" he yelled above the roar of the engines. *"Tell the men to stay the fuck awake back there!"*

"Yes, sir!"

Chief Boatswain's Mate Trask folded up the map and descended the steps to the main deck while Lieutenant Woodward pulled the wheel to his left. *P T–114* turned and bucked sideways against the waves as it headed toward shore.

"I hear them coming," said Longtree, his ears perked up.

"I think I do too," said Bannon.

Butsko hadn't been hearing too well since the Japs kicked the shit out of him, but he knew Longtree and Bannon had good ears. "Okay," he said, "get ready to move that boat onto the beach."

The other men in the squad stood around the inflated rubber boat and held it by its rope gunwales. They were perched at the edge of the treeline, and Butsko took out Bannon's flashlight, pointing it out to sea. He eased the button forward and pressed it three times. A few seconds later he saw a light flash three times out at sea, and now he could hear the sound of engines too.

"Hey!" Frankie La Barbara said. "Here they come!"

"Move out the boat and keep your voices down," Butsko said. "There might be Japs around here."

The men picked up the inflated boat and dragged it out of the woods and across the sand. Butsko walked behind them, looking to the right and left, holding Craig Delane's submachine gun ready to fire. The Japanese girl walked near Butsko and he kept an eye on her, too, because he figured she was going to pull some shit before long.

"Look!" said Sergeant Jukichi, pointing to the light flashing out to sea.

"Get down!" said Captain Mizushima.

They all flopped onto their stomachs, and Captain Mizushima tried to figure out what was going on. A boat was out there; were the Americans going to land some troops? Was a major invasion going to take place? He should report what was happening to headquarters, but what should he report? He had no idea of what was going on.

"Look!" said Sergeant Jukichi again.

Ahead of them, not more than thirty yards away, they saw a group of Americans carrying an inflated rubber boat toward the water. Now everything became clear to Captain Mizushima. The American patrol was leaving, probably with valuable information, and he couldn't let them get away. But he also had to try to take them alive, so that Colonel Tsuji could find out what they knew. Captain Mizushima racked his brain for a feasible plan of action, and when none presented itself, he decided to take action to stop the Americans at least.

He pulled his samurai sword out of its scabbard, leaped to his feet, and shouted at the top of his lungs, *"Charge!"*

Butsko spun around and saw Japs charging with fixed bayonets. *"Hit it!"* he screamed.

The GIs dropped the boat and fell to the ground, whipping their submachine guns around and opening fire on the charging wave of Japanese soldiers. The air filled with a hail of their bullets, and several Japs tripped and went tumbling across the sand, streaking it with spirals of blood.

173

"Get down!" said Captain Mizushima.

The Japanese soldiers dropped to their stomachs and aimed their rifles at the Americans, whom they outnumbered by more than two to one. Meanwhile the Americans and Japanese soldiers could hear the P T boat speeding closer to shore. Butsko looked to his right and couldn't see it yet, but it sounded close and he wondered how in the hell he was going to get his men out of there.

"Sullender!" yelled Sergeant Jukichi. *"Sullender or die!"*

Butsko wiped his nose with the back of his hand. "Anybody got any hand grenades left?"

Nobody said anything.

"Okay," he said. "You'll just have to make a break for it. I'll stay behind and try to cover you."

"Huh?" said Bannon. "How're you gonna cover us?"

"I just gave you an order!" Butsko yelled. "Leave your fucking ammo clips behind and get going when I say the word! After you get out on the PT boat, it can use its machine guns to cover me! Ready: one—two—three—*Go!*"

Butsko opened fire on the Japanese soldiers in front of him, swinging his submachine gun from side to side and trying to keep them pinned down, but the Japanese soldiers could see the Americans carrying their boat toward the water, and a few of them managed to fire some wild shots through the hail of bullets Butsko was sending their way. Two of those bullets hit the big rubber boat, and air whistled out of the holes.

Bannon realized in an instant that the boat was going to be useless. "Let it go and swim!" he yelled.

The GIs dropped the shrinking boat and ran toward the water as bullets whizzed all around, but the Japanese had difficulty aiming through the one-man barrage Butsko was putting out. His submachine gun shook every fiber of his body, but he kept the trigger depressed and his bullets skimmed over the sand toward the Japanese. His bolt went *click* and he ejected the empty clip, ramming in a new one and resuming his fire.

His submachine-gun bursts made it difficult for the Japanese soldiers to advance and aim, but they fired back anyway, trying to kill Butsko and stop the Americans who were running into the water. One Japanese soldier sighted on an American in the water and pulled the trigger of his Arisaka rifle. His rifle fired, kicking into his shoulder, and he thought he saw an American soldier fall. Raising his head a few inches to get a better look, a .45 caliber bullet from Butsko's submachine gun slammed into the side of his helmet, piercing the metal easily and scrambling his brains. He went limp on the ground, blood pouring out of the big crack in his skull.

The Japanese bullet had struck Homer Gladley's chest, and the big, powerful man stumbled in the coral beneath his feet. He tried to regain his footing, but the pain was too much for him and he dropped into the water.

Bannon saw him go down and rushed through the water to grab his arm. He saw the front of Gladley's shirt covered with blood and knew it was a bad wound. Shaw took hold of Gladley's other arm, and he and Bannon carried Gladley deeper into the water, toward the PT boat roaring at them.

"There they are!" shouted Chief Boatswain's Mate Trask.

PT–114 was speeding toward shore, and Lieutenant Woodward stood up to get a better look. Ahead in the darkness he saw men wading toward him in the water, and behind them were flashes of light. Easing off on the throttle, the sound of his engines died down and he could hear rifle shots and submachine-gun fire. But he didn't know who was firing at whom. He picked up his binoculars from the control panel and looked at the beach, and just then a bullet shot a hole through his windshield.

He flinched and looked through his binoculars again. He saw a group of men lying on the beach, shooting at the GIs wading toward him in the water.

"*Thornton!*" he shouted, pointing toward the beach. "*Hayes! Put those fifties over there!*"

The two sailors swung around the big fifty-caliber machine guns mounted on the PT boat and aimed them toward the beach, pressing down on the thumb triggers and filling the night with thunder. The big bullets, nearly twice the size of ordinary machine-gun bullets, flew to the shore like angry gnats, every fifth one a tracer. The bullets chewed into the Japanese soldiers and *whump*ed into the sand.

Now the Japanese soldiers were completely pinned down. The ground shook as every fifty-caliber bullet rammed into it, and the bullets were landing with the frequency of a downpour.

"Sergeant Jukichi!" screamed Captain Mizushima. "Call headquarters! Tell them to send planes!"

Sergeant Jukichi, lying next to him, picked the headset off the field radio on his back, and a big fifty-caliber bullet hit him on the shoulder, ripped through his rib cage and tearing apart his heart. He slumped soundlessly to the ground, and Captain Mizushima reached for the headset, when another bullet hit the radio and shattered it.

Captain Mizushima hugged the sand, his teeth chattering. Three inches more to the left and the bullet would have blown his head apart. He looked around and saw dead and wounded Japanese soldiers all around him. His mind presented him with two major alternatives: He could lay where he was and let the Americans get away, which would be ignominious, or he could order a charge and try to stop them.

For an officer like Captain Mizushima, only one choice was realistic. He recalled an old Japanese aphorism: *Duty is as heavy as a mountain, but death is as light as a feather*. Drawing his sword out of his scabbard, he leaped to his feet and shouted, *"Banzai!"*

Most of his men who were still alive jumped up and followed him through the rain of bullets. Some were felled immediately, and the others rushed toward the Americans in the water, their bayonets fixed on the ends of their rifles and firing from the waist.

"Banzai!" yelled Captain Mizushima, swinging his sword through the air. *"Get them!"*

The two fifty-caliber machine guns on *P T–114* ripped the charge to shreds, and on the sand Butsko peppered them from the side with submachine-gun bullets, but still the Japanese kept charging, their numbers diminishing every second, until Captain Mizushima and five other survivors got behind the

176

Americans in the water and Lieutenant Woodward had to stop the machine guns for fear of killing the Americans wading out to his P T boat. Suddenly the beach became quiet, and *P T–114* bobbed gently on the waves.

Butsko saw what had happened and knew the men in the water were in trouble. They had no more ammo and the Japs would have them at their mercy. Stuffing a clip of ammo into his belt, he scrambled to his feet and ran obliquely toward the water, so that he could shoot down the Japs from the side without the danger of his bullets going astray and hitting any of the men in the First Squad.

Butsko charged across the sand like an angry bull as the Japanese soldiers splashed through the surf, firing wildly from the hip, trying to get close so that they could kill the Americans with their bayonets. As soon as the angle was right, Butsko pulled the trigger of his submachine gun and two Japs were hit in their sides, dropping into the water. Butsko charged directly at them now, screaming and hollering for blood, remembering his hours of torture in the jungle and recalling the Bataan Death March.

The surviving Japanese soldiers turned to meet this new threat, but they were no match for the torrent of submachine-gun bullets. One by one they shrieked in pain and collapsed into the water until only one was standing, his bandy legs knee-deep in the surf: Captain Mizushima himself.

Butsko recognized him, and it was as if an electrical charge went through his body. His eyes bulging, his teeth clenched together, he continued his charge and aimed at Captain Mizushima, who raised his sword to cleave Butsko in half. Butsko pulled back his trigger and the bolt shot forward.

Click!

The submachine gun was empty and he didn't have time to reload. His forward motion carried him within range of Captain Mizushima's sword, and the stalwart Japanese officer swung downward, screaming, *"Banzai!"*

Butsko gripped his submachine gun in both hands and raised it above his head, catching the blade on the middle of the barrel. Captain Mizushima pulled back his sword to swing at Butsko from the side, and Butsko smashed him in the face with the

177

butt of his submachine gun. Captain Mizushima was dazed and stumbled backward, tripping on the coral and falling into the water.

Butsko saw Captain Mizushima lying at his mercy in the water and lost total control of himself. This was the Japanese officer who'd beaten and kicked Butsko on the Bataan Death March and had killed Sergeant Clyde Drake and many other men. Tossing his submachine gun to the side, Butsko dived for Captain Mizushima's throat.

The water revived Captain Mizushima, who saw Butsko flying through the air at him. He lashed out quickly with his foot and kicked Butsko in the chest, but gravity brought Butsko down on top of Captain Mizushima nonetheless, and he grabbed for the Japanese officer's throat. Captain Mizushima shot his thumbs forward, to gouge Butsko's eyes out, and Butsko had to raise his hands to protect himself.

He blocked Captain Mizushima's thrust and delivered a short right jab to Mizushima's jaw. Mizushima was stunned by the punch, and Butsko hit him again, this time with a left hook. Dazed but still game, Mizushima punched Butsko in the mouth, and Butsko slammed Mizushima in the nose, tearing cartilage and breaking bone and sending blood squirting into the air, but Captain Mizushima was so full of adrenaline that he didn't feel a thing. He reached up and grabbed Butsko's thick neck, and at that moment Butsko lost his balance in the surf and fell to the side, flailing with his arms and breaking Captain Mizushima's grip on his throat.

They rolled over and around in the water, clawing and punching each other, spitting into each other's faces as the waves crashed into them. Butsko was frustrated and furious by his inability to finish the wily Japanese officer off, and he heard the men of the First Squad charging through the water to help him out.

"Get away from me!" he bellowed. *"I can handle him myself!"*

Captain Mizushima tried to push Butsko's head under the water and drown him, but Butsko was too strong for him. Captain Mizushima, on the other hand, was too fast and tricky for Butsko. Finally, Butsko realized that the only thing to do was steady himself and then simply overwhelm the son of a bitch with sheer brute power.

Butsko stuck out a leg and stopped himself from rolling around with Captain Mizushima. Butsko caught his balance, pulled back from Captain Mizushima, who clawed wildly at the air, and then lunged forward, throwing hard punches and putting all his weight behind them.

He hit Captain Mizushima with a left jab that snapped his head back and then landed a hard overhand right that made Captain Mizushima see stars. Captain Mizushima lashed out with his foot, trying to kick Butsko in the balls, but Butsko pivoted neatly to the side and received the blow on his outer thigh, jabbing with his left again and then turning and throwing a haymaker with his right. The punch landed on Captain Mizushima's broken nose and made his legs buckle. Butsko straightened him with a left uppercut, hit him with a hard right hook, then a left hook, and finally threw an incredible overhand right to the mouth that sent Captain Mizushima sprawling back into the water.

Butsko was on him like stink on shit, punching and kicking in a wild fury. Captain Mizushima had only a glimmer of consciousness left, and he raised his arms weakly to protect himself, while Butsko crouched low and pounded him again and again in the head, his thunderous fists breaking bones and knocking the Japanese's jaw loose from its hinges.

Captain Mizushima was out like a light, but Butsko couldn't stop. All his anger and hatred of the Japanese—and of this officer in particular—erupted out of him like a volcano, and he shrieked madly as he punched and kicked the limp, broken body of Captain Mizushima. He picked up Captain Mizushima, held him high over his head, and threw him down into the water. Then he dived on him, grabbed him by the neck, pushed his head underneath the surface, squeezing with all his strength. Captain Mizushima's neck became compressed in Butsko's hands and then something snapped, and Butsko knew the Japanese officer was dead, air bubbles and curls of blood streaming from his battered face up through the water.

Butsko loosened his grip and stood up, gasping for air. He stumbled on the coral and Frankie La Barbara put out a hand

179

to steady him. Butsko looked around and saw the men of the First Squad looking at him. In the distance Bannon and Shaw were carrying Gladley toward the P T boat, which was backing up toward them.

Butsko took a deep breath as the waves washed the mangled corpse of Captain Mizushima away. "Let's get the fuck out of here," he said to the men around him.

SEVENTEEN . . .

The Japanese convoy had made its final course change and now was heading directly to its debarkation point. The decks of the transport ships were crowded with Japanese soldiers carrying rifles and full field packs, looking ahead toward Guadalcanal only a few miles away now. On the perimeter of the convoy were eight destroyers, and in front was the battleship *Aoba*, bristling with guns and covered with thick slabs of armor.

On the bridge Admiral Tamaki and General Ooka looked at Guadalcanal through their binoculars.

"It won't be long now," Admiral Tamaki said. "We'll be in position within thirty minutes, and all your men should be ashore in an hour or two. Then you will be able to win great victories for the Emperor. I'll bet you can hardly wait."

General Ooka didn't know whether Admiral Tamaki was being sarcastic, so he thought he'd play it straight. "That is true, sir. We are most anxious to go ashore. The Forty-eighth will turn the tide of battle here on Guadalcanal, mark my words."

"How strange," said Admiral Tamaki. "The commander of the Shunsake Regiment told me the same thing when I unloaded him and his men here less than a month ago. He's dead now, and his regiment was almost completely wiped out."

"So is much of the Japanese fleet," General Ooka snapped back. "The war is showing a hard face."

His anger was not lost on Admiral Tamaki, who was more

mature and less emotional. Admiral Tamaki thought General Tojo and a clique of army officers were responsible for getting Japan into a war that the admiral believed Japan couldn't win in the long run, and in his eyes General Ooka was a representative of the same fanatical saber-rattling sensibility. But Admiral Tamaki said nothing, because if his opinions became widely known, he would be relieved of command and disgraced, and besides, it was more enjoyable to watch General Ooka turn red with anger.

Admiral Tamaki watched the coastline of Guadalcanal and decided it was time to make final preparations for the troops to go ashore. Lowering his binoculars, he turned to his executive officer and said in a calm voice, "Prepare to lower the landing boats and the nets."

"Yes, sir."

Admiral Tamaki turned to General Ooka. "Kindly inform your men that they should make ready to go ashore."

The three Packard supermarine engines of *PT–114* idled as the boat rocked in the water and its crew pulled the soaking GIs aboard.

"Easy with him," said Bannon as four crewmembers lifted Homer Gladley out of the water.

"This guy's as heavy as a horse," said Seaman First Class Irwin Thornton from Corpus Christi, Texas.

"He's as big as one too," added Gunner's Mate Third Class Jerry Riggs from Tampa, Florida.

Lieutenant Woodward called down from the bridge, *"Hurry up, you guys! Let's get the fuck out of here!"*

Shaw was pulled out of the water next, and after him came Bannon, who kneeled beside Homer Gladley, who was lying on the deck. Gladley was pale and the front of his shirt was soaked with blood. His eyes were closed and he didn't appear to be breathing very much. Pharmacist's Mate Third Class Ray Musco bent over Gladley and took his pulse, then opened his medicine bag and took out a packet of sulfa, tearing it open and sprinkling it over the wound.

"How is he?" Bannon asked.

"I don't think the bullet hit anything vital. If we can stop the bleeding, he'll be all right until we get back."

Musco poured on more sulfa, coagulating the blood and disinfecting the wound. O'Rourke limped across the deck, holding his chest.

"I think I got a broken rib, Doc."

"I'll see you after I finish this guy."

O'Rourke sat down and leaned against a gunwale. Craig Delane sat opposite him with a half smile on his face that irritated O'Rourke.

"Can I get you anything?" Delane asked.

"Naw," grunted O'Rourke.

"Anybody got a dry cigarette?" Delane asked.

A sailor handed him one and lit it with his Zippo. Thornton and Riggs pulled the Japanese girl onto the deck and then followed her with their eyes, because the water had plastered her dress to her curvaceous body.

"Wake up down there!" yelled Lieutenant Woodward from the bridge. *"Let's go!"*

Thornton and Riggs reached down and pulled Longtree out of the water, and next came Frankie La Barbara, winking and blinking and clicking his teeth. "Hey!" he said. "Shit! Fuck! Piss! I never thought we'd get out of there. Who's got a cigarette!"

The crew of *PT–114* passed around cigarettes while Lieutenant Woodward and Chief Boatswain's Mate Trask scanned the horizon through their binoculars to make sure no trouble was approaching. The three engines purred smoothly and *PT–114* rocked gently in the waves.

Thornton and Riggs dragged Butsko onto the deck, and he was a fearsome sight, still showing the signs of beatings and the battle he'd had with Captain Mizushima. He took two steps and collapsed next to Gladley.

"How is he?" Butsko asked in a low raspy voice.

"I've stopped the bleeding," replied Pharmacist's Mate Musco. "I think he'll be okay."

Butsko rolled over and went limp against a gunwale. He closed his eyes and had difficulty opening them up again. The fight with Captain Mizushima had taken the last ounce of his strength, and he felt as if he were going to die.

"Hey, whatta we waiting for!" yelled Frankie La Barbara, walking up and down the deck like Groucho Marx. "Let's get this show on the road!" He looked at the Japanese girl shivering next to Longtree, who tried to warm her by hugging her close to him.

Frankie knew he should sit down and shut up, but all the demons were loose inside him and he couldn't. "Wow!" he said, looking at the girl. "I never knew a Jap bitch could be so pretty. Hey, let's have a fucking *gang bang* on the way back!"

Bannon tensed, because he could see the muscles twitching in Longtree's face. Longtree pulled out his bayonet and jumped to his feet. Frankie looked around for an ax or a baseball bat, but of course neither was around, so he yanked out his own bayonet and got ready. Longtree let out an Apache war whoop and charged across the deck while Bannon leaped forward, tackling Longtree and bringing him down, the bayonet slashing through the air.

Shaw and Craig Delane dived on Longtree and pinned him to the deck, but they were having trouble holding him, so Shilansky and Thornton also piled on.

Frankie danced around on the balls of his feet and whipped his bayonet through the air. "Lemme at him!" he yelled. "I'll kill the son of a bitch!"

Lieutenant Woodward jumped down to the deck and stormed toward the GIs. "What the hell's the matter with you men!" he shouted. "Knock it off!"

"I'll kill the son of a bitch!" Frankie said, hopping around. "He won last time, but I'll cut his fucking throat this time!"

"Settle down!" screamed Woodward.

"Lemme loose!" hollered Longtree.

Butsko opened his eyes, saw what was going on, shrugged, and closed his eyes again. He didn't care if Frankie and Longtree killed each other, and in fact at that point he thought it might be a good idea.

"Now listen to me!" Woodward said. *"We're not leaving here until everybody calms down!"*

"Aw, shit," Frankie said, putting his bayonet away. He looked at Longtree, who was squirming under five bodies. "He just saved your ass, Chief."

Longtree fought to bring himself under control. A warrior

184

should not go nuts the way he did. He took a few deep breaths and loosened up. "Okay," he said, "I won't kill him until we get back on land."

Bannon and the others let Longtree up. Longtree sat beside the Japanese girl again and put his arm around her, and Lieutenant Woodward returned to the bridge, where Chief Boatswain's Mate Trask was looking east through his binoculars.

"Sir," said Trask, "I think I see something out there."

"Where?" asked Woodward raising his binoculars.

"Toward the horizon in the direction I'm looking. I think I see some ships out there."

Lieutenant Woodward looked through his binoculars in the direction Trask indicated. He was younger than Trask and had excellent eyes, and he saw a number of dark shapes on the horizon. They might be clouds or an optical illusion, or they might be something else, like the Tokyo Express.

"I think maybe we'll go have a look," Lieutenant Woodward said. "Notify the base that we've picked up nine men, one of them wounded, and we're on our way back, but don't tell them we're taking the long way back. Got it?"

"Yes, sir."

Chief Boatswain's Mate Trask descended the steps to the deck, and Lieutenant Woodward sat in his chair, easing the throttle levers forward. The engines burbled and the PT boat moved forward in the water. Lieutenant Woodward steered to the left and headed for the dark shapes on the horizon, then pushed the throttles forward all the way, and *PT–114* leaped forward, its engines screaming as it accelerated like a rocket over the water.

Frankie La Barbara glanced from left to right quickly. "Hey!" he said. "Ain't we going the wrong way?"

Farther down the coast Colonel Tsuji stood on the sand and looked at the convoy through his binoculars. He'd watched the ships approach and now it appeared that they were dropping anchor. Soon the Forty-eighth Division would start coming ashore. He looked at his watch; it was two-thirty in the morning. *Only a half hour late*, he thought, *but all the troops ought to be ashore long before daybreak*. He smiled as he thought of

185

the many interesting ways he could deploy the Forty-eighth Division on Guadalcanal.

Colonel Stockton paced back and forth in his office, puffing his pipe, anxiously awaiting word about Butsko and his men. He glanced at his watch: It had been over an hour since he'd spoken with Commander Ames. Surely the PT boat should have picked up the men by now. Had there been trouble? Maybe the PT boat had broken down?

The phone on his desk rang, and he dived on it. "Colonel Stockton speaking."

"This is Commander Ames. You'll be glad to know that my PT boat has picked up nine of your men and they're on their way back. One of your men has been wounded fairly seriously, but he should be all right, provided he gets to a doctor within a reasonable length of time."

"Do you know his name?"

"No. They kept the message brief so that the Japs wouldn't pick up their signal."

"I understand," said Colonel Stockton. He looked at his watch. "They should be back pretty soon."

"Within an hour, I'd say."

Colonel Stockton hung up his phone and stared through his window at the moon. "Thank God," he whispered.

"Land the troops and equipment!" said Admiral Tamaki, standing on the bridge of the *Aoba*.

His executive officer order saluted and passed the order along. The convoy was anchored in the moonlit waters about a half mile from shore, and this would be the most dangerous part of the trip, because if the convoy was attacked, it couldn't maneuver or fight while it was unloading men and equipment.

General Ooka looked at the transport ships through his binoculars and soon saw increased activity on the decks. Landing boats were being lowered into the water, and nets were thrown over the sides of the ships so that the men could climb down. The troops lined up in front of the nets, waiting for the order to go over the side.

It was a hot night and the portholes of the bridge were open. The humid night air wafted against General Ooka's face as he watched the preparations for the landing. He thought he heard an engine running in the distance, but then it stopped, and he figured it must have been one of the motors on the *Aoba* that had just been turned off.

Lieutenant Woodward cut the throttles of *PT–114,* and the boat hunkered down in its own wake. His Red Sox baseball cap backward on his head, he raised his binoculars to his eyes and gazed ahead while Chief Boatswain's Mate Trask, next to him, did the same.

"It's the fucking Tokyo Express!" Woodward said. "It looks like they're getting ready to unload! Tell Crouse to radio the fleet immediately and then come right back up here—we're going to attack!"

"Yes, sir!"

Trask jumped down the stairs, passing Butsko on the way to the radio shack. Butsko climbed the stairs and looked at Lieutenant Woodward in disbelief. "Did I just hear you say you're going to attack all them ships?"

"That's right, Sergeant. Tell all your men to get below."

"But, sir," Butsko said, "I've got a wounded man back there and he's got to get a doctor!"

Woodward turned to him, looking ridiculous with his Red Sox baseball hat on backwards. "Are we supposed to stop the war just because a man is wounded? I said get below, Sergeant! That's an order!"

"But, sir," Butsko said, "there are about twenty ships out there, and one of them looks like a battleship!"

Lieutenant Woodward's eyes were shining with excitement. "It *is* a battleship, and I've got four torpedoes that can send it right to the fucking bottom! Now get below, Sergeant! I'm not going to tell you again!"

Butsko looked into Lieutenant Woodward's eyes and could see pure maniacal intensity. He knew he could never change the young officer's mind, so there was no use in trying. And if there was going to be a fight against Japs, he didn't want to miss it.

"Sir," he said, "I don't think I can make my men go below. They're not sailors and they'll get sick down there. Besides, it looks like there's plenty of room up here. Ain't you got

187

something they can shoot Japs with?"

Lieutenant Woodward knew he'd found a kindred soul. "As a matter of fact we have. We've got carbines below and lots of ammunition. You and your men can help yourselves."

Butsko jumped from the bridge to the deck. "Bannon!" he yelled. "Get two men and come with me!"

While the GIs went below to get the carbines and ammunition, Chief Boatswain's Mate Trask returned to the bridge. "I got through to the fleet, sir. They're on the way."

"Battle stations!" Lieutenant Woodward screamed, pushing the throttles forward all the way with the hell of his hand.

The engines snarled and *PT–114* charged forward toward the Japanese convoy in the distance. The deck and walls shook from the sudden burst of power, and the hull came up out of the water and planed across the waves as sailors put on their helmets and flak jackets and manned the fifty-caliber machine guns and torpedo tubes. *PT–114* raced as straight as an arrow across New Georgia Sound, leaving a long white trail of foam behind it. Bannon, Shaw, and Frankie La Barbara hauled crates of carbines and ammunition onto the deck and ripped them open. They hung bandoliers of ammunitions around their necks and carried carbines to positions along the gunwales, loading up and getting ready as *PT–114* bore down on the Japanese convoy. They flicked the levers that permitted the carbines to be fired on automatic, like submachine guns.

"Enemy patrol boat off port bow!" screamed Ensign Nakamura.

Horrified, Admiral Tamaki swung his binoculars and saw the lone PT boat streaking out of the night toward the *Aoba*.

"Stop it!" he shouted. *"Open fire!"*

Many of the gunnery officers on the *Aoba* had already seen the PT boat and were zeroing in on it. They opened fire immediately and many fired wildly, hoping that a screen of explosions would keep the PT boat away. Machine gunners aboard the *Aoba* also opened fire, and within seconds the destroyers in the vicinity fired artillery shells and machine guns at *PT–114*, whose unswerving course was toward the *Aoba*.

Tons of shells exploded in the water all around the PT boat, but still it kept coming at such a furious speed that it was difficult to take aim at it. Admiral Tamaki watched helplessly as the PT boat sped closer.

"Full speed ahead!" he yelled. *"Hard left rudder!"*

Geysers of water were blown into the air around *PT–114*, and machine-gun bullets whistled all around it, but Lieutenant Woodward sat solidly behind the wheel, his teeth on edge, watching the big battleship pulling away and destroyers moving toward them firing their big guns. Explosions nearby sent torrents of water cascading onto the deck of the PT boat, and the men hung on to anything they could to keep from being washed overboard.

"Torpedo tubes one and two, prepare to fire!" Lieutenant Woodward screamed, shifting his course so that the torpedoes would hit the big battleship broadside.

"Torpedo tubes one and two—FIRE!"

The two torpedoes shot out of the tubes and dropped into the water, where they streaked toward the *Aoba*.

Lieutenant Woodward cut the wheel to the left, heading for the opening made by the departure of the *Aoba*. Ahead of him was the heart of the convoy, with Japanese soldiers scrambling down nets to their landing craft.

"Torpedo tube three—prepare to fire!"

Lieutenant Woodward aimed for one of the transport ships unloading Japanese troops. He looked to his left and right to see what was around him, and along the gunwales of *PT–114* the men from the First Squad turned their carbines toward the Japanese soldiers on the nets. The Japanese soldiers heard the approach of the PT boat and turned around fearfully, their worst fears coming true as the fifty-caliber machine guns on the PT boat opened fire, raking the soldiers with bullets.

Butsko and his men stood up and fired their carbines from their hips at the Japanese soldiers on the nets. The Japanese were smashed by the hail of bullets and fell like dead flies to the water below. Some dropped to the decks of the landing boats, smashing skulls and bones.

"Torpedo tube three—FIRE!"

The torpedo shot out of its tube and splashed into the water, beginning its journey toward the transport ship. Lieutenant Woodward steered sharply to the right and sped past the transport ship as the GIs on the port side of the PT boat joined those on the starboard side and fired their submachine guns at the Japanese soldiers still on the nets.

Butsko aimed lower and poured a stream of bullets into the row of landing craft, blowing apart soldiers already in them. In the distance they heard two loud nearly simultaneous explosions. Turning in the direction of the sound, they saw orange blasts on the side of the big battleship and men and metal being blown into the air.

"Direct hit!" yelled Chief Boatswain's Mate Trask.

The battleship leaned over, due to the impact of the explosions, then righted itself as a huge fireball rose from its deck.

"I'm gonna finish that son of a bitch off!" yelled Lieutenant Woodward, cutting the wheel to the left again.

PT–114 veered away from the transport ship as the GIs kept firing at the remaining Japanese soldiers on the nets and on the bridge of the ship. Gunner's Mate First Class Fuller, manning the thirty-seven-millimeter automatic cannon on the stern of the PT boat, blasted holes in the hulls of the landing boats and the transport ship itself.

Meanwhile every Japanese gun and cannon in the vicinity was trained on the speeding PT boat, and bullets whistled in all directions as water exploded all around it. A Japanese destroyer plowed toward it, all guns blazing, and Lieutenant Woodward zigzagged across the water, leaving huge *S*-shaped trails behind him.

"Smoke screen!" shouted Lieutenant Woodward.

A crewmember turned on the smoke generator and black smoke belched out of the funnel. Lieutenant Woodward made the stern of the PT boat wag from side to side, spreading the smoke around, and sped back toward the battleship, hidden by the cloud of smoke.

Japanese gunners fired wildly into the smoke and at the sound of the retreating PT boat, and one of the bullets hit Gunner's Mate Third Class Jerry Riggs in the stomach. He jumped into the air at the impact of the bullet and then fell back against the steel wall that was supposed to protect him.

Bannon saw him fall and in a second was bounding up the ladder to the fifty-caliber machine gun. Fastening himself to the shoulder bars, he wrapped his fingers around the handles, aimed at a transport ship on his right, and pressed the thumb triggers. The machine gun thundered and trembled on its pedestal, and Japanese soldiers fell from their nets to the sea below.

Another tremendous explosion echoed across New Georgia Sound, cracking apart the transport ship that Lieutenant Woodward had fired upon. Its bow and stern rose in the air while its central portion sank into the water. It looked like a huge flaming *V* as it settled slowly into the sea, soldiers and sailors jumping off of it into water covered with burning oil.

Frankie La Barbara leaned against the gunwale of *PT–114* and fired his carbine gun at the transport ship Bannon was shooting at. He grinned as he saw Japanese soldiers cringe on the rope netting and then let go, dropping into the water. Gunner's Mate Third Class Thornton shot holes in the hull of the transport ship as the PT boat sped by, heading for the stern of the big battleship turning in the water.

"I'm going to send that son of a bitch to the bottom!" Lieutenant Woodward shouted into the howling wind. *"Torpedo tube number four—prepare to fire!"*

He veered hard to the right and made sure the throttles were all the way forward. *PT–114* shot across the water like a bullet, leaving a huge plume of spray behind it. Three destroyers spotted the tiny craft and headed toward it, but Woodward was sure he could beat them to the punch. He swung hard to the right and gained on the battleship, intending to hit it on the same side he'd hit it before. When he was abreast of the huge ship, he steered to the left and drove in for the kill.

Lieutenant Woodward stared straight ahead and saw fire and smoke billowing out of the hull of the battleship. Bannon and the other GIs raked its bridge and decks with machine-gun fire as the battleship fired machine guns and cannon at the speeding PT boat. Water spouts from explosions fell around the PT boat, rattling Bannon's teeth, but he kept his thumb triggers depressed and saw his tracers making long orange lines directly into the bridge of the battleship. Machine-gun bullets ripped into the plywood hull of the PT boat, sending splinters flying into the air, but Lieutenant Woodward was a man possessed and stayed on course, wanting to get as close as he could so that his last torpedo couldn't miss.

The battleship loomed closer, a monstrosity of metal and

fire in New Georgia Sound. Japanese sailors could be seen running on the decks amid flashes of light from the battleship's guns.

"Torpedo tube four—FIRE!" screamed Lieutenant Woodward.·

The torpedo shot forward into the water and dropped beneath the surface.

"Torpedo away, sir!" yelled Torpedoman Second Class Len Fulton.

"Yowie!" hollered Lieutenant Woodward, cutting his wheel to the left.

PT–114's hull skidded over the water as it turned away from the battleship. Lieutenant Woodward looked ahead and his jaw dropped as he saw three destroyers, all guns blazing, bearing down on him. He steered back into the center of the convoy as the GIs and sailors aboard the PT boat fired at all the ships around them. Bullets whizzed through the air, smacking into the plywood boat. A shell landed twenty yards away and the PT boat was knocked onto its side, everybody hanging on for dear life, but then it righted itself and kept on going. Japanese soldiers and sailors from the sinking transport ship swam in the water, and *PT–114* ripped into them, sending them flying through the air in huge sheets of water.

Barrrooooommmmm! sounded the explosion on the battleship, the night becoming momentarily bright in the blast. Men and cannons were blown into the air, along with the guts of the huge ship. A violent shock passed through every rivet of the *Aoba,* and then it listed toward the side in which two gaping holes had been blown in its hull.

Japanese destroyers roared from all directions toward the PT boat, all guns blazing. There were so many explosions and bullets that Lieutenant Woodward could barely see.

"Sir, we'd better get out of here!" yelled Chief Boatswain's Mate Trask.

"Smoke screen!" shouted Lieutenant Woodward.

Black smoke poured out of the funnel, and Lieutenant Woodward looked for a clear path through the destroyers closing in on him from all directions. He ran a circle through the smoke to confuse the destroyers and then made a run for one

192

of the openings, realizing grimly that the PT boat wasn't at its top speed anymore. He figured it was taking on water, and if he didn't get away quickly, the destroyers would blow him out of the water.

"Hang on!" he screamed, gritting his teeth and heading for the path between two destroyers.

Bullets and shells rained down all around *PT-114* as it streaked through its smoke screen. It came out the other side and everybody opened fire on the destroyers, raking their bridges and decks with bullets. A blast of machine-gun bullets from a destroyer knocked off the top of *PT-114*'s bow, and a shell explosion nearby lifted it out of the water, but it kept on going.

Bannon, sweat pouring from his face, held the thumb triggers of the fifty-caliber machine-gun down and saw his tracers sweeping across the bridge of the destroyer to the left of *PT-114*. Japanese bullets splattered across the deck of the tiny PT boat, and one of them hit Gunner's Mate Third Class Thornton in the head, blowing it away.

Butsko found himself splashed with blood. He turned and saw Thornton lying in a clump at the base of the thirty-seven-millimeter cannon. Jumping to his feet, he ran across the heaving deck, climbed the ladder, and dived behind the cannon, leaning into the shoulder bars. He'd never fired a thirty-seven-millimeter cannon before, but he found the trigger buttons and pressed them. The cannon rocked on its pedestal and shells fired into the superstructure of a destroyer, knocking down its mast and sending massive chunks of metal flying into the air.

PT-114 sped toward the opening between the two destroyers, and the Japanese fire became more intense. The PT boat roared closer and then passed between them, as bullets ripped apart the control panel in front of Lieutenant Woodward's eyes. A piece of wood hit him on the cheek, tearing it apart, and he flinched, causing the PT boat to veer toward one of the destroyers.

Chief Boatswain's Mate Trask jumped on the wheel and brought it back on course. *PT-114* passed between the destroyers and headed for the open sea as more Japanese bullets tore into its hull. One of the big Packard engines shuddered, and there was a horrible grinding sound below decks. Lieutenant

Woodward opened his eyes and felt *PT–114* slowing down.

"Come on, you son of a bitch!" he screamed, banging on the throttles.

The PT boat lost speed, and he figured he'd lost an engine, but he had two left and each could put out 1200 horsepower, enough to outrun any destroyer in the world. He heard a shell whistle over his head and realized it was going the wrong way. Peering ahead, he saw flashes of guns on the horizon and realized the US Navy was on the way.

He hunched over the wheel and aimed the PT boat toward Lunga Point. Behind him the destroyers turned back to protect their convoy, because they too had seen the approaching American fleet.

"We made it!" Lieutenant Woodward hollered, jumping up and down and banging his demolished instrument panel. *"Yowie!"*

Below on the deck of *PT–114* the sailors and GIs stopped firing. They stood up on shaky legs and turned to look behind them. The convoy was brightly lit by fires on the battleship, and the transport ship that Lieutenant Woodward had torpedoed had disappeared beneath the water. Shells from the approaching American fleet poured onto the Japanese convoy, which was still trying to unload troops.

"They're fucked!" Frankie La Barbara said, throwing punches at the air. *"They're fucked!"*

EIGHTEEN . . .

On the shore Colonel Tsuji watched through his binoculars as the American fleet tore into the Japanese convoy. The Americans sent up flares and the battle was as bright as day as American ships pounded those of the Imperial Japanese Navy, which had been caught in a terrible predicament. The Japanese warships couldn't leave until all the troops were unloaded from the transport ships, but it was difficult to unload the troops during the battle. American planes had appeared from Henderson Field and dive-bombed the Japanese ships relentlessly.

Approximately twenty percent of the Japanese soldiers had made it to the beach so far, and they were soaked and exhausted, some burned badly by the oil fires. Many were wounded. They huddled together all around Colonel Tsuji as Japanese medics scurried about and treated their wounds.

Colonel Tsuji felt sick in the pit of his stomach and thought he might vomit. He swallowed hard as he realized that the Japanese Forty-eighth Division wouldn't make much of a difference in the battle for Guadalcanal. But there'd be other nights and other convoys. The Americans wouldn't intercept all of them. Japanese strength on Guadalcanal would be built up somehow, and then they'd attack the Americans again and drive them into the sea.

He tried to convince himself of this as a barge motored

toward the beach, carrying four tanks and soldiers. He trained his binoculars on the battleship *Aoba,* which appeared to be sinking in New Georgia Sound. The night was a catastrophe, but the war wasn't over by any means. There'd be other nights and other battles. The Imperial Way would emerge victorious in the end.

Then the bile rose up in his throat and he couldn't swallow it down. Dropping his binoculars, he ran toward the bushes to spew out the bitterness of defeat.

"Abandon ship!" shouted Admiral Tamaki.

The mighty *Aoba* listed forty-five degrees to starboard and water covered its foredeck. Sailors struggled to put out fires, and gun crews still fired their weapons at American ships swarming around them. An American shell hit the *Aoba* amidships, and the battleship shuddered at the blow. Gun turrets were blasted apart and sailors thrown into the sea.

The order was passed along to abandon ship, and General Ooka hung on to a rail to keep himself from falling onto the slanting deck. He looked through the shattered glass at sailors leaving their posts and running through flames toward the lifeboats. Two more American shells slammed into the *Aoba* with such violence that General Ooka was thrown to the deck, where he rolled down the incline until a bulkhead stopped him. Shaking his head, he staggered to his feet.

Admiral Tamaki, his face ashen, was hanging on to a brass rail. "General Ooka, I have given the order to abandon ship! You must go!"

General Ooka looked at Admiral Tamaki and felt great sorrow. He wanted to say something, but there was nothing appropriate at a time like this. He didn't like the admiral, but he wouldn't have wished such a disaster on anyone.

Admiral Tamaki trembled as he gripped the shiny brass rail. *"Long live the Emperor!"* he shouted.

"Long live the Emperor!" replied the ship's officers who were crowded onto the bridge.

Admiral Tamaki glowered at them. "You all must go!"

"We wish to stay with you, sir!" said Ensign Nakamura.

"I have ordered you to go!"

The ship's officers held on to rails and made their way out of the control room, and finally General Ooka was alone with Admiral Tamaki.

"This is my ship and I am still in command," Admiral Tamaki said, his voice faltering. "I have ordered you to leave, General Ooka. What must I do to make you leave?"

General Ooka's guts churned with emotion. "Do you have a last message for your wife, Admiral Tamaki?"

Admiral Tamaki looked away. "My heart is with her right now, and she knows everything. Long live the Emperor."

"Long live the Emperor," General Ooka replied, pulling himself toward the door. He gripped the side of it and stepped outside, to see the *Aoba* sinking quickly. Water covered all the lower decks, and crewmembers rowed away in lifeboats. He heard the roar of engines overhead and dropped to his stomach as a squadron of Hellcats appeared, strafing the superstructure of the battleship. Bullets slammed into metal over General Ooka's head, and then they passed as suddenly as they'd come. He pulled himself erect again.

He made his way to the ladder and climbed down. After three steps he heard a shot on the bridge and stopped, closing his eyes. Admiral Tamaki had put a bullet in his brain, he realized, but there was no time to mourn. He continued to descend the ladder, reached the next deck, and looked around. The ship was going down fast, and he knew he'd have to get away from it or else it would suck him under. Holding the rail, he pulled himself to the side that leaned over the water and looked down. It would be a thirty-foot drop, and the sea was full of slabs of wood and swimming sailors. He threw one leg over the rail, then the other, hung on, and then jumped.

He kept his feet close together, one hand protecting his groin and the other covering his face. His hat flew off his head and he thought he'd been falling for an awfully long time, when his feet hit the water and he dropped like a rock beneath the surface.

The oil and salt burned his eyes, and he struggled against the water, fighting to return to the surface. He dared not open his eyes, and his hand struck something solid, then his head broke the surface and he heard screaming.

Treading water, he looked around at sailors flailing the air and water as dark triangular shapes circled around them. *Sharks!* he thought, his blood turning to ice. He kicked with his feet and swam away with all his strength, seeing a crowded lifeboat rowing away from him. He opened his mouth to shout "Wait for me!" but then caught himself. Even at a moment like this, a Japanese general should not beg for help.

"It's General Ooka!" yelled a sailor on the stern.

The lifeboat turned in the water and headed for him. He looked back and saw the water boiling with shark fins at the spot where he'd seen the screaming soldiers. Looking at the lifeboat again, he kicked his legs and swam toward it, trying to hold down his mounting hysteria. The boat came closer and hands reached down to him. He held his arms up and they grabbed him, pulling him aboard.

His stomach and legs scraped over the gunwale and then he was safe in the boat. Sailors squeezed to the side and made room for him. The boat was so full, the water was only inches below the gunwale.

"Are you all right, sir?" asked a young lieutenant.

"Yes, I believe so."

"There she goes!" somebody shouted.

General Ooka turned around and saw the *Aoba* sinking beneath the surface of the water. The bridge was nearly completely submerged, and General Ooka thought of old Admiral Tamaki floating around inside with a bullet in his head. The water covered the bridge, then only the upper portions of the superstructure were visible. The sailors pulled their oars with everything they had, and huge bubbles broke on the surface around the *Aoba*. Then there was a terrible crunching sound and it disappeared beneath the waves.

General Ooka looked around at burning Japanese ships turning the sky red. The sea was covered with lifeboats and the bobbing heads of soldiers and sailors. The American fleet was retreating; there was no more work for it to do. General Ooka closed his eyes and willed himself not to cry, but the tears came anyway. The sailors in the lifeboat looked away so they wouldn't see his embarrassment.

The Forty-eighth was the first division he'd ever commanded, and now it was gone. Somehow, some way, he must avenge their deaths. He was still alive, and he'd move heaven and earth to obtain another command. Then he'd show the Americans what war was about. He'd attack and attack again until there was nothing left of them except broken bones and a river of blood.

I'll show them no mercy, he said to himself, trembling with emotion. *I'll kill them all.*

The horizon glowed red from burning Japanese ships as *PT—114* motored toward its dock at Lunga Point. Sailors on the dock threw lines aboard as it came alongside, and crewmembers fastened them to cleats. On the bridge Lieutenant Woodward cut the engines and gazed, bleary-eyed, at ambulances, jeeps, and a truck. A crowd walked out onto the dock, and Lieutenant Woodward saw Commander Ames in his tan summer uniform with his collar unbuttoned.

Lieutenant Woodward turned his Red Sox baseball cap around on his head so that the bill faced forward, then stood up groggily. He turned around and descended the ladder to the deck where the GIs were handing down the wounded to medics.

Colonel Stockton walked beside Commander Ames, and as he drew close, he could see the men from his recon platoon jumping down to the dock. They staggered around as if drunk, bumming cigarettes from everybody nearby, and one of them held up his arms to help down a pretty Japanese girl. Colonel Stockton wondered where in hell she came from.

Colonel Stockton spotted Butsko and walked toward him. He wanted to congratulate him or say welcome home, but somehow that seemed too corny. Butsko looked like he'd been through a meat grinder, his face gashed and one of his hands held in front of him as if it was bothering him. Colonel Stockton put his hand on Butsko's shoulder.

"I never thought I'd see you again," he said.

Butsko's eyes were bloodshot and at half mast. "I never thought I'd see you either."

"What's wrong with your hand."

"It's all fucked up."

"I'll get one of the doctors over here."

199

"That's okay. Some of the men are hurt worse than me."

Medics carried the dead and wounded away on stretchers, loading them into the ambulances. The men from the First Squad milled around, waiting for somebody to tell them what to do. Sailors looked at the P T boat, which was torn apart in numerous places, and they wondered how it had made it back. Some stared at the Japanese girl, shivering with apprehension, Longtree's arm around her shoulder.

Commander Ames walked up to Lieutenant Woodward. "You look like you've been through hell."

"We have."

"What the hell happened?"

"You'll never believe it."

Colonel Stockton looked at the Japanese girl. "Where'd she come from?" he asked Butsko.

"The men found her in the jungle. She'd run away from the Japs."

"We'll have to send her to Headquarters for questioning. Is she dangerous?"

"She hasn't been yet, but you never can tell about fucking Japs."

Colonel Stockton turned around. "Lieutenant Harper!"

"Yes, sir!" Lieutenant Harper ran toward him through the crowd.

Colonel Stockton pointed to the Japanese girl. "Take her to General Vandegrift's headquarters for questioning."

"Yes, sir."

Lieutenant Harper walked up to Longtree and the girl, and Longtree knew what was coming.

"She speak English?" Lieutenant Harper asked.

"No, sir."

"I'm afraid she'll have to come with us." He motioned for her to follow him.

She looked fearfully up at Longtree's face, because she wouldn't move unless he told her to. Longtree felt sick, because he didn't want her to go, but he couldn't fight the whole Army. "Go with him," he said softly, pointing to Lieutenant Harper and then motioning into the distance.

Her eyes filled with tears, and she moved to kiss him, but

200

he stepped back because he knew if he kissed her, he'd never be able to let her go. She understood and lowered her head, moving with resignation to the side of Lieutenant Harper. They walked away, and Longtree saw her delicate shoulders quaking with sobs.

"Aw, fuck," he said, sucking on his cigarette.

Colonel Stockton and Butsko moved to the side to let Lieutenant Harper pass with the girl.

"Watch her," Butsko growled.

Lieutenant Harper nodded. Colonel Stockton saw no point in keeping the men on the dock any longer. "Sergeant Butsko," he said, "tell your men to load onto that truck. You'd better stay with the medics."

"Yes, sir." Butsko turned around. "Bannon!"

"Hup, Sarge!"

"Get over here!"

Bannon ran over and stopped in front of Butsko. He stood, lanky and loose, glancing nervously at Colonel Stockton, whom he feared.

"You saved my ass," Butsko told Bannon. "Don't think I don't know that. The others wouldn't't've lifted a finger to get me if you hadn't made them. Load the men onto the truck over there. I'll speak to you later."

"Hup, Sarge."

Bannon ran off to pull his squad together. He lined them up in a column of twos and marched them toward the truck.

"Isn't that Corporal Bannon?" Colonel Stockton asked.

"He's the best man in the platoon," Butsko mumbled. "He fucks up once in a while, but he's the only one with any brains."

"Let's go, Sergeant."

Colonel Stockton walked toward the medics with Butsko at his side. He wanted to tell the doctor personally to return Butsko to duty as soon as possible.

Meanwhile the First Squad loaded onto the deuce-and-a-half truck. They sat on the benches and the driver put up the tailgate, then walked toward the cab and got in. He started up the engine and drove off into the jungle, heading toward the lines held by the Twenty-third.

In the back of the truck the soldiers closed their eyes and

bounced around every time the wheels hit a rock or a pothole. Frankie La Barbara fell off his seat and collapsed onto the steel floor of the truck, fast asleep. Bannon rolled from side to side, his submachine gun on his lap and his jaw lolling open, dreaming of tracer bullets flying through the air and bombs bursting in the sky.

Look for

HIT THE BEACH!

and

RIVER OF BLOOD

two more novels in the new RAT BASTARDS series from
Jove
available now!

Also watch for

MEAT GRINDER HILL

coming in January!